NOT Strictly BALLROOM

Dance Lovers Collection

Book 1

JEM WENDEL

Published by Larking About Press

Edited by Jennifer Green and SJ Buckley

Cover designed by Stephanie Dempsey

ISBN: 978-1-916758-08-7 - v1. Standard Paperback

ISBN: 978-1-916758-09-4 - NSFW Paperback

ISBN: 978-1-916758-10-0 - Discreet Paperback

It's Not Strictly Ballroom...

This year Darcy's dreams may finally come true - he has a chance at winning the National Ballroom Championships, something he has worked for and wanted, with his family's support, for as long as he can remember. But after his dance partner leaves to pursue her dreams as a Marine Biologist, Darcy's world is turned upside down... until he dances with his best friend, Nick.

Darcy's dream, future, and family's dance school are in trouble, and his mum convinces him that winning could give them the publicity they need to save it. However, that means he cannot dance with Nick... A ballroom competition has never witnessed two men dancing as a couple, and they would never be crowned champions.

The night of the competition changes everything and what Darcy thought were his dreams come crashing down and splitting his family apart. Can Darcy rebuild his future with Nick by his side?

"You have me,
every step of the way,
side by side."
-Nick

NOT *Strictly* BALLROOM

Dance Lovers Collection

Book 1

JEM WENDEL

Author's Note

Thank you for reading Not Strictly Ballroom. It's a project that I've planned to write for a long time.

I wanted it to be so much more than a retelling of the film and it breaks out of the narrative, whilst still keeping some key recognisable elements.

I didn't want to make the story about the inclusion of new steps as in the film, but more about highlighting the rarity of same-sex dancing partnerships. Same-sex dancing couples have been permitted in British ballroom dancing for several years and there is a UK Equality Dance Council. However, we have yet to see them on the podium of top level competitions.

Though there are many ballroom dancing competitions in the UK, most notably the Dance Festival held at the Winter Gardens in Blackpool, The National Ballroom Championships mentioned in the book are purely fictitious.

Content Warnings: Shitty parent, Mention of divorce.

This book is intended for adult readers. It contains scenes of sexually explicit material between male characters. If this is not for you then please do not read my books.

Language Notes & Glossary

Not Strictly Ballroom is written is British English which means that some words are spelled differently - such as s in the place of z as in apologise. Similarly u is used such as in colour or favourite. Practice/practise - both are used in British English depending on if they are being used as a verb or a noun.

Also in some cases, different grammar rules are followed.

GLOSSARY - for some words and terms which may confuse non-British readers.

Bank Holiday – official holiday day in the UK, started by financial institutions, hence the name

Copse – small group of trees

Love Hearts – British brand of candy with hearts and messages

Motorway – fast road with limited access/exit points (expressway)

Paper round – paper route

Pork Scratchings – snack – pork rinds

Privy – outside toilet

School dinner lady (lunch lady) – In the UK, dinner is interchangeable for lunchtime and a later meal which we also call teatime

Tannoy – English slang for PA system

Treacle - molasses

Yorkshire Dialect

The book is set in the Northern county of Yorkshire. I have included a few phrases of Yorkshire dialect for one of the characters. I have also taken some liberties of what an internet search might tell you of the dialect as there are regional differences within the county. The book is set in the North-eastern area of Sheffield, and as such, the phrasing is consistent with that area. It is a place I grew up in and I can still speak it very well if required.

Words you will see:

Tha and thee – these are used in place of you, usually tha is plural and thee is singular – but most often tha is used for both, except in certain phrases

Dus thee – do you

Aye – Express assent, yes

Summat – Somewhat

Reyt – Right

Owt – Anything

Nowt – Nothing

T' – this is often used in place of 'the' or 'to the' and is written in front of the noun. However in speech, especially where the book is set, the 't' would be sounded at the end of the preceding word.

Time After Time - Mark Williams, Tara Morice
Moves Like Jagger - Maroon 5, Christina Aquilera
The Weeping Song - Nick Cave and The Bad Seeds
Kinda I Want To - Nine Inch Nails
Just A Kiss - Lady A
I Want Candy - Bow Wow Wow
It Is You (I Have Loved) - Dana Glover
More Than Words - Extreme
Just Like Honey - The Jesus and Mary Chain
Breathless - The Corrs
Honey - Rook Monroe
Love is in the Air - John Paul Young
Show Me Heaven - Luke Evans
Dance With Me - Orleans
Open Arms - Journey

Dedication

For everyone who has loved and will love Strictly
Ballroom - thank you Baz Luhrmann

Chapter 1

Darcy

As the first few notes of the music drift across the dance floor, my heartbeat slows from the nervous staccato it's kept up for the last half an hour. I take a deep breath and exhale, allowing the tension in my body to ease and my jaw to relax. I roll my shoulders in readiness. Briefly closing my eyes, I let the rhythm infuse my soul, and break into a joyful smile. This is what I live for. This is what I'm made for. This is my life.

I extend my hand to my partner and wait for our number to be called so I can escort her onto the dance floor. The competition has begun.

The next couple of hours pass in a whirlwind of dance steps and costume changes. From the full-flowing skirts and formal suits of the traditional, to the slinky and sexy outfits of the Latin American dances, all are adorned with enough sequins to fill a swimming pool. I've been dancing with Julia for the last decade, since we were old enough to enter the junior competitions. We usually place well and have won several trophies, but never the National Ballroom Championships. It's the one prize that has eluded us, and if we do well in today's competition, we'll be going to the Nationals in a couple of months. It's a path I've been on for as long as I can remember. What'll happen after that, I don't know, but this has been the entire focus of my existence.

We're on the final costume change, just one more dance to go. I'm exhilarated, the adrenalin of the moment coursing through my veins. I love the atmosphere of the competition, the opulent surroundings, feet flying over wooden dance floors under crystal chandeliers. We're currently in the lead and will surely make the Nationals this year. Something has always happened in previous years, either in the heats or after qualification, that has prevented us from securing a spot. Usually sickness, or injury to myself or Julia, had conspired to keep us from them. But this year it all feels good. It's going to be our year—everyone says so. It's even a mantra at home. *It's Darcy's year!* As if saying it enough times could manifest it happening. I don't know if that contributes to how I'm feeling now, but I'm going to dismiss it. As I walk onto the dance floor for the final time today, I glance over at my mum. My teacher and biggest supporter. She'd never won the final herself back in the day, when she still danced competitively with Dad, but I know she's as excited as I am at the possibility of me getting to the Nationals this year. Some people say she's a pushy mum, but that would only be true if this wasn't my dream as well, wouldn't it?

"This is it." I laugh as I take Julia's hand one more time. "We can do this." I expect to see my elation and excitement mirrored on her face, like it has been for every competition we've entered, but it's not. Instead, her face is a mask, her mouth a grim line. I've known Julia for most of my life and we've spent a lot of time together, dancing. We even dated for a while when we were eighteen. Luckily, we realised that was a mistake fairly quickly, and didn't damage our friendship or dancing relationship because of it. We laughed it off as exploration and something we needed to get out of our systems. I feel like we've grown apart a little bit, as Julia has been away at university for the last few years. But she still loves dancing, and comes back for the competitions, practising with me when she's back for holidays.

"What is it?" I hiss, a hard knot of something cold forming in my stomach. Surely she wants this as well. If not, I'm positive she would have said so over the last ten years. Her brow creases briefly into a frown, and she gives her head a little shake. The announcer calls our number and I see her face set into a performance smile, so I make mine do the same. But somehow, the sparkle of the competition has dulled a little and I can't shed the feeling that something bad is about to happen. This is our year, I repeat to myself, hoping there's power in the incantation.

As we dance, I try to ignore the small niggle at the back of my brain, to dismiss it as something trivial. But it doesn't go away and I let my body shift into automatic. The dance steps are as natural for me as breathing. Julia still has her face set into a smile, but refuses to look at me, which is so out of character that my steps falter as we move out of a turn and into a promenade. Just for a second, before muscle memory kicks back in and takes over again. To most people watching, they wouldn't have been able to tell that I had misstepped. *Most* people. I hope the judges hadn't been looking at that precise moment as they would've been able to tell. Of course, Julia notices it. There isn't another person who is so in tune with me and I with them. She glances at me, and I see a veil of sadness and resignation over her eyes. Confusion crowds my thoughts, but now is not the time to confront her. I remember why I'm here and try to act like the professional I'm supposed to be. We finish the dance with no further problems, but I don't have the same exhilaration I felt when we started it. Applause reverberates around us, and instead of enjoying it, it jangles a discordant rhythm in my ears. I ignore the other couples and tug Julia after me. I want to know what's going on. As we reach the barrier, my mum is there waiting.

"What was that, Darcy?" she demands. I knew she'd have seen my mistake. I evade her, as I don't want her disapproval and displeasure weighing on me now. I'll have enough of that to deal with later. She might be my biggest supporter, but she is also my biggest critic. I pull Julia through the throng, and she doesn't resist, allowing herself to be towed behind me, my mum following with her face a moue of disappointment.

I reach a quiet spot backstage, if it can be called quiet, but at least we aren't being jostled.

I turn to face Julia, and she looks at me, biting her lip. Before I can say anything, my mum cuts through again.

"What is going on?" Her voice is tinged with anger.

"Mum, leave it." I direct it at her but turn back to Julia and echo my mum using a much softer tone. I'm quiet in contrast to my loud mother—she's dramatic enough for both of us. "What's going on?"

Julia presses her lips into a line and looks away before turning back. "I can't go to the Nationals," she says quietly. But it's loud enough for my mum to hear.

"What?" Her voice is a falsetto stab that draws the attention of those around us. "You've been working for this your whole life. You and Darcy. It's going to be your year. It was your dream."

I stare at Julia, feeling numb. I don't know how to process the news.

"No," Julia replies to my mum with an edge of steel. "It was never my dream, was it, Sheila? It was yours." She gives me a sad look before turning and disappearing into the crowd. My mum is left gaping like a fish.

"You come back here and explain yourself," my mum shouts after her, and I hear the crowd murmuring around us. I don't want her to create a scene right now, and that thought galvanises me into action.

"Mum. Stay here. I'll find her and figure out what's happening."

"Yes, go find out what nonsense she's talking about." She recovers enough to spit out. I sigh, hoping she won't follow. Not everyone appreciates my mum's drive and determination.

I track Julia down and find her sitting on a bench close to the changing rooms, picking at the sequins of her dress.

"I'm sorry, Darcy," she says as I approach.

"Tell me what's going on, Jules." She huffs a sad smile at my familiar use of the name I've called her for years. I sit next to her and swivel my knees round so I can face her.

"I've accepted a research position. To study whales. I leave in three weeks," she says with a sigh.

My mouth goes dry and I can't conjure up any suitable words. I know how much something like this means to her. She's been studying marine biology, and this is what she wanted. My stomach roils and bile bubbles up. I swallow, forcing it back down. I'd known this moment would come, eventually. I just hadn't thought it would happen yet. I'd hoped it wouldn't. She's only just graduated and come home. I never believed she'd be leaving again so soon. I don't want to sound like a selfish prick, so I swallow to moisten my mouth so the words will come. "I'm really happy for you." I am happy for her, but turn away, unable to look at her. Not just yet. She reaches for my hand.

"Why didn't you say anything?" I ask, wanting to know if this is something she's been holding on to for a long time.

"I only got the call yesterday. I didn't tell you, as I never imagined I'd be accepted. Competition is really tough. I thought I was going to apply for dozens of positions and wait a year or so before getting a place." She gives my hand a little squeeze.

"It sounds perfect Jules, you'll be amazing at it." And she will be. It's her dream. Whereas my dreams have come crashing down around me to lie in tatters at my feet.

"I am really sorry, Darcy. I know how much this means to you." I give her a small smile. I'm grateful she doesn't sneer, as some people do. Dancing isn't considered something worthy, like marine biology and conservation, but to me and my family, it's all we know.

"Can you come back? For the competition?" I ask hopefully, but knowing it would be unlikely.

"I'll be somewhere on a boat in the Arctic Ocean by then, Darcy. I can't come back." Her voice is soft, but even so, it firmly hammers another nail into the coffin of my future. I nod. I'd known that would be the answer, but I had to ask.

"You'll find another partner for the Nationals, you'll see." She makes it sound so reassuringly easy, but partners experienced enough to win national championships don't just appear out of nowhere, and most of the people we know are already partnered up. For a partner to become available, it would take something awful, like an accident, and I wouldn't wish that on my fellow dancers.

"No, I won't," I reply sadly, as she gives my hand another squeeze. I can't bear her sympathy any longer, not for a situation of her making. I don't blame her, not totally. She has to follow her dreams. It just so happens she's destroyed mine in the process.

Announcements start coming over the tannoy, and the hubbub of people increases. The winners are being announced. Julia stands and pulls me to my feet.

"C'mon. Let's go find out how we've done." In the end, we're placed second. We were the leaders going into the last dance, so the judges must have seen my mistake. Not that it matters now. Second is good enough to qualify for the Nationals, but it doesn't look like I'll be going. It might be a long time before I find another partner—if I ever do—so the fact that I didn't even win this, my last competition, seems like another bitter pill to swallow.

Julia had travelled with us to the competition, but she finds another way home with some friends. I can't blame her, as my mum keeps up her complaining and cursing of Julia for the several-hour drive back up the motorway.

I sit and look out the car window, still not feeling anything except that I have no future. My phone buzzes and I stare at the screen, not knowing how to respond to the text from my best friend, Nick.

Nick: Hey champ! I bet you slayed them all :)

Chapter 2

Nick

"Does it do something if you look at it?"

The words pull me out of my reverie, and I chuckle, putting down my phone which was clearly not going to do anything the longer I stared at it.

"Not that I know of," I reply to my gran. I sent the text to Darcy a while ago and now I'm worried as I haven't received a response. There's no point sending another. He'll respond when he sees it.

"I thought you were asleep." I turn to her. Her small frame is enveloped by a large, comfortable chair, her feet resting on a low footstool. I'm keeping her company this Sunday afternoon, or I was until she fell asleep. I'd usually be at the dance school on Sundays, but with everyone attending the competition, it's not open today. Mum was adamant that she didn't want any help making Sunday dinner and practically shooed me out of the kitchen with a broom. I certainly didn't want to go to the Working Men's Club with my dad, so I offered to keep an eye on Gran for a while.

"I was, and now I'm awake." I like how she states the obvious. "I reckon the dryness of my throat woke me up." She follows that with a small, wolfish grin. She may be old, but she's still feisty. I can take a hint as well as anyone, so I rise like the dutiful grandson I am, and head to the kitchen to put the kettle on.

With tea brewing in the pot, and a plate of biscuits nestled next to Gran's Sunday china, I carry the tray back into the front room. Gran has never been taken with "fancy speak," as she calls it, and doesn't use the words lounge or parlour. It's the front room, as opposed to the back room which is the kitchen. The house is a typical, stone-built two-up two-down terraced house, the likes of which paint the landscape of most industrial northern towns. Now serving as a disquieting reminder of the decline of the cotton mills, coal mining, and in my town's case, the steel industry. There are two rooms downstairs, and two bedrooms upstairs, with one reduced in size to make room for a bathroom, as the houses predate indoor plumbing. It follows the usual pattern and is a mirror image of my parents' house, situated next door.

"Thanks love. Ooh, blue today. It suits you." Gran smiles as she takes the china cup I offer.

"Thanks, Gran." She's referring to my nails. I like to have a splash of colour now and then. I'd paint them more often, but the paint remover I use at work acts as an effective nail-polish remover, so I don't usually bother. This weekend I'd given in to the urge.

"Now tell me what has you watching your phone and sighing." She directs her shrewd gaze at me.

"I wasn't sighing," I protest. I truly wasn't. I would have remembered if I were. Gran smirks and I ignore it.

"I just wanted to know how it went today. Darcy had a big

competition to qualify for the Nationals. It's not like him to not get back to me."

"I'm sure everything is fine, dear. Why aren't you dancing today? You do competitions as well, don't you?"

"Not at this level, Gran. This is for the Nationals. I'm nowhere near good enough to go to them."

"I'm sure you are Nicholas." She gives me a knowing smile and I love her confidence in me. It's misplaced, of course. I'm an alright dancer, but I do it for the joy of it. I don't practise enough to be at the standard required for the top competitions. If I'd been born into that life, like Darcy, maybe it would be different. It was due to my gran that I dance at all, something I'll be eternally grateful to her for. I'd been asking for lessons for a long time, but had never been allowed.

"It's just a phase," and, *"I can't understand why you want to waste your time on this stuff."*

No, my parents didn't understand at all. How I loved the music, the movement, and the costumes. Gran had given me some money for my birthday when I was twelve years old and I'd asked for dance lessons. I'd been surprised that my parents had agreed, and I think they thought I would get it out of my system. But as soon as I'd had a taste, I wanted more.

I'd bugged them for more dance lessons after that, but the only answer I received was, *"I'm not paying for dance lessons,"* or, *"We don't have the money for those."* It was true, my parents weren't well off. My father had had to find his own way after losing his job at the steelworks. He set himself up as a painter and decorator, while my mum was working part-time as a school dinner lady. Times were hard. I knew that, but I rarely asked for anything. In the end, I'd got myself a paper round to pay for my lessons. They'd allowed that, probably pleased that I was industrious enough to find my own way. My dad wasn't deliberately cruel, he just didn't understand what appeal it held for me. It was outside his experience. There is a part of me that wonders whether the money would have been found if I'd asked for football lessons. Football was something my dad understood—something he considered worthwhile.

The house phone cuts shrilly through the quiet—three rings, my mum's signal. Time to fetch my dad from the club. Sunday dinner is nearly ready. She's just next door and could've just hollered, but that wasn't my mum's way.

"I've just got to go to the club. I'll be back soon with your dinner," I say to Gran, rising. She could come round to ours to eat her dinner, but she isn't as mobile as she used to be and finds the steps down from the house too much of a trial. That's the problem with living on a steep hill. Accessibility wasn't a consideration when the houses were built. It'll only be a matter of time before she needs to move somewhere better suited for her needs, like a bungalow, but she's trying to be independent and won't be rushed into it, nor do I want her to be anywhere else but next door.

I give her shoulder a squeeze, then pick up the tray of teacups and take it through to the kitchen before heading out. A cold wind whips round, and I pull my jacket tighter to me. The weak spring sunshine is unable to counter the chill. I look across the valley at the woodland and hills beyond as I head down the road to the club, already knowing my dad will complain about the walk back up.

It's quite a bit later when my phone finally buzzes in my pocket. I'm washing up after dinner when I feel the vibration. I dry my hands and head upstairs to my room. My stomach churns as I take out my phone to view the message. I don't know why I feel this way. Darcy and I message each other often, almost every day. It's what best friends do. And there are often long gaps between messages if we're busy, so I have no idea why this one seems so important, or why I've been in a state of nervous tension all day. It doesn't make any sense. I put it down to the fact that the competition is important to Darcy, and as his best friend, I'm always pleased for him when he does well. I want him to do well. I'd sent off some supportive messages to him this morning, before the competition. But still, to wait this long after something so huge is unusual. It isn't like him to be silent, and the knot of worry that's been sitting in my stomach all afternoon is now throwing itself around, like a washing machine on an intensive spin cycle.

Darcy: We came second, we got through to the Nationals.

Nick: That's fantastic D, I said you could do it.

Tomorrow we can celebrate.

Darcy: . . .

I watch as the three dots dance on my screen, disappearing and reappearing, bouncing up and down, creating their own form of torture. I don't know if Darcy is typing and erasing, or if it's a really long message. I stare at the screen. Gran is right, it doesn't make any difference, but that doesn't mean I'm not willing the message to appear. In the end, it's a simple message.

Darcy: I can't go to the Nationals.

I explode up off the bed in surprise, cursing loudly and shooting off a message that echoes what I just shouted.

Nick: WTF!!!

An icy hand of uneasiness traces its finger down my spine. Has something happened? Is this why it took him so long to answer? It's amazing, the horrendous scenarios a brain can conjure up in the briefest slivers of time. Within seconds, I've imagined the worst, and given in to some fantastical notion that there's been some sort of accident on the drive back up, resulting in Darcy never being able to dance again. That he's lost all his family. I try to control the shakes that my hands have taken on and send a text back. My fingers don't work and I have to delete several letters before I manage to type a coherent message.

Nick: What happened? Are you ok? Is everyone ok? Tell me you're ok?

My heart rate returns to something close to normal, but it takes a moment for me to draw a steady breath. I'm not willing at the moment to examine why my brain went for the worst-case scenario and I still need to know the details, so I reply quickly.

I take a moment to breathe and compose myself, letting the overwhelming sense of relief seep through me. After what I'd conjured up, this seems a trivial thing, but I know the blow to Darcy will be deep. We've talked about it enough. I remember how, when he talks about it, his eyes light up with a brilliance that shows the green of his irises, like polished sea glass. I dismiss the image, confused why my best friend's eyes are something that lingers with me.

I hate the tone of his text. His quiet resignation. But that's Darcy. He'll be hurting inside, but he always puts on a brave face. Sometimes I wish he'd let his feelings out, but I wonder if he's just spent too long hiding them. His mum has outbursts enough for the both of them. I can just imagine what the journey back would have been like for him. We text for a little longer. He doesn't seem hopeful that he can find anyone else, and I don't blame him. Great dancing partners don't grow on trees. I'm looking forward to seeing him tomorrow so I can see how he's really doing.

Chapter 3

Nick

"You done in here?" My dad pokes his head round the door of the room I'm working in.

"Just a few more minutes." I run the brush along the last section of skirting board. Painting and decorating might not be exciting, but it's a job, and better than working at a fast-food drive-through or something. I didn't get good enough grades to go on to further education, let alone university, though if I had, I would've been the first in my family to do so. We Richardsons are working-class stock, the backbone of Britain, my dad would say, and he's proud of that. We don't need fancy bits of paper to get by.

For as long as I can remember, at least since I discovered dancing, that was all I'd wanted to do when I grew up. But as much as we Richardsons don't get university degrees, we also don't work in the arts. I had a few blazing rows about that one with my dad. It wasn't all about him wanting to make sure I had a proper job. For him, it was about pride. He'd followed his father and grandfather into steelmaking, and then had to pick himself up after redundancy from the industry he'd thought he had a job in for life. He'd managed to forge himself a new future as a painter and decorator. I remember that he never had a prouder moment than when he added "and Son" to his business cards and the signwriting on his van. He'd created a legacy for me, and enjoyed thumbing his nose at an industry that had cast him out. That he worked hard meant he could also hold his head up high in the Working Men's Club, where he spent a lot of his spare time.

For me though, I still want to dance, but sometimes, we don't get to do everything we want, and so I content myself with going as often as I can.

I finish the last brush stroke and, picking up my stuff, I head out to the van. I don't mind the work. It isn't hard, and I can usually listen to music on my earbuds. But today I'm restless. I want the working day to be over so I can go see Darcy. To find out how he really feels. I've never been to the Nationals, even just to watch, as they're held in different cities every year. But this year they're being held here, in Sheffield, at the City Hall. For Darcy to not even be able to compete in his home city would be an even bigger blow. I'm looking forward to watching the big competition, the most prestigious of the dancing calendar, and not being able to see Darcy is a disappointment to me, too.

I take a quick shower to wash off the grime of the day, scrubbing at the paint splatters I invariably end up covered in. I lament my nail polish is already disappearing. Usually, I can't stand seeing it chipped and worn and would remove it completely, but today I have more pressing things on my mind. Same with my hair. It's super short at the sides—sometimes I shave it—but the top is long and I usually style it over my eyes. Today, though, I grab a beanie and shove it on. It'll have to do.

"Don't you want any tea, love?" my mum calls, as I clatter down the steep, narrow staircase and into the kitchen, pulling my coat on as I go.

"I'll grab something later." I lean down and press a kiss on her cheek before pulling open the back door. I see Mrs Smith, our neighbour on the other side of Gran, opening our back gate into the yard. No one uses their front door round here. The front door usually means official business, or trouble, as my dad calls it. Everyone uses the back door. We've no garden. Steelworkers, who these houses were built for, didn't have time to garden. The yard was for the privy. Ours has long since gone, with the introduction of indoor plumbing, and the brick building is used as a garden shed and the washing line. The wall between our yard and Gran's had been removed years ago, and my mum makes use of the larger space by filling it with flower pots. The daffodils have more or less finished, but the crocuses are just starting to show themselves. There's also a table and chairs—a metal bistro set that one of Dad's customers was throwing out to make way for a more modern wicker set. Dad painted it in bright colours, and it lends a cheery feel to the yard.

"Hi Mrs Smith." I call out to her from the top step. No doubt she's heading round for a brew and a gossip with my mum.

"Hello, young Nick." She'd started calling me "young Nick" when I would do odd jobs for her as a young boy—another way I could earn a bit towards paying for dance lessons. But I think she'll be calling me young Nick forever, even though I tower over her now. "You still dancing?"

"Yes Mrs Smith, I am." When I bounce down the steps, grab her hands, and twirl her around, she gives a girlish giggle. "Sorry, gotta dash. Mum's inside if you want her." I release her and turn towards Gran's house.

Mrs Smith giggles again and heads up our back steps, calling out, "Doreen, you'll never guess who I saw earlier." I laugh at the comfortable predictability of it. I quickly check that Gran has everything she needs until Mum or Dad come round later, and head down the road.

I let the steepness of the hill carry me down at a fast walk, to the bus stop on the main road at the bottom. I can drive, but I don't own a car. We only have Dad's work van and he doesn't often let me borrow it. I'm saving all my money to try to buy a house so I can move out. It's a bit crowded at my parents' with three adults in that space. I know that larger families did and still do occupy them, but it still seems like we all live on top of each other, and that's one of the reasons I spend so much time out of the house or at Gran's place. It's also another reason why I don't date. Not seriously, anyway. Not, bringing-a-guy-home type of seriousness. If I need to scratch an itch, I'll go out to a nightclub. Maybe hook up there or at his place, if he has one. Not that I've found anyone I would want to take home with me yet, but then I don't look either. Maybe when I save up enough money for a deposit and get my own place, I can think about it then. So, I manage without a car. We have a good bus service in the city anyway, so it's not too much of an issue, and the bus that runs along the bottom of our street takes me to the dance school, anyway. I can walk it, but it takes thirty minutes and I don't want the journey to be any longer than necessary. I'll most likely walk back later, though, if it's after the last bus has run.

I say hello to the couple of people also waiting for the bus, and they ask how I am and how my mum is, promising to call round soon. No doubt she'll be going to see them, too. The friends' network in our little suburb is very active.

Luckily, the bus is on time and we pile on. I sit, willing it to go faster, and ignore my knee jiggling in impatience. As soon as it stops at the right place, I erupt from it and walk as fast as I can up the road to the Franklin School of Dance.

The Franklins *are* dance, certainly in this corner of the city, and are well known throughout the whole county. Sheila and Arnold Franklin had been very successful dancers in their youth, and set up the school when they settled down to start a family. The building was erected in the seventies and is at one end of a small parade of shops. It has a couple of large dance studio rooms, a kitchen, toilets and showers, and a reception room with a small office off it. Upstairs is a large apartment that the Franklins—Sheila, Arnold, and Darcy— live in. Darcy's sister Claire, older than him by a couple of years, lives elsewhere in the city. She'd decided that she wasn't going to stay in the family business of dance, and went to work for a media and events company. The shops on the parade are a strange mix of convenience store, pizza place, hairdresser, and vape shop. The rest are empty or boarded up. It has certainly passed its heyday.

"Nick! Nick!" Sheila's wail greets me as I enter the reception room looking for Darcy and only finding his mum instead. "What are we going to do?"

"I don't know," I reply. "Where's Darcy?"

"In his room, sulking. Yes, go talk some sense into him. He says he won't dance at the Nationals even if we do find another partner for him. Tell him he must dance." I frown at her pushiness, but it's not really surprising. I head towards the door marked "Private," that leads upstairs. I close it behind me with Sheila's final remark following me though. "And tell him there's a class in ten minutes."

I track Darcy down in his room. He, too, is still living at home, part of the same generation for whom home ownership seems unattainable. He is sitting on his bed, knees drawn up, his bear—Bearlero—locked tightly in his arms. I bought it for him a few years ago for his birthday, laughingly telling him he could pretend it was me when I wasn't there. Trust Darcy to name him after a dance. That he went to it for comfort sends a warmth blooming in me. I don't take time to register it, and the feeling is doused by his dull eyes and slumped shoulders. He doesn't even look up as I enter, seemingly staring at a point on the wall opposite. I sit down on the bed next to him, shuffling back to lean against the wall. I put an arm round him and he leans into my side, still not looking at me, still no words. One reason why Darcy is my best friend, apart from our love of dance, is that he doesn't mind this closeness. I'm not sure most straight guys would be okay with their gay friend putting their arms round them and holding them close without thinking something of it. But Darcy has always accepted me for who I am, never questioned it, or my motives. He always seems just as comfortable hugging as I am, and it's never awkward.

He doesn't speak for a long moment, and I don't ask him anything, allowing him the comfort of being tucked into my side, processing his own thoughts.

At length he sighs. "I'm done with all this."

I'm sure he doesn't mean what he's saying. The Darcy I know would rather stop breathing than give up dancing. I squeeze him a little tighter.

"I mean, I just don't think I can go back out there again. I don't feel it anymore."

I look at him and he tilts his head towards me, dejection weighing down the corners of his mouth.

"Give it time. You'll find someone to dance with. It'll work out."

He gives a half-hearted shrug. "Now you sound like my mum."

I slap my hand to my chest. "You wound me, D." It raises a slight chuckle from him. I proceed, in the best imitation I can do of his mum's tinny tones. *"Darcy Franklin, you get back out there and you dance, do you hear me?"*

I see the faintest glimmer of a spark in his eyes, and he presses his lips together as if to suppress a giggle.

"Darcy, get down here now. You have a class." I feel him shudder as her real, steel-honed voice booms up the stairs.

"I could never do it that loudly," I say, and he huffs a small laugh. I take my arm from round his shoulders, scoot forwards on the bed, and then look back at him.

He tips his head back and bangs it against the wall. "Urgh. I really don't feel like doing this right now. Can't they just let me wallow in my misery a little longer?"

That he shows a bit more spirit pleases me, as that's more the Darcy I recognise.

"You know that if you don't appear in approximately thirty seconds, she'll be up here giving you 'the speech,'" I say conspiratorially.

That finally gets me a smile—a small one, but I'll take it. Sheila's speeches are as legendary as they are awful, and always delivered at full volume.

He sighs resignedly and I hold out a hand.

"Come on, I'll help you." I would help anyway. I always do if I'm around. I learned early on that if I stayed around and helped in the classes, I'd get extra dance practice time. Over the years, I've learned both male and female parts, as there were never enough partners to go around and being able to do both helps. I'm almost as much of a fixture at the dance school as the sign above the door. He takes my proffered hand and I pull him up before we head downstairs to stave off his mum coming to find him in person.

Chapter 4

Darcy

I get through the beginners and improvers classes without really taking much in. I certainly don't remember any of them. Except for Nick's help. His unwavering support and ready smile charming everyone, young and old alike. I don't know how he does it. He looks ridiculous dancing in his beanie, which he refuses to remove, claiming his hair isn't fit to be seen. He's always been like that, taking care over his appearance. I'm far more relaxed about mine, unless I'm getting ready for a competition of course, but most days I run my fingers through my hair and that's as good as it gets.

The last customers are leaving, and Mum's just finishing up the private lesson. She's been teaching a couple who are practising for their wedding-day dance. We get a lot of couples like that, wanting to make that first dance memorable on their special day.

Dad has already gone upstairs. The arthritis in his knees prevents him from dancing anymore, so he normally chauffeurs us to competitions, and does a lot of the cooking and other household chores.

"Nick, will you stay for supper?" my mum asks. He often stays for something to eat after classes, but today I see him waver for a second. He probably thinks my mum will keep up her current complaints about Julia and the Nationals. It is likely, so I mouth a "please" at him, and see the corner of his mouth twitch before he turns back to my mum. "I'd love to, Mrs Franklin. It smells delicious. What is it tonight? Is it Mr Franklin's famous mac 'n' cheese?" He's a consummate charmer. My mum leads him upstairs while I lock up the studio. When I join them in the kitchen a few minutes later, he's already sitting on one of the stools at the breakfast bar, beer in hand, talking to my dad about the best way to make cheese sauce. I grab a beer from the fridge and then start setting the table in the dining part of the open-plan living space.

My mum doesn't disappoint in her predictability throughout supper, and continues to prattle on at length about the situation. I don't bother joining in or, even worse, offering an opinion. There's no point, and it just prolongs the diatribe. My shoulders sag as the sombre hues of desolation settle over me again and I stare down at my food, not tasting any of it, until I feel the bump of a knee against my leg. Only Nick is sitting close enough to do that. I look up and he gives me a small smile. My mouth twitches in response and I'm rewarded with a bigger smile. He bumps my leg again, but doesn't move it away this time, and I feel the pressure of it, lending me strength and fortitude. I'm grateful and can finish the rest of my dinner. At length, my mum runs out of breath, or rather, things to say, at least for now.

"What do you think, Nick?" she asks him, and he looks up from his plate, startled, as if he were miles away.

"I . . . err, Mrs Franklin, I think it will all be alright," he offers tentatively. I don't think it matters what he says as long as it's a general agreement.

"Well, we shall see. All that work for nothing, though!" She sits back, looking peeved, and I fear she's gearing up for another round. I can't take any more. I need to get out of here. Do something different for once. I can't listen to it for a moment longer.

I rise and start gathering the empty plates and dishes, taking them over to the dishwasher. I place my hands on the counter and lean heavily on them, taking a few deep breaths. The overwhelming air of perpetual disquiet is more than I can take. I need to get out of the house, to get some air.

"I'm going out," I announce, pushing off from the counter and turning round to face them.

"Out? Where?" my mum exclaims. She isn't concerned about me, more that she'll lose an audience. I pity my dad sometimes, but he always seems content, and I think he likes to spend more time in the kitchen nowadays. It's his sanctuary. He gets up, and brings some more dishes over and sets them on the counter.

"I'll load the dishwasher. You go on out," he says, then leans close and speaks quietly, so only I can hear. "She'll calm down in a few days, don't worry."

"Thanks Dad," I say equally quietly, and he nods in acknowledgement.

Nick rises. "Thank you for supper, Mrs Franklin, Mr Franklin. It was a treat, as always."

"You're welcome dear." My mum smiles at him.

"Next time I'll teach you how to make a red-wine sauce," my dad tells him.

"I'll look forward to it, Mr Franklin," he replies, and we head towards the back door, grabbing coats as we go. The back door leads out onto a small balcony with steps down to the ground level, so we don't have to go back through the studio to get out.

"How do you do that?" I ask, as I follow him down the steps.

"Do what?" he asks.

"Just seem to be able to talk to anyone?"

"I don't know." He shrugs. "I guess I spent so much time as a kid listening to my mum and her friends talk about anything and everything."

I reach the backyard and tip my head back, spreading my arms wide. I embrace the feeling of not being cooped up in the house, listening to my mother go on like a stuck record. I just hope the batteries will wind down soon. I let out a sound —half groan and half cry.

"Do you want to go up to the park and shout it out?" Nick asks.

I agree, and we head on to the street and along the shops.

"Hold on," Nick says when we reach the convenience store, and he ducks inside. I find him in front of the chocolate stand.

"Well, we did leave before dessert." He makes a mock sad face when he catches me watching him and I chuckle. Nick has the worst sweet tooth I know. He hovers over the assortment of chocolates for a few more seconds before selecting a couple of bars and a bag of gummy sweets.

We turn towards the park. At the end of the shops is a piece of wasteland. There's been nothing on it for as long as I can remember, it's just full of overgrown brambles and litter, but now a hoarding has been erected. I stop and look up at what it says. "Land acquired for development," is in large writing across it, along with the developer's name: D. H. Gregory.

"How long has that been there?" I ask.

"I've no idea." Nick stands beside me, the sweets already

open. He offers them and I take a cola bottle. "I've not seen it before." He stuffs a sweet into his mouth.

"Hmm. What do you think they're building?" I muse, mostly just asking out loud.

"Houses probably," Nick offers, seemingly unconcerned. "Aren't the government always going on about how they're going to build so many new homes?"

"I guess." I shrug, dismissing the small, disconcerting feeling I have at just not having noticed it before. "C'mon." I dip a hand into Nick's sweet bag, not at all surprised that they're mostly gone. I've no idea how he can demolish a bag so quickly. I pull out a fried egg and pop it in my mouth, chewing slowly as we make our way to the park.

Dusk has given itself over to full dark as we make our way through the gates and follow the path. We leave the streetlights far behind at the entrance, but we've no need of a light to find our way. We've been following the same route for as long as we've been friends. Our eyes soon adjust to the gloom and we can see well enough. The tarmacked path wends its way through the grassed area, a small copse, and a bridge over a brook until we emerge at the top of a hill that overlooks parts of the city. There is a play park, and we enter it, sitting side by side on a set of swings. We idly swing backwards and forwards for a few minutes, enjoying the silence.

"Ready?" Nick grins at me.

I nod, beaming back at him. We rise and then stand on the swings, bending our knees to push them to get them moving, daring each other to go higher. We've been doing this for years when something has got either of us down, and I feel a warm sense of gratitude that Nick suggested it.

We swing as high as we can, and when we reach the apex of the swing, Nick lets out a howl. The next time, I holler in answer. We continue like that for a while, each cry getting louder and more frenzied, until we sound like a couple of demented madmen. Eventually, I have nothing left, and I let the swing slow until I can jump off. I'm panting and my legs feel wobbly, so I collapse onto the grass for a rest. I lie on my back and hear Nick drop next to me.

"Feel better?" he rasps, clearly as out of breath as me.

"Much better, thank you." I stare up at the sky. There's no cloud cover, so the stars are shining down in all their glory. I love this view. Looking up at something which is far bigger than we are.

"It puts it all in perspective, doesn't it?" I say, suddenly feeling very small and insignificant.

"What does?"

"That." I wave up at the sky. "Out there could be a million other worlds, all full of people just going about their business, or alien races, all exploring and discovering new things. And here we are, a tiny speck on a small world spinning round a ball of fire. I'm worrying about what will happen in a stupid dance competition, when we're just two of a few billion people, clinging to a rock hurtling through space. Everything I do seems so trivial. It feels ridiculous when you think of it, doesn't it?"

"Hey." Nick lifts onto one elbow to look down at me. "Don't you ever think your dreams are unimportant, D. The stars shine brighter knowing you're under them." He takes a breath. "You bring a lot of joy to people. Not only with your dancing but your teaching, too. Allowing people a time in their week when they can forget their troubles. Where they can set aside that they've had a shitty day at work and be someone else for a little while. Never belittle what you do, D."

His words barely register. Instead, I'm struck by his eyes—how they glitter darkly, reflecting the small amount of available light, and looking like they hold the secrets of the galaxy. It feels like I'm noticing them for the first time, and I want to lose myself in their unfathomable depths.

"D? Are you okay?" I blink as his words bring me back to the present, and he has a curious expression on his face.

"Um, yes. I must have spaced out there for a moment." My cheeks heat up as I think he might have caught me looking at him, and I can't explain it to myself, let alone anyone else. I'm glad it's dark, so he doesn't notice the deep shade of red they must be. "Sorry."

"No worries." He's still looking a bit puzzled. Then he smiles and reaches into his pocket, pulling out the chocolate bars he bought earlier and holding them up.

"Which one?" He grins as if it's even a question, and I reach for the Snickers.

"Heathen." He laughs and sinks back onto the grass beside me. The sounds of us eating are the only thing punctuating the silence.

 Chapter 5

Nick

"Doesn't she have any rhythm?" At the sound of the voice whispering in my ear, I turn from watching through the kitchen window that looks out onto one of the studio rooms where Darcy is dancing with a possible replacement for Julia.

"Claire!" I whisper loudly, and she draws me into a hug. I've known Claire as long as I've known Darcy, and although she's not my sister, she's probably the closest I have to one. Having been a fixture at the Franklins' for a long time, I've been treated to the same big-sister teasing that he has.

"How's it going?" she asks, releasing me.

"As you see." I cock a hip and flippantly gesture with my hand towards the window, earning a grin from Claire as she peers out to watch.

"Hmmm." She sounds non-committal, which isn't much like Claire. She normally has an opinion on everything. She's a lot like her mum in some ways, not that she likes to be reminded of that. But far too much like her to remain at the dance school. She'd made it very clear dancing wasn't going to be her career and put herself through university. She now works in media and marketing.

"How many have there been already?"

"One so far. This one, and then there are another three today."

We scoot across the kitchen to the other side, which looks out to the other studio room. The windows slide open and serve as hatches to pass drinks and refreshments straight out into the rooms. Once a month, the dance school hosts a social tea dance for the older generation and endless pots of tea are a necessity.

The other candidates are warming up or talking with whomever they brought along with them. They look alien in their unfamiliarity, and I can't imagine any one of them dancing with Darcy.

"Jeez, she looks older than Mum." Claire points to one of the candidates and giggles. I suppress a laugh and wander back over to the other side to watch Darcy some more. Claire joins me.

"Poor Darcy." She sighs. "Did my mum take it very badly?"

"What do you think?"

She looks at me with a grimace that tells me she knows *exactly* how it's been.

I let out an exaggerated gasp. "Wait? Have you stayed away this week even knowing what she'd be like?"

Claire's sheepish grin tells me I've hit upon the truth. She normally visits a couple of times a week, but I haven't seen her and Darcy hasn't mentioned her visiting at all this week.

"You coward!" I hiss. "You *know* what it's been like."

"I'm sorry, but you know how she is. Just having her hollering down the phone at me was bad enough."

"You don't need to apologise to me, Claire, but you need to say sorry to Darcy." I'm more than miffed with her. She's cut from the same cloth as her mother, thick-skinned, but Darcy is much more like his father, quiet and unassuming, and it's been hard for him. "You knew how this would be. He could have done with some support."

"He had you." Claire shrugs, as if that was enough.

I glare at her as I head to the sink to fill the kettle for a pot of tea. There is nothing as important as being supported by your family, but her words burrow their way into me, nestling deep inside.

Yes, he does have me. I'll always be there for him.

Inadvertently, my thoughts turn to the other night, like they have too many times in the last few days. When we were in the park, I'd been looking down at him. Darcy had stared up at me with the strangest expression on his face and he'd looked so vulnerable, his soul so open, that for a brief moment, I'd wanted to kiss down the white column of his throat.

But that is so very wrong, for lots of reasons. The first is that he's my best friend, and it's not normal to want to kiss your best friend. And he's straight. So wanting to kiss my straight best friend is definitely *not* something I should be doing. I push the thought deep down inside, refusing to allow it any chance of resurfacing. The last thing I want to do is make things awkward between us. Our friendship is the most important thing to me, and there's no way I'm going to ruin it for something that happened in a moment of weakness under a canopy of stars. It's an occurrence I can't let happen again.

Darcy pushes through the door to the kitchen and heads straight to the fridge. After roughly pulling the door open, he grabs a bottle of water, twists off the cap, and downs half of it in one go. It's only then that he turns and sees Claire and me standing by the window.

He narrows his eyes. "How long have you been here?" he directs at Claire.

"Look Darcy, I'm sorry." She walks over to him. "I shouldn't have left Mum to you all week."

"No, you shouldn't." His face darkens, and he continues through clenched teeth. "Have you any idea what it's been like? Well, I guess you do or you would have been here days ago."

"You can handle it," she replies, and he gives her the biggest "are you shitting me" look I've ever seen.

"Well, you're fixing it now, aren't you?" She gestures towards the studio he just exited. He drops his head back and looks towards the ceiling, letting out a wail of exasperation. *"Urgh."*

"That good, huh?" she asks, earning herself another glower. "You can't expect to find someone straight away, or to be immediately in sync with them," she says.

Darcy downs the rest of the water and aims the empty bottle towards the bin. It goes straight in; our hours spent idly throwing things in the trash weren't wasted.

"Now you sound just like Mum." He pushes past her and heads back out to the studio. She screws her face up as she turns back towards me. She looks as if she's about to say something cutting, but I guess the look on my face stops her. She'll get no sympathy from me. I'm always going to take Darcy's side, and she knows that. Instead, she sighs and rejoins me at the window. We watch the next few candidates dancing with Darcy and fall into an agreed but unspoken truce about her behaviour, joining forces to pass comment on the dancers.

"She looks like she's never worn a pair of dance shoes before."

"Can someone actually have two left feet?"

"It's 'grab-a-granny' time."

To be fair, they weren't all bad and certainly not as awful as we made out, but we were just egging each other on to be more outrageous. I was more concerned about Darcy; by the end of it, he wasn't dancing well either. A casual observer probably wouldn't notice though, as he was always step-perfect.

There's a difference between playing a symphony note-perfect, and playing it with the feeling and passion that elevates it into something exceptional.

It's the same with dancing, which is why Darcy is so good. He imbues his dancing with a fluidity and flair that makes him distinctive. I've spent hours watching him, trying to work out how he does it and emulating it for myself. So I can tell when the spark has gone, and he's just going through the motions, even if those movements are still absolutely correct.

Eventually it's over, and Claire and I enter the studio. I wince a little at the volume of the exclamation from Sheila as she spies Claire. I want to talk to Darcy, but I'm caught up in the confusion of ushering the candidates out of the building with promises of being in touch soon to let them know. Sheila locks the front door and shepherds Claire upstairs, keen to have a new audience to tell her woes to. A quiet settles over the studio, the silence a stark reverence in contrast to the cacophony of a few moments previously.

I head back through the kitchen, grab a cold bottle of water, and head out to the studio. Darcy is standing looking out of the window, his posture a depiction of despondency. His shoulders are slumped as if he's curling in on himself. I hold out the bottle of water and he looks at me, a sad smile ghosting across his lips as he takes it and goes back to looking out the window. I reach out with my other hand to rub his neck and stop, hovering my hand just above his nape. It's a gesture I've done dozens of times. I've never shied away from a touch or a hug; it's been a huge part of our friendship. My brain spirals into thinking about *why* I've halted. Am I thinking Darcy might interpret it differently? Do I mean something else with the gesture? I dismiss both thoughts immediately. The first, Darcy has no idea what's been going through my mind, and the second, on the grounds that I'm certainly not allowing any more thoughts along those lines to happen. I take a breath and force my hand onto his neck, giving it a rub, and focusing only on how it makes me feel like a good friend when he leans into it and I feel the knot of tension I detect there begin to ease.

"Thank you," he says after a few minutes, and his grateful smile makes my stomach flutter slightly. "Is it wrong to not want to dance with any of them?"

"I don't know?" I shrug and release his neck, and he starts some shoulder rolls. "What's the problem with them?"

"I can't explain it." He sighs. "It's like we're dancing to a different beat. I didn't feel in tune with any of them."

"It's still early days. If you think of how long you danced with Julia, that harmony didn't happen overnight; it was something you grew together."

"I know, which is why I don't think we'll find anyone suitable in time. I might as well give up the whole idea." A shadow darkens his face and I grab his arm as he walks past me.

"Don't give up, D. There'll be someone for you, you'll see."

"I wish I had your confidence." He huffs wryly. I release my hand and he goes over to the sound system. He punches a few buttons and then looks back at me with a cheeky smile. I love it when he looks like that, and haven't seen enough of it lately. Also, as I know Darcy almost as much as I know myself, I recognise what he's doing.

The first few notes of the song, "Moves like Jagger," reverberate through the room and, as I get into position, Darcy takes his place beside me. He flashes me a smile and I return it with a nod of acknowledgement. This is our song, our dance. Whilst the Franklin School of Dance is renowned for its tuition of ballroom dancing—which is Darcy's and my first love—it's no surprise that we love all forms of dance. There was also the phase we went through as teenagers, of imagining ourselves in a boy band. We developed this dance back then and have occasionally added to it. It's for fun, and always brings me joy to dance. It's not strictly ballroom, though it has some roots in jive and swing; we've incorporated other dance elements into it. It's very much freestyle, and we mostly dance side by side rather than together. We'll often use it as a warm-up, or just to let off steam. Or, like now, when I think Darcy's reason is to loosen up and remember how his body feels when he's dancing for the love of it.

The routine ends with us facing each other, one arm flung out, the other with our fingertips touching. The music dies away and we stand there. My chest is heaving from the exertion and there's a sheen on his brow. Something fizzles between our fingers and there's an expectant charge in the air. I watch him as he looks back at me silently, his expression unreadable. I notice his throat as he swallows, and the overwhelming urge to kiss it returns tenfold. I can't let this happen, and yet I cannot move away. I feel this indescribable pull towards him, and I fight the desire to take that step and discover what his lips taste like, with every fibre of my being. Appalled at the very thought of it, but powerless to do anything to break off. He isn't moving either and his green eyes lock onto mine, a question poised ready to spill forth.

"Darcy, Nick!" Claire's voice cuts through the weight of tension that hangs between us, cleaving it so cleanly I can feel the sharp edges catch on my skin, raising goosebumps. I gulp a breath in like I've been starved of air for a week. I turn away. I can't face Darcy right now, scared he'll see the shame of my thoughts written there.

"Oh, there you both are," she says brightly. "Nick, are you staying?"

"I—I can't. I have to—to go," I stutter, my mind scrambling as I grasp desperately for a coherent sentence. "I have to go do a thing, for, erm . . . my gran."

I walk to the kitchen, not looking back. I grab my hoodie and exit through the back door, allowing my legs to carry me as my brain spirals in a loop that I've just fucked up big time.

Chapter 6

Darcy

"What just happened?" My sister's words barely register.

"Huh?" All I can think is that Nick is leaving and there's a Nick-shaped hole in the shimmering space he just occupied.

"Dad says dinner is ready."

"Huh?" Coherent thought clearly isn't happening right now.

"Food. Darcy. Dinner." Claire stands right in front of me, and as she slowly comes into focus, the sluggishness in my brain diminishes. I shake my head, trying to clear the last of it and concentrate on what she's saying, ignoring the chilling feeling creeping through my body that whatever caused Nick to leave is somehow my fault.

She gives an exasperated sigh and practically drags me upstairs. By the time we reach the top, I can almost function again. Enough to pass without too much comment at least, though I can still see Claire glancing at me, and I don't think I can get much past her. I could be headless and my mum wouldn't notice, and it's not like I've been the most dynamic person all week. But this feels different from the heavy ache that's been gnawing at me since Julia's news. The ponderous uncertainty of my future. This is sharp and spiky and has hooks that snag at my organs with every breath I take.

Luckily, given the activity of the day, I'm not required to comment much, but my mother has an opinion on all the dancers. Whether it be that they're too tall, too short, too old —my sister sniggers at that one—or just that they can't dance well enough. I don't have a great aversion to any of them. It's just that none of them felt right. There wasn't that spark I needed to feel in order to truly love what I do. To give myself over to the rhythm, to feel the beat in my soul. Today I was just dancing; I might as well have been teaching a class. That was, until I put on our song, the dance Nick and I made up together. I want that feeling when I dance, the exhilaration of every cell in your body working in harmony. The rhythm becoming the pulse that flows through your veins. That's what I need if I'm going to win the Nationals, but no one I've danced with has come close.

"I have some news," Claire announces over dessert, cutting Mum off from launching into another round of disparaging dissection of the day's potential dancers. I'm starting to get a headache and mouth a thank you to my sister.

"I've mentioned that Seven Hills Media is covering the Nationals." She waits until she has the attention of all of us. Seven Hills Media is the company my sister works for and they've been contracted for the competition. "Well, the project manager has gone on maternity leave earlier than expected. And . . ." She pauses for dramatic effect. "I've been promoted to take her place. That means I'll be in charge of all the publicity and marketing on the day."

"That's amazing!" I gently punch her arm in a brotherly way, as I'm too far away to hug her.

"That's great news. Well done," Dad says, looking proud. He's a staunch supporter of my sister's decision to do something else with her life. A stance that made for a tense time in our household for a while, as Mum couldn't conceive of anything other than that her children were going to dance. I don't think it was the only reason my sister moved out, but I know it was a contributing factor. I can't blame her for wanting to distance herself and concentrate on her own studies, but it wasn't an option for me. I also wanted to dance, and I was well aware having Sheila Franklin as my mother was an advantage in the dance community, even if there was a price to pay for that.

"So you'll be at the Nationals." Mum looks up. No congratulations that, after just a few years working for the company, my sister has been given a managerial position at a prestigious event. No, my mother only thought of herself. "You could dance with Darcy. Why didn't I think of that before?" She was in full flow now. "That will be perfect. You two can dance together, as you'll be there anyway. And how exciting, to have both my children in the Nationals."

"Mum! Have you been listening?" Claire shouts to make herself heard. "I'm the *project manager*. I'll be far too busy to dance, even if it were allowed—which it isn't because we are the ones organising the media. Any involvement or taking part by any of the employees would be considered an unfair advantage. And even if it were allowed, or I wasn't involved. I'm. Not. Dancing. Not with Darcy, not with anyone. I don't do that anymore!"

"Well, I think you're very mean." Mum sounds peevish. "I was just asking you to help your brother out. This was his year. And think of me. Am I going to have no children dancing at the one event I couldn't win? It's all I ever wanted for you and it's here in our city. It was all supposed to be so perfect." She descends into a wail, resting her head in her hands and rubbing her temples. I'm reminded that this too was a reason Claire moved out; they often locked horns, usually over the dinner table.

"Urgh." My sister pushes her chair back from the table and rises. "Now I remember why I didn't come back." She storms out the kitchen door, the force of her exit causing it to bang an exclamation mark to her outburst before it swings back into place.

My dad rises to fetch my now-snivelling mum a glass of water. In the ensuing uneasy calm, the air hangs, cloying and oppressive. I don't want to go out onto the balcony where my sister is no doubt pacing, because I'll be treated to her thoughts on the subject—like mother, like daughter—so I retreat to my room.

I curl up on my bed, trying not to feel anything and feeling far too much. I have a family at war with each other, a dream that will never happen, and a friend who . . .

Who, what?

The clash of the last few minutes has at least successfully prevented me from pondering Nick, but now that I'm alone, the events from earlier flood back to me.

I felt alive when we danced. Maybe it was because it's familiar and comfortable to me, but somehow, it felt different. Maybe it was just a welcome relief after dancing all day with indifferent partners, but it also felt much more than that. It was something ethereal that I couldn't grasp, like chasing fireflies, the meaning just beyond the tips of my fingers.

I replay the last few moments of the dance in my head. We'd finished dancing and, I don't know how, but I felt the same sensation as I had the other night in the park. I hadn't been able to look away from Nick, lost in his aura. My fingers had tingled where they'd touched his. My mouth had dried out, and I'd swallowed, trying to moisten it. I'd been about to ask something; I can't remember what it was now. Then Claire had appeared and Nick had left like he couldn't stand to be in my presence any longer. I don't know what I did, but the feeling still digs its claws into me.

There's a knock on my door.

"Go away," I croak, but it's my sister, so she ignores it.

"Hey." She enters the room and sits down on the bed next to me. "What's up?"

"I don't know." I shrug, picking at the fur on Bearlero, only now aware that I'd been squeezing him tight for comfort.

"I'm sorry about that." She jerks her head towards the door, referring to the earlier argument. "But you know how she is and I couldn't stand it anymore. She just wasn't listening."

"You know how important this is to her." I try to stand up for Mum, at least a little.

"I know, but it doesn't give her the right to try to organise us into making it happen by whatever means necessary."

I smile in response as I agree with her.

"I'm going now. Want to walk me to the bus stop?" she asks, and I sit up. Some fresh air might help.

"Sure."

I grab my jacket, as there's still too much of a bite in the spring air to go without, and we use the balcony to exit to ground level.

As we walk along the parade of shops, I see that another one of them has shut—the vape shop. The windows are boarded up, and a sign's been erected. It says it's "Under Development," by the same company that's on the hoarding on the waste ground.

"Have you seen this?" I ask Claire, but she shrugs.

"Things change all the time. It's about time someone did this area up." I guess it doesn't affect her where she lives. I dismiss it. I have enough to worry about right now.

"So, what's happening with you and Nick?" She springs the question on me out of nowhere.

"Um, nothing." I don't know where she's going with this, and as I'm also confused, I decide to go for a casual response.

"Hmm, it didn't look like nothing," she drops in.

"We were just dancing," I offer. Well, it *is* the truth.

"I didn't see any dancing," she says slyly. "I saw you looking at him like he was a long, cool drink on a hot summer's day."

"What? No!" Whatever she's implying is definitely not a thing. I'm not sure what *did* happen, but it wasn't that. Because that . . . that implies I fancy my best friend and it certainly isn't anything like that. I ignore the hollowing sensation in my stomach that her words invoke. It's not happening.

I hope she drops it, but then, she is my sister, and she has the tenacity of a tiger whose jaws have locked onto their prey.

"Are you and Nick . . . ?" She just leaves the sentence hanging, unfinished and heavy with suggestion.

"No, no, and no." Now I'm nearly shouting at her. We reach the bus stop and thankfully there's no one else waiting. She smirks at me.

"You know," she says softly. "I had my money on you and Nick getting together long before this. It's about time."

"That is *so* not happening. Why would you even think that?" I'm saying the words, but my insides are churning in uncertainty.

"Oh, I'm sure you've been in love with him since you were sixteen."

"You're ridiculous," I spit out, and because I don't want to hear any more, I walk away and leave her at the bus stop.

Whatever she says isn't true. I am not even into guys. Absolutely not.

Oh God, a dreadful notion surges through me. Does he think I looked at him like that? Does he think I fancy him? I know Nick is good looking, that's a given, and he is lovely and charming. He could have anyone he wanted—and probably does. Does he think that I want that from him? That's so messed up. He's my best friend. Okay, there have been a couple of strange moments lately, but surely that's just the stress I'm under right now. But if he thought that, then no wonder he couldn't get out of there fast enough. I've scared him off. I walk home with heavy steps, wondering how to make right the things I've messed up between us.

Chapter 7

Nick

I pace my room for the umpteenth time. I feel cooped up in here, but I don't know what to do with myself. I'd spent some time with my gran, but I wasn't good company. Everything inside feels discordant, like a puzzle where the pieces have been fitted together incorrectly. I cannot be having these feelings about my best friend. It's not fair to him. There must be something wrong with me.

Perhaps it's because I haven't been with anyone for a while. Perhaps all I need is some dick. Pent-up sexual frustration, and I focus on my best friend. It's sick, really. It's been a long time since I've been out and had a hook-up. That's what I need to get this out of my system.

I pick up my phone and punch out a message to Riley, one of my friends I met through going to the club. He and his boyfriend Kieran are probably my closest friends, apart from Darcy.

Nick: Are you guys going to be at Brazen tonight?

I wait a few minutes for a reply.

Riley: OMG! Nick, is that you? I thought you'd fallen off the face of the planet

Nick: Haha. Still around, just been a bit busy

Riley: Whatevs

Riley: Yeah we'll be there from ten. Kieran says hi

Nick: Say hi back. I'll see you later

I feel better now that I have a plan. It's simple. Go out, get some dick. Be able to face my best friend again without embarrassing myself.

I shower thoroughly and choose my clothes carefully. White skintight jeans and a netted tank top in blue. I deliberate about underwear. If I'm going out, I like to wear lace. I have some nice lacy and silky pairs. It was embarrassing the day that my mum found them. Living in a house like this, it's difficult to have secrets, and my mum had gone ferreting around in my room for some washing. I remember coming home from work one day and she followed me into my room when I went to get changed.

"Mum, I need to get showered. I'm going out in a bit."

"Are you going to wear these?" She held up some lacy black briefs. My face heated to what felt like a hundred degrees as I snatched them out of her hand.

"Mum!" I was appalled she'd found them, as I thought I'd hidden them well. I had no idea what to say to her. I was eighteen at the time and not as comfortable with myself as I am now.

"I have two things to say," she said, leaning against my door frame. I remember looking at her, horrified and scared.

"One. Probably best to not let your father know. This might be a step too far." She was right. He'd accepted I was gay in his own, quiet way. Sometimes it's hard to know what he's thinking, but he doesn't mention it and I don't flaunt it. I know lots of friends who'd had much worse experiences, including being kicked out and cut off from their families, so I didn't push it.

"And two, don't wear these, love. They feel cheap, like you've got them off the market. Let me get you something nice, eh?"

I was still embarrassed, but I remember sagging onto my bed and my mum sitting next to me rubbing my back while I sobbed onto her shoulder. It was the first time I'd known she fully accepted me. I think that for the two years after I'd come out to them, I'd been holding in a lot of tension, wondering if they were hoping I'd get over it, or if it was just a phase, which had been a refrain I'd heard a lot as a child. From then on, I knew my mum was on my side, and whilst I didn't shove it in my dad's face, I didn't feel I had to hide who I was, tiptoeing around their disapproval.

My gran was a different matter entirely. I remember telling her I was gay and her reply was, "Of course you are dear. Now go put the kettle on, and we'll have the blue china today to celebrate as I'm glad you've finally told me." I must have stared at her for a full minute with my mouth open before she gave me her trademark grin and said, "I think we'll have the chocolate biscuits as well, don't you?" And that had been that. She told me later that she'd known for a long time. I wish she'd told me. It might have saved me a lot of teenage angst.

In the end, I don't bother with underwear. I'm not going to find someone who'll appreciate it, and it's just going to get in the way of what I have planned and slow me down.

I style my hair, applying wax to get it to fall over one eye and adding spray to get it to hold. I notice the small piece of sea glass I have in a trinket bowl on the dresser. I pick it up and run my fingers over it, remembering when Darcy had given it to me, having brought it back from a visit to a beach. The Franklins don't have holidays, so he'd have been in a competition. Most likely Blackpool, Brighton, or Bournemouth. I don't know where, since they all sound the same to me. I remember telling him it's the exact colour of his eyes, and how they shone when I said so. I sigh and place it back in the bowl, reminding myself that I'm doing this to preserve my friendship, and ignoring the slight unease I feel in my stomach. I return to getting ready by applying some makeup—eyeliner and some blue round my eyes. I add a bit of glitter to my cheeks, and some lip gloss. I even paint my nails: neon yellow to show up in the dark club. I haven't been to Brazen for a few months, so Riley's comment was justified, but I feel excited. It's just what I need right now.

My friends are creatures of habit, so I know exactly where I'll find them when I enter the club. Kieran squeals and launches himself at me, and I hug him back. Perhaps it has been too long. Kieran is short and slim, with ginger curls and a freckled nose. He looks a lot younger than his twenty-three years. Riley, in contrast, is tall and well built, a bear of a guy. He gives me a quick hug and then disappears for a few minutes, reappearing holding three bright blue drinks. I don't usually drink alcohol when I'm out, preferring water because I need to take in a lot of fluids as I dance a lot. But maybe it wouldn't hurt to dull the edges a little tonight. It's sweet and syrupy, which is good, as I prefer them that way.

It's difficult to be heard over the music but we manage to shout our latest news to each other. Riley says that when the weather is a bit warmer, they're planning a trip up to the Slippery Stones—a natural swimming pool in Peak National Park, just a short drive out of the city—and asks me to join them. I love it up there and haven't been for a while. I nod enthusiastically in agreement. Then I shake my head when Riley offers to fetch another drink. Instead, I drag my friends to the dance floor. I spend the next couple of hours just giving myself over to the beat of the music, the heat, the darkness, and the writhing bodies. I'm enjoying myself, but I haven't forgotten my main purpose. A couple of people dance with me; one of them, a tall guy probably in his thirties, jerks his head and gives me a smile. I understand his invitation well enough. He's handsome, but not what I'm looking for tonight. I shake my head and he smiles and shrugs, turning back to the melee to try his luck somewhere else. I get caught up in the music again for a while before I notice someone is dancing with me. He's dark haired, a few inches shorter than me, and looks *very* fine in his shorts and tight T-shirt. He mirrors my moves for a while, dancing closer and closer. He turns and pushes his ass towards me, so I grab his hips. He flashes me a cute grin over his shoulder and deliberately pushes back into me, both of us gyrating in sync to the music. The effect of his ass rubbing against me and the increased friction from wearing no underwear soon has me very hard. Something that's not lost on him as he looks back at me again with a suggestive smile. This is exactly what I want—some easy, no-strings way to release my tension. I give him a nod and he takes my hand as we head towards the bathrooms. Thankfully, there's a cubicle free, as I don't want to spend time canoodling or, even worse, having to make conversation while we wait. I push him inside and close the door behind us, leaning back against the door. My breathing is fast and shallow, partly from the vigorous dancing, but also in anticipation. I tip my head back as he drops to his knees, licking his lips. This is definitely what I need. He undoes my jeans and releases my cock. It had been uncomfortable in my tight jeans and I hum in contentment that it feels good to free it.

He chuckles. "Mmm commando, I like it." I look down at him. He flickers his eyes up at me, his mouth heading straight to take me in.

Time. Stands. Still.

His eyes are green and opalescent, not the bright sea glass of my dreams. I hadn't noticed the colour in the darkness of the dance floor, but here, under the harshness of the strip light, all is laid bare. I can see what I'm doing in stark reality, with no filters, and it feels very wrong, like the high-pitched wail of a tuneless violin.

My chest constricts and I can't draw in air.

I push his head away from me, not wanting him anywhere near me. I scramble to push my cock back into my jeans whilst spinning round, fumbling with the door lock in my haste to get out of there.

I barely register his shout. A pissed-off call of, "*You fucking tease!*" I can't blame him, but I don't turn back. Instead, I push through the crowds, feeling like I'm trying to move underwater. Eventually, I burst out of the entrance and into the street. I feel groggy, and I use the wall of the building as support until I reach an alleyway that runs along the side. I bend over, hands on my knees, and lose my dinner and the sweet blue drink, which doesn't taste half as nice coming back up. Once I've lost the contents of my stomach, I lean on the side of the cool stone building. I feel like shit and just want to go home. I head out onto the street to look for a taxi, and once inside, fire off a quick message to Riley. He sends one back that'd he'd seen me disappear and guessed I was having a good time. I throw my phone down on the seat next to me. I haven't the energy to explain right now.

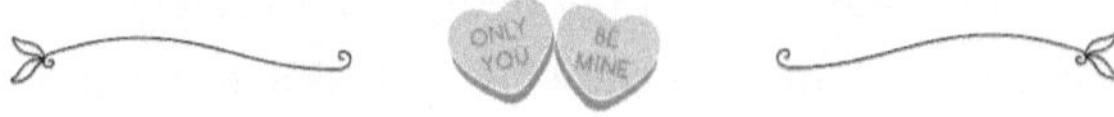

But what can I explain? Who runs out on getting their cock sucked? A dickhead, that's who. All I could think of at that moment was Darcy. Darcy and his clear green eyes, even though there's never going to be a time when he looks at me like that. The shock I felt was that it was him I wanted. At that moment, I wanted Darcy to be the one on his knees before me. Anyone else felt like I was cheating on him.

The taxi pulls up outside my house, and I pay the driver. I try to be as quiet as possible as I unlock the back door. I pull my clothes off and throw them in the wash basket, stepping into the shower to try to scrub the feeling of repulsion off my body. I'm disgusted at the truth that I want my best friend and almost cheated on a relationship we can never have. I climb into bed feeling no better, but at least my skin no longer crawls.

I toss and turn for at least an hour, sleep drawing further and further away. As much as I try not to think of Darcy, the more difficult it becomes, and in my weakness, the tender and sweet moments creep up on me. They lie in wait for me, showing me a technicolour movie of our more memorable moments every time I close my eyes. My cock, answering only to the base need inside me that wants Darcy, is hard and aching. My head fights back, as there is no way I'm rubbing one out over my best friend. Sleep eludes me, mocking my refusal to give in. I struggle to lie in a comfortable position while my head battles with my body. Time stretches and I lie on my back, rigid, my jaw clenched, refusing to touch myself. In the end, something else takes over and, in an attempt to find some comfort, I turn over and punch my pillow in desperation. The next minute I'm on my knees, head in my pillow, my hand wrapped round my cock, powerless to stop myself now I've started. I squeeze my eyes shut, my pillow dampening from the tears as I try to not hear my slapping flesh painting the sound of my failure. Release comes quickly, and I groan piteously, exhaustion claiming me as I collapse into a pool of self-loathing.

Chapter 8

Darcy

"Darcy, are you even listening to me?" My mum's pitch rises when she's stressed, and she's right, I'm not listening. "The first class is in half an hour. You need to be ready."

I return to pushing soggy cereal round my bowl. I slept badly last night, Claire's words reverberating round my head. I'd been adamant that what she said was nonsense, but somewhere in the night, or it could have been the early hours of the morning as I'd lost track of time, something shifted. I don't know what, why, or how, but it's like I'm viewing my life through a prism and the aspects of it are being refracted at different wavelengths into a spectrum of colours.

Not that it helps, as confusion circles me like a prowling wolf, waiting to pounce on another level of uncertainty of the truth. I abandon breakfast; the thought of eating makes me feel nauseous. Instead, I shower and get ready, hoping that a morning of teaching classes will distract me from my thoughts.

Whilst it keeps me occupied, it does nothing to diminish my being on high alert, nerves stretched like piano wire. Every time the door opens, I'm hit with a duality of hope and dread.

Hope that Nick appears, as there's nothing more I want than for him to come tell me everything is all right as he's done for me time after time.

Dread that he will never come back and I've lost him. This thought opens a chasm of ache in my chest that widens every time the door goes and it isn't Nick.

"Will you show me that again, please?" I pull my thoughts back to the guy standing in front of me. Justin. He and his partner, Mark, have been coming to classes for a few weeks now.

"I'm sorry," I say, apologising, and admonishing myself for being unprofessional. I stand by his side and slowly show him the step again.

"Thank you." He tries again, getting it this time, and I help the next couple.

The class finishes and I'm sure Nick isn't going to appear, though feeble hope has my eyes darting to the door as the clients exit.

"Can we ask you something?" It's Justin who's trying to gain my attention again. He and Mark are holding hands, looking excited.

"Sure, what is it?"

"Would it be possible for us to have private lessons? We're enjoying these, but we're getting married soon, and we'd like to do something special for our first dance."

"Congratulations, and of course we can help with that." They look good together and I like the idea of teaching them a dance routine. Normally, I'd hand the special clients over to my mum, but something makes me want to keep Justin and Mark for myself. I open the appointment diary, noticing that it looks quite empty. Normally, it's hard to fit extra clients in and we've been known to have a waitlist. As it is, I pencil in an appointment for a couple of days' time.

I lock the door after them when they leave, and go upstairs. I still can't stomach food, so I head to my room instead. The atmosphere feels oppressive, and for once, I wish I could get away from this place and leave it all behind for a while. A look out the window and all thoughts of going out for fresh air are ruined. The weather has turned from the promise of spring in the last few days, and now the clouds are dark and rain tracks its way down the windows. I stare out at the rain for a while; the weather matches my mood, but I can't settle. I take out my phone and look at it, willing it to do something, angry at it when it doesn't. I fling myself onto my bed, staring up at the ceiling for a while. My phone remains silent. I grab my earbuds and select "shuffle" on my playlist. It seems only fitting that the first song up is "The Weeping Song."

I'm still confused about a lot of stuff, except for one thing: I *need* Nick. I'd like to see and talk to him, but I need to at least hear from him, even if it's just to tell me to go away. I value our friendship above all else.

With that certainty strengthening me, I reach for my phone and tap out a message.

Darcy: Hey

Chapter 9

Nick

When I eventually gain consciousness, I feel no better. In many ways, I feel much worse.

I grab my phone, and my first disappointment is that there are no messages. I don't know why I thought there might be some, but maybe a tiny nugget of hope deep inside thinks this is salvageable and things can be normal again. The second cause for chagrin is that it's one o'clock in the afternoon. Which makes the first reason cut even deeper. I hate sleeping the day away; I'm an early riser and like to be occupied. A work ethic I've inherited from my dad no doubt. Sleeping past nine a.m. usually makes me feel groggy, with an overwhelming sense of being behind on something for the rest of the day. I contemplate giving up completely and staying where I am until tomorrow. But also, when I'm awake, that's it. No going back to sleep for me. There's also the problem that I'm stuck to the bedsheets. *Urgh.* I peel myself off them, strip the bed, and shower.

Peering into the mirror, I see I look like shit. Well, at least it's an outward sign of how I'm feeling right now. I clean my teeth to try to eliminate the sour taste in my mouth, but it's only partly successful.

I notice my nails, their neon brightness a gaudy reminder of a poor decision. I remove the colour before heading downstairs.

"Ah, there you are, love." My mum looks up from where she's checking the Sunday roast in the oven. The smell of the cooking meat and fat brings up a wave of bile that I swallow back down.

"Hi, Mum."

"I didn't hear you come in last night, so it must have been late. I looked in on you earlier, and you were dead to the world so I let you sleep. Did you have a good night?"

"Hmmm." I grunt a non-committal answer, hoping she doesn't require a real answer.

"Do you want anything to eat, love?" She smiles at me. It's a comforting smile, and I would appreciate it if I could be comforted right now.

"Maybe later." She's used to me being out, usually at the dance school, so I know that it's not a problem for me to have leftovers later.

"Okay. Will you fetch your dad then, please?"

"Is he at the club?" I didn't fancy a walk down the hill and back.

"He's next door. Gran had a leaking tap he said he'd fix for her."

I nod and go to the back door. My body feels uncoordinated, so I force it to negotiate the steps, managing them successfully. The fact that I consider using some steps as a small win today shows how low I've sunk. But movement is helping and I step up to Gran's back door, feeling at least more together.

My dad is just finishing up fixing the leak and I despatch him back home, following him to collect some dinner for my gran.

I place it on the table for her in the kitchen, and fetch her a drink and some cutlery. I'm still not hungry so I go into the front room and sink onto her couch, pulling out my phone. Still no messages.

Eventually, I hear the kettle boiling, and Gran makes her way through from the kitchen.

"Would you make the tea, dear?" she says before she sits in her favourite armchair.

"Of course." It'll give me something to do, anyway.

"And bring the biscuit tin. I baked some cookies this morning," she calls after me. Another layer of irritation with myself adds to my dark mood. I love baking cookies with Gran and I could have helped her this morning. Her chocolate chip oat cookies are my favourite.

I fill the teapot, set out the china cups, add the biscuit tin to the tray, and take it through. I put it down on the table and pour her a cup. I pour a cup for myself, grab a cookie, and then slump back onto the couch. Gran takes a sip of her tea and then sets the cup down.

"What is it?" She turns her keen eyes on me.

"I'm fine," I mumble, refusing to look at her.

"Nicholas, don't you lie to me. Something's hurting you, and keeping it bottled up won't help." The stern note in her voice makes me wince.

"Talking about it won't make it any better." I pick at a thread on my jeans and still won't make eye contact with her.

"You never know unless you try." Her tone is softer this time, and I know she's probably right, even though I don't want to talk about it and I can't see a way out of it.

"I think I've messed things up with Darcy." I open with. She's met Darcy several times. When she was more mobile, she'd sometimes come to watch my dance lessons.

"Why do you think that?" she probes.

"Because I can't help myself wanting to be more than just friends. It's become awkward, and I ran out on him yesterday. I can't just act normal around him. It's wrong to want your best friend, but I can't help it, and I hate it." I drop my head into my hands, not wanting her to see the tears that have been close to the surface all day.

"Does Darcy know any of this? How does he feel?" she asks.

"I can't talk to him about it," I whine. She doesn't understand.

"Why not?" The way she asks makes it sound so simple.

"Because then it will make it even more awkward." I sigh. "I just need to get over it so we can go back to being like we were."

"If you told him . . . What are you most afraid of?" Gran continues.

I take a deep breath. "That I'd lose him. He's not like me, Gran. He's not into guys, which makes this so messed up. We couldn't be friends like that, him wondering about me all the time. I can't tell him. I'll get over it and everything can go back to being normal again."

"Then you'll always live in fear," she says.

"What do you mean?" My plan is good. It's the only way.

"You'll always be wondering whether he knows, or if he'll find out. You'll always be afraid to get too close to him. My

Reggie always used to quote an old proverb his grandfather taught him—that a life lived in fear is a life half-lived—you cannot carry on like that, Nicholas."

I don't believe her. I'm not risking it all by telling him. I scowl, ready to dismiss her, when my phone buzzes on the table.

Gran looks at it and then at me, giving me a soft smile.

I snatch it up, cradling it in my hands, almost too nervous to check it now that it has a message.

Darcy: Hey

I breathe a sigh of relief.

Nick: Hey

Darcy: I'm sorry

What does he have to be sorry for? It's *me* that's sorry.

Nick: I'm sorry too

My breath catches, and knowing that I'd made him feel that way by making it weird causes the tears to well up. I respond in our time-honoured way.

I take a deep breath. It's time to get over myself and make this work.

We message for a couple more minutes and I tell him I'll be at the dance school in a couple of days. I feel relieved that we're talking. All I need to do now is make sure it doesn't get weird again.

Chapter 10

Darcy

"Let's try that again," I say, encouraging Justin and Mark back into their starting positions.

They carry on for a few more minutes until Mark sighs.

"I feel like we're just stuck on the same thing. I know we need to practise the basics, and I promise we will." He shoots a grin at his fiancé, who meets it with his own smile. I can't help smiling at the joy they radiate. Mark continues. "But it's hard to see what we're aiming for and how it will all fit together."

"Can we see you do it?" Justin chimes in. I think for a minute, indecision preventing me from moving. I glance towards the door. There is a way, but am I prepared to do it?

Nick arrived earlier, and was now helping my mum with her class. Despite our messages the other day, it was awkward, and we didn't get past a stiff hello before my mum claimed him. I'm hoping we can talk later, but I could do with his help now if Justin and Mark want to see what they're looking to achieve.

"I'll be right back," I say, and before I can change my mind, I head towards the other studio and poke my head round the door.

"Nick, do you have a minute?" He's currently showing an elderly lady how to waltz.

He checks with my mum, who waves him away.

"Please excuse me, Mrs Carter. I'll be back soon." He releases his partner with his trademark charm and a smile, and warmth blooms in my chest as, for a moment, I can see a glimpse of how things have always been for us. How much I've missed that smile and how my sister might have been right. But as he turns towards me, his face becomes guarded and the prism shifts, refracting a different view. I push that away, trying to remain professional for now.

I don't speak, but beckon him to follow me, not trusting what I would say right now. Back in the other studio, I introduce him to Justin and Mark.

"They want us to show them what it looks like."

He nods, his mouth a thin line as I put on some music. I face him and hold up my arms. My heart cinches as I see him hesitate before he moves forward, putting one hand in mine and the other on my shoulder. It starts badly, maybe not enough for Justin and Mark to notice, but we both know, and I see him wince. I call a stop.

"I want to try something for a minute," I tell Justin and Mark. "Can you join us?"

They stand and come over. I pair Justin up with Nick, and I take Mark. "Let's do a few basic steps for a while and then we'll try again."

I'm hoping Nick will loosen up a bit. The dance I'm teaching them is mostly based on the rumba, one of the most sensual of the dances. I resolutely ignore the feeling I have that he'd rather not be in the same room as me. This time, things are better and Nick starts relaxing. Justin says something that makes him laugh, and my chest loosens a bit. Mark is good fun and I start enjoying myself, too.

"Can we watch you again now?" Justin asks when the music ends, and Nicks agrees.

"Oooh, can you dance to our wedding song?" Mark asks excitedly. "That's what we're working towards."

"Of course. What have you selected?"

"Love is in the Air." Mark almost bubbles over with glee. I catch his excitement, as I love the song myself and it's great to dance to.

This time, Nick steps forward without hesitation and I see the glimmer of a smile still on his lips.

This time, as soon as the music starts, we move freely. Everything feels different. It feels . . . right . . . It feels like home. As the song progresses, we become more in tune with each other. With every step we take, I feel more complete. Everything that had been missing with the dancers who'd tried out, is here in this dance with Nick, and I don't want it to end. As the last notes die away, we're facing each other, and I feel the same tingling I'd felt the last time we danced. Nick is looking at me in the same way and the moment seems to stretch.

"Oh, that was wonderful." A clapping sound breaks the spell. I'd forgotten anyone else was in the room, and I turn, almost in a daze, to Justin and Mark.

"That was amazing," Justin says, echoing Mark's words.

Nick thanks them, but excuses himself. I feel the edges of my euphoria dull as he leaves the room, but it feels different from the last time he left, and this time I have a plan. I just need to check something out first.

As soon as Mark and Justin leave, having booked in for another session, I race upstairs and switch on my laptop. Hastily checking out information for the Nationals. I hear the other lesson finishing and clatter back down to the studio. My mum is saying goodbye to the clients. When they've left, she closes the door and calls out.

"Dinner in ten. Darcy, do you want to ask Nick to stay?"

I wonder where he is. I poke my head into the kitchen, but he's not there. I find him in the changing room. He's sitting on a bench, changing into his trainers.

"Hi," I say, keeping my distance but leaning back against the door.

He looks up, but his face is neutral, and I can't read it.

"Hey." He returns to tying his laces.

"How have you been?" I ask, and I'm saddened to see him shrug. We've never kept secrets from each other, and have talked about how we've felt with each other many times. I guess remaining friends is easier to promise remotely, via text, than saying it face to face. But now I've felt how good it was when we danced together, I'm not willing to give it up without a fight. I take a deep breath.

"Will you dance with me?" I blurt before my nerve fails me.

"We just danced." A frown crosses his face.

"At the Nationals. Will you dance with me at the Nationals?"

He stands and faces me. "We can't dance at the Nationals," he says with a derisive snort.

"Why not?"

"Surely it's not allowed."

"I've checked. There's nothing in the rules that says we can't dance together."

He starts pacing. Nick is never still, but pacing is his stress response.

"I'm not good enough," he says roughly.

"You don't believe that any more than I do. You saw those candidates; you're way better than any of them." He doesn't slow his pacing, but his face crumples slightly. I feel like he's slipping away from me and that makes me desperate.

"Nick, tell me you didn't feel something when we danced. Look at me and tell me," I demand.

"I can't dance with you." He doesn't even turn around.

"Why not?" I'm almost yelling.

He eventually comes to a stop in front of me, so close I could touch him, pain written across his face as he answers.

"Because every time I get near you . . ." Anguish threads through his words. "I want to kiss you."

I stare back at him, seeing those eyes, capable of holding the universe, look dark and haunted and I want to make them shine again.

"What if I want you to?" I whisper.

His shoulders sag.

"D." It comes out as a sigh. "You don't know what you're asking. We could never go back to being just friends."

"Look at us." I gently raise a hand and waft it between us. "Don't you think we've already messed that up?"

He closes his eyes briefly and releases a heavy breath, like he's fighting an internal battle. He moves closer, and I lock my eyes on his, seeing a hunger that makes my knees go weak. I'm grateful for the support of the door behind me.

"Are you sure?" he whispers. My stomach flips, seeing that he's still Nick, still so courteous.

"Please," I breathe back, and I see a tiny curl of his lips as they meet mine.

It's soft, gentle, and over too soon. He pulls away slightly and looks at me, licking his lips as if he's tasting me there. Then he breaks out into his usual grin and kisses me again.

This time, it's needy and possessive and steals my breath. I kiss back with a hunger born from years of longing erupting through the cracks created by my sister's words. It's not enough. I grasp his hips and pull him so he's pushing me up against the door. I feel his tongue questing, and I open up, wanting him to devour me. Wanting nothing more in this moment than to feel like this forever.

Slowly, breathless, with heaving chests, we break apart. Nick rests his forehead against mine and gives a low chuckle.

"I don't know if this is the stupidest or most incredible moment of my life."

"We'll make it incredible," I whisper, and seal the promise by fusing my mouth to his again.

Chapter 11

Nick

I can barely concentrate through dinner. Darcy invites me to stay and I don't feel like letting him out of my sight just yet. I can't quite believe, after what I've put myself through recently, that he wants me, too. So, just in case it's all a terrible dream, and I wake up tomorrow feeling like I do now but with an oblivious best friend—and if that happens, I don't think I could ever face him again—I'm sticking by his side for as long as I can to make the most of it.

If his parents notice our flushed faces and kiss-bruised lips, they don't say anything. More noticeable is the difference in Darcy; he's lost the faded look he's been wearing since Julia gave her news. He looks like his colours have come brighter in the wash. Maybe it's just me who's seeing him that way. His mum probably wouldn't notice anything, but I see his dad give him a couple of curious glances. Not in a bad way, or frowning. If anything, he looks pensive, hopeful almost. At one point, Darcy knocks his knee into mine and I look at him.

He gives me a small, secret smile, and my heart flips over in my chest. I glance back at his parents and his dad is watching us. I give him my widest smile.

"This is great bolognese, Mr Franklin. You'll have to teach me the recipe one day."

"Thank you, and I can show it to you anytime," he says with a smile that reaches his eyes, and follows it with a few quick nods. "I'd like that."

I feel like I've passed some sort of test, even though this should be like any of the many previous occasions I've had dinner with Darcy and his parents.

There is tarte au citron for dessert, and just knowing this would have been incentive enough for me to stay for dinner. I won't tell Darcy . . . though maybe I will, as he'll think it funny and he would totally understand. Something settles deep in my core that I have someone who knows me on that level. That I didn't lose him like I feared, but I got more than I'd ever hoped. I want to do a whole lot more with him—deliciously sinful things. Now that Darcy's reciprocation has freed me from trying to keep a lid on my desires, ideas crowd my head. I take a deep breath. I need to stop these thoughts quickly. They're wholly inappropriate for the dinner table, and I'm getting hard and uncomfortable in my jeans. A subtle nudge from Darcy's knee brings me back into focus after I must have been staring at my plate for too long. Keeping my head down as my cheeks heat, not wishing for anyone to ask what I've been thinking, I take a spoonful of the tarte and it tastes as good as it looks. I swear the man's culinary skills are wasted on his family.

As soon as we're finished, I help clear the table. I'm both desperate to get Darcy alone again, and also wanting to prolong the anticipation of it. As soon as we're in his room, I kick off my shoes and throw myself headlong onto his bed. It's a move I've made hundreds of times before and he chuckles at me. This time though, I lie on my side and invite him to join me. He lies on his back next to me, but he's tentative about it and I draw back slightly, wondering if I've pushed it too far.

"What's wrong?" I frown down at him, trying not to let worry cloud my thoughts.

"I—I don't know what we do next," he says, and a crease crosses his brow. I've never noticed before how adorable it is.

"Well, I'd really like to kiss you again. If that's okay?" I say, and receive an enthusiastic nod and a smile. "We'll figure it out, D. We have all the time in the world."

"Okay," he whispers, as he turns to face me and snakes his hand across my hip, which I take as encouragement to kiss him. This time he tastes of the sweet and sharp citrus of the tarte, and damn, if he's going to start tasting of my favourite foods, I might believe there is a heaven and I've just landed there.

"*Hmmmm.*" Darcy lets out a sigh and snuggles closer against me, his head resting on my shoulder. I marvel at the freshness of the excitement rippling through me, whilst slipping into a warm familiarity like we've been doing this forever.

"So, will you dance with me at the Nationals?" Darcy asks, flicking a glance up at me.

I falter. He can't possibly mean it.

"I told you, I'm not good enough."

"And I said that was rubbish. Weren't you listening?"

"I might have been a bit distracted." I huff, not really wishing to revisit the revulsion I've had for myself for the last few days.

"I'm sorry." I barely hear the words.

"Hey, none of that. You have nothing to be sorry for. I was hating myself for fancying you. Wanting to hit on my straight best friend. It's not cool, man. I thought the only way to deal with it was to stay away from you. But the truth ate me up inside."

"I thought I'd chased you off." He flashes those eyes at me again, shining green under dark lashes, and it fairly takes my breath away. I'm a sucker for them and always will be. "I thought you'd picked up on my thoughts towards you. I have to admit, I wasn't sure what the thoughts were at first, but I believed I'd somehow repelled you. You, who could have anyone."

"Hey." I crook my finger under his chin and lift it gently so he has to look at me. "I don't want just anyone, D. I want you."

I lean down and place a gentle kiss to his lips, just briefly, and feel him smile against me.

"It was Claire who helped me sort out what I was feeling," he says when I release him.

"Oh, what did she say?" I'm all shades of curious now. Claire is, well, a typical big sister; she gives a lot of tough love. She means well, but she speaks plainly.

"She said she was sure I'd been in love with you since I was sixteen."

What? I swallow. Has he?

"Um, I don't know what to say." I truly don't know how to process that nugget of information, if it's true.

"I've been thinking a lot about this." Darcy seems to gain a bit more confidence in my own unease.

"I don't really know how to sort this out in my head. I haven't really been attracted to anyone at all. I've only ever been with Julia, and we agreed early on that it was a mistake that would hurt our dancing partnership. I've never really had the opportunity to meet anyone else, and if I had, who would be happy with their boyfriend dancing with another girl? I wasn't attracted to guys, either. I guess I considered that a relationship wasn't for me somehow, like I wasn't normal. But Claire's words brought out that the only person I've really felt anything for is you. This wanting to kiss you, wanting to do . . . more." His little pause cracks my heart and I squeeze him a bit tighter. "That's new, but I was so scared. No, I *am* scared that it won't be enough for you."

This time, when he looks at me I can see the unshed tears brimming in his eyes, and my heart splits open. I can't believe what a precious thing he just trusted me with. An admission of himself that I don't think he would have told me before. Even with our best friends, we keep some parts of our natures bottled up, frightened to say things we can't even admit to ourselves.

I don't respond for a few seconds, but I tighten my hold and he turns to lie against me, wrapping his arm around me.

"You will always be perfect for me, D. We've got this, just like we always have. This is us, just becoming even better."

I understand at that moment that it might take Darcy some time for anything more physical, and despite giving in to my thoughts of what I'd like to do with him, I already know there's not going to be anyone else for me. I ignore the pang of disquiet that the memory of my last Brazen visit invokes; it will fade in time. And time is what we have. I have all the time in the world to help him figure it out.

His tears dampen the shoulder of my T-shirt as I let him

sob it out, holding him tightly. I wipe away a few of my own which have spilled down my cheeks.

Eventually, he lifts his head slightly to look at me.

"Feel better?" I ask, and he shrugs a little.

"I should be happy, but right now I feel drained." I get that. It's been an emotional few days, so he's bound to feel wrung out, and I can't say I feel any better.

"Well," I start, trying a smile on for size. "You were just trying to convince me to dance with you."

This time, I get a more positive response and, with dancing, I know we're on a more stable topic. He sits up fully and crosses his legs. I'm sorry for the loss of contact, but he does seem more animated. I raise myself up, too, and lean my back against the wall.

"You're easily as good as, if not better than, any of the dancers we've seen try out."

"But I'm just an amateur." It's true, I've only been in a few competitions and always at the lower levels.

"But that's because you haven't had the right partner." Darcy is more confident now that he's in familiar territory. "If you'd had the right partner, then you would've been able to dance in the open competitions."

"I dunno." I'm not convinced.

"C'mon Nick, you've been dancing for what? Eight or nine years now?"

"Eight years, seven months," I reel off. I really only know that level of detail, as it was my birthday when I first had lessons, so it was memorable. It gets a laugh, though.

"Exactly. Yet there are people competing in the open competitions who have only been dancing three or four years. Honestly, you are much better than them."

I tip my head back against the wall, trying to imagine a reality where I could dance in an open competition. It's something I'd thought of as a concept, not believing it could actually happen. And here was Darcy, offering it on a plate. I don't want to let him down. I could ruin his chances.

"I have no experience." Is what I finally sputter. "I don't know if I can do it, D."

Darcy rests an elbow on his knee and cups his chin as he thinks. Then he breaks out into a grin.

"There are the North Midland regionals in Chesterfield in a few weeks. Why don't we dance there? It's the next competition before the Nationals that's close enough to get to. That will help you get some experience. And then we can announce that we'll dance at the Nationals. It'll be our secret."

I blow out a breath. It certainly sounds much more manageable to dance there than the city hall, at the most prestigious event on the calendar.

"Yes, alright," I reply. "I'd love to try it." He launches forward and plants a kiss on my lips.

"Woohoo, this is going to be fantastic!" His joy is infectious and I grin at him, but I also don't want to let him down.

"But please, can you still try out with other people? Just in case I can't manage to dance in front of so many people."

He frowns, but says fine in a way that conveys he doesn't believe I could let him down.

I leave shortly after, as I have work tomorrow with my dad. It's a job that's across town, so we have to start early, but I'm not allowed to head home until I've promised to return the next evening so we can work on our dance for the regionals.

I call at the convenience store on my way to the bus stop. I pick up my usual gummy sweets and also a packet of Love Hearts, laughing at myself for being in the mood for their sentimental messages right now.

Chapter 12

Darcy

The sun is gracing us with some warmth today, a reminder that summer is just round the corner. I'm glad to get out of the house and studio for a while, and elect to walk to the library instead of taking the bus. As I walk, I enjoy seeing gardens coming into bloom. Walking also affords me thinking time and I hoist my bag a bit higher on my shoulder.

I feel a little apprehensive about Nick . . . well, not Nick as such, as I've known him so long. It's rather, what am I supposed to do? Which sounds clinical, but really, I have very little experience. That Nick has so much more than me makes me feel a bit uneasy and naïve. It's not a position I'm usually in as I've been the one giving knowledge and helping others since I was young—too young, perhaps, as I was helping with the dance school as soon as I could. Nick has probably had a lot of partners, not dancing, but sexually. And I haven't. I told him that the other night, and he was so sweet and Nick-like, but despite his words, I feel like I'm not good enough. I'm sure he'll want more than I can give. Whatever *that* is, I don't know. I've never really considered it until now. Nick has me feeling sensations I've never felt before and there have been several times I've got hard just thinking about him. Especially when I think of his kisses, or how he looks dancing. I've never noticed how sexy his smile is until now.

This has resulted in me jerking off, with his face in my thoughts. At first, it felt odd, almost as disquieting as admitting that I fancied my best friend in the first place, and I felt a dirty pleasure doing it. But then I remember the way he kisses me and I no longer have a problem with it. I'm more amazed at the *frequency* he can affect me. I don't know if it's normal, but usually it's several months between getting any thoughts or desires that make me feel like that. I might ask Nick about it. The thought of asking for relationship advice from my best friend, and that it's about him, has me stifling a giggle as I enter the library. I'm not sure that giggling would be considered library-appropriate behaviour.

The old Georgian building that houses the library sits squarely within the park that would have been part of its grounds before the city flowed round the boundaries and subsumed it. Libraries come in all shapes and sizes, but this has to be one of my favourites. The heavy wooden door opens into a large entrance hall. The main part of the library is straight ahead, filling what would have been large reception rooms. The children's section is off to one side and upstairs are offices and a reference section. There is a gentle hush I like, and a peace settles over me as I check in my books at the desk and move into the quiet world of stories and other lives.

I like books that involve myths and legends, gods and heroes. There are a couple for me to collect, but I scour the shelves for anything new. I also like to read biographies, usually about dancers of any type, but also movie stars, sportspeople, and others who have achieved their goals through hard work and dedication.

I guess I'm lucky in that my career was set out for me, and I'm pretty sure I would have chosen it for myself, though I know that I'm privileged to have the support of my parents. A career to walk into. Sometimes, I think about what I would do if I couldn't dance anymore. There might come a time when I can't dance any longer. Like my dad. The arthritis in his knees is premature through dancing, and is a risk for me, too. I think of how much he loves his cooking. I've often wondered if he prefers that to dancing, as he has always been interested in creating and perfecting dishes. Maybe he would have been a restaurateur if he hadn't been a dancer. Thinking of my dad sparks an interest that I'd like to learn to cook. I am fairly proficient at basic stuff. I mean I can cook beans on toast, but I'd like to know how to create something more complicated. I wonder if my thoughts are because I know how much Nick loves to eat. I remember how much he liked the lemon tart my dad made the other day. I'd like to be able to make that for him. It could be fun, and I don't think I've challenged myself like that before, certainly nothing outside of dancing.

I'm diverted by how easily my thoughts turn to Nick—he's my best friend, and if I'm honest, my only real friend. I haven't had a lot of opportunities to make many friends in my life. I have a few acquaintances from the competition circuit, but we only ever see each other at events, so it's more a friendly rivalry than a friendship, and it's not like we hang out together. I know Nick has a few other friends as he's mentioned them before. Maybe he'll introduce me to them sometime.

I collect my reserved books from the library, and a biography about an ice dancer which looks interesting. Then, on a whim, I pass the cookery section and see a recipe book of desserts and puddings, so add that to my pile as well.

The bus is just about due when I leave the library, so I hop on it to get back. It's tight, as time always passes a lot quicker than I think when I'm browsing the shelves. I'm due to help Mum with the senior classes this afternoon. I'm so late that I end up having no time for lunch. As soon as I jump off the bus, I pop into the shop for a bar of chocolate to tide me over for a little while and give me some energy. My attention is arrested as I leave. The waste area now has wooden boards enveloping it and a set of new signs showing a development of houses that they're building. Maybe Claire was right and they are doing up the area.

After an afternoon of wartime favourites and telling Mrs Herringsworth that the Charleston was perhaps a bit too ambitious for her—not that it stopped her trying, much to the amusement of her fellow dancers—the senior classes are finished for the day. The seniors love them, and the dances of the forties are becoming quite popular again. There seems to be a growing number of forties events springing up the length and breadth of the country, according to Mr and Mrs Hamilton, who spend their weekends travelling to them. They've started turning up to the dance classes in forties clothing and they look great. Some of the other clients have asked them where they got them from. I wonder if doing a themed evening of dancing and entertainment is something we could do. It might bring more people into the school.

I'm famished, as I've used up a lot of energy today and haven't eaten enough, but I need to shower first. Nick isn't coming over tonight and, whilst I'd love to see him, I'm really beat. I'll text him instead, tell him about my idea, and he'll tell me if it's any good or not.

I feel refreshed once I've showered and dressed, and I walk into the kitchen where my dad is starting to cook dinner.

"Can I help you today, Dad?"

He stops and turns to look at me. I can see the surprise on his face but he doesn't make anything of it right now, which I'm grateful for.

"Of course you can, son," he says with a smile. I know he'll be asking why, later, but for now it's enough that he lets me help. It isn't difficult, and he just has me prepping some vegetables while he explains what he's doing.

Soon the casserole is in the oven and he puts me to work preparing a salad while he cuts some crusty bread.

"So what's brought this on?" he asks. Following it up with, "I'm just curious."

"Well, I never help out and I feel like I ought to." I shrug, trying to look nonchalant. "Instead of leaving it up to you all the time."

He regards me for a long minute. "This doesn't have anything to do with the large appetite of a certain handsome blond friend, does it?" He's being coy, but we both know who he means, and the truth of it is that it does. I feel my cheeks heat as I give him a smile back. His returning smile is tender. He's pretty astute, my dad.

"Well, then," he says. "I can certainly give you some help there, and I know a few recipes you could try."

"Really? Thanks Dad. I picked up a book at the library today and wondered if you'd help me try some of them out."

"I'd like that." He beams back at me and I feel I've started to create a bond with my dad that I never had before. Whilst my mum's been my biggest supporter, I don't think we've ever felt a deep bond, but in that moment, I feel like my dad is on my side.

The food is delicious and I'm proud that I had a hand in it, even if it was only a bit of preparation work, but I enjoy the way my dad explains things to me. Cooking has a whole different vocabulary, a bit like dancing has, and I want to know more. I want to learn what all the terms mean and I ask for another lesson the following day.

"What do you know about the new building development?" I ask my parents after dinner. "There's boarding erected around the site."

I see a look pass between my parents, but it's my mum that answers. "All we know is that they're building some new houses. Let's hope they will be people that want dance lessons." Her tone is glum, and I wonder if this has anything to do with the reduction in bookings we've had recently.

"How bad are things?" I look between them. "Mum, Dad?"

"They're fine, Darcy," Mum says, her smile brittle. "Of course they are. You're a draw for customers. They want to dance with you, and you're going to dance in the Nationals. That's going to be a big help; really put us on the map. You just concentrate on that."

She gets up, announcing that she's going to have a bath, so I know I won't get anything more from her right now.

"Dad?" I enquired, after Mum had swept out of the room.

"Your mother's right, son. We'll be fine."

I feel a small niggle of worry, but the dance school is all we have, so they wouldn't say it was fine if it wasn't. I try to put it out of my mind and go to my room to text Nick.

Chapter 13

Nick

I watch the paint adhere to the wall as I run the roller over it, the white obliterating the awful acidic-lime colour underneath. I like how paint can do that, can wash over, like a do-over. Though, in this case, due to the brightness of the garish colour we're covering, it's going to take a couple of coats. I mean, who thought that colour was suitable?

This is a big job, repainting the whole house in a week. The new owners want to move in as soon as possible, so we're working hard, putting in long hours and days so it will get finished this week. My dad even drafted one of his friends in to help us, so we'd get finished on time. Alan is an old friend of my dad's from his steelworking days. Alan managed to hold on to his job longer than most, but was still another casualty of the rise in overseas steel. Most of the steelworks in Sheffield now make specialist steels. Alan says he's applying for a job at the Stocksbridge works, where there has just been an injection of investment money, but for now he's helping

Dad. I can hear them in the room next door. I don't think I've heard my dad talk so much. I guess no one really understands him like his old friends. Their voices rise and fall, occasionally bursting into laughter as they recall fond and not-so-good memories of when they worked together.

I return to concentrating on my work. Because of the long hours I haven't been to see Darcy all week and I can't wait to see him again, not only because we need to practise our routine for the competition in Chesterfield, but also because I want to see him more. But the money from this job is worth it —just. It will all go into my savings. I've nearly saved up for the deposit on a house, and with what I earn working with Dad, I should be able to make the mortgage repayments. I don't need anywhere big or flashy, just somewhere to call my own, with some privacy. I'd rent, but the rental prices are so high I can't rent and save for a mortgage at the same time, so it's worth living at home for a bit longer.

Until now, it hasn't been much of an issue, but now I find myself wanting some privacy. Never before have I really wanted to bring a person home, be with someone for any length of time, but I want that with Darcy. His place is worse than mine, so that's not going to happen anytime soon, but yes, a place of my own where I can be with Darcy would be fantastic.

I'm still reeling from him wanting me. I put myself through a couple of weeks of hell while I struggled with realising that he was who I wanted in my life as more than just a best friend.

I can't believe that he fancies me, too. I feel a little sad that he was upset that he doesn't have much experience. I kind of figured that he wasn't really a horny kind of guy. I am, but I also don't think that will be a problem. It's clear no one else is going to do it for me. I nearly made that mistake and I'm not going to do it again. So we'll figure it out, and I'm looking forward to seeing what Darcy enjoys. I think there is more in there than he even knows himself, and I want to be the one to help him discover it.

"How's it going?" My dad looks in on the room I'm working in, startling me into action as I've been dreaming off into space for the last few minutes.

"Um, not bad." I dunk the roller in the tray to gather more paint, as if that was the action I was in the middle of.

"Do you want a brew?" If he notices he doesn't say anything.

"Thanks, that'd be great," I answer.

He's back within a few minutes and puts the mug down on the dust sheets that cover the empty room. At least the house is completely empty, which makes the job a lot easier.

"Dad?" I ask before he gets to the door.

"What is it?" he asks, his hand resting on the door handle.

I falter. I don't know how to ask this. I guess I can just go ahead and ask in a straightforward way.

"Is it alright if Darcy comes over sometimes?" I start with, and because I'm suddenly very nervous, I start babbling. "For tea. You know Darcy, don't you? My friend, he dances. Well, I'd like him to come over, and well, I'm seeing him now. Is that alright?" I've talked myself to a stop and run out of breath. It does feel odd to ask, as I'm an adult, but it's my parents' house and I wouldn't want to make them feel uncomfortable in any way. My dad thinks for a long minute. He can never be rushed, and my heart won't stop hammering in my chest the whole time.

Eventually, he speaks. "Are you asking me if it's alright that Darcy comes over, or if it's alright that you're seeing him?"

Did I really say that, but okay, in for a penny . . .

"Um, both I guess."

A pained expression crosses my dad's face, and then he looks at me.

"Well, in the first instance, I appreciate you asking, lad, and yes, it would be fine. In the second instance. Would you have asked me if it was a girl you were seeing?"

I felt stunned, but my dad was right.

"I guess not," I say, and it has always irked me that queer people feel they have to announce their sexuality.

My dad gives a little nod of his head. "Thought not. You don't have to ask my permission for that either, lad. All I've ever wanted is for you to be happy."

My dad isn't an easy man to love. To respect, yes. He's always been fair and just. But love, that was for my mum, who always gives her hugs freely and has a kind word for everyone. My father is the silent type, but I don't think I've loved him more than I do at this moment.

I choke back the lump that forms in my throat from his words, and reply. "Thanks, Dad." He nods again and tells me to, "Hurry up or that paint'll dry in the tray before you get a chance to put it on the wall."

He's typical of his breed—the silent Yorkshireman. But he doesn't lie, so I believe him when he says that it's okay. I didn't expect a hug, but an admission of acceptance? That's something. I'll work on asking Darcy round, which excites me and keeps me entertained for the rest of the day.

I'm too tired to do much after work, but after showering and having had tea, I decide to sit with Gran for a while. I'll help her up to bed later, as well.

"Is that you Nicholas?" She calls out from the front room as I open the back door. I chuckle. She's the only person who calls me by my "Sunday" name, and she's the only person who I allow it from, not that it would make any difference if I asked her not to.

"Yes, it's me, Gran," I answer.

"Well, put the kettle on, on your way through." I laugh, as I'm already at the sink, filling it up. If I know anything about my gran, it's that she can't go half an hour without a cup of tea. I flick the switch, and leave it to do its thing while I go through to the other room. It's dark, so I turn the light switch on.

"Why are you sitting in the dark?" I ask, as I head over to the chair where she's sitting and peck a quick kiss on her check, something else she'll not let me get away with not doing. I'd rebelled once as a teenager, and received a very curt reply that she'd lost the only person who'd given her kisses far too early and I would have to do. I never missed it after that because she did lose Grandpa early. I can barely remember him; I must have only been about five or so.

"I couldn't be bothered to get up to switch the light on," she replies, and I feel sad that this was the case.

"Is your hip playing up again?" I ask, knowing that it's sometimes painful for her.

"I'm not getting any younger, dear."

"I know, Gran, but sitting here in the dark . . ."

"I can still see the television," she protests. It's true, the television is almost always on.

"What are you watching this time?"

"*Vera*. I like this series."

I laugh. What is it about old ladies and murder? She used to read all the stories when her eyesight was still good enough. She was always reading or watching Agatha Christie and, as I spent a lot of time with her, I got to watch them, too. I can still recall most of the plots now.

I hear the kettle boil, and go through to make up a teapot. That was another thing Gran's a stickler for: tea in a teapot, a china one, and *always* in a china cup. I'm quite happy with a mug anywhere else, but my gran refuses to have them in the house, claiming that tea never tastes good in anything other than china.

Setting the tray down on the low table, I pour her a cup. I'd brought a few biscuits from the tin as well. Otherwise, she'd only be sending me back for them.

"So how are you? Work busy?" Gran opens with. But I know her better than that.

"You know it is, Gran." My mum will have been round earlier and told her all about the job we were currently working on. "What is it you really want to know?"

She has a twinkle in her eye. "How did it work out with you and your young friend?"

I knew that's what she was really after. She's the biggest gossip and I know where my mum learned all her tricks from. I just need to decide how much I'm going to tell her.

"Well, you were kind of right." She gives me a knowing smile and I let her have that point. "I did tell him how I felt."

"And?" she prompts. "You're not moping around here like a lovesick puppy anymore, so I guess it went alright."

"Gran! I was *not* a lovesick puppy," I exclaim, possibly more shocked than anything else.

"Were too." She takes a sip of tea and smiles at me over the rim of her cup. I'm not rising to her bait. She got me too many times with that trick as a kid. I shake my head at her as I take a long gulp of my tea. I'm going to make her wait. I make a deliberate show of picking up my cup and then, after I've drunk, putting it slowly back down again.

"I taught you too well," she sighs eventually, and I can't help but grin at her. She's the best and I love her.

"Well, I think it went well, really well, Gran." I eventually put her out of her misery. "He admitted he liked me, too." I don't dwell over the thought that he may have been into me for a long time. That was in both our pasts and not something we can do anything about now.

"So, did you kiss him?"

"Grandma!" This time I give her a full title. "Wash your mouth out, this instant," I tease, and see her giggle.

"Spoilsport," she says with a wrinkle of her nose. And I mimic her, mouthing her tried-and-tested saying, *"I was young once; I've seen it all."* I very much doubt she's seen everything I've done before, but I'm not going to test that theory by bringing up those sorts of activities.

"Okay Gran, yes we kissed, but that's all. And any future things we may or may not do are completely off limits."

She giggles again.

"Did you put my mum through the same treatment?" I wonder what my mum would have said.

"Oh, no." Gran looks affronted. "No point. It would have been boring, anyway. You, my dear, are far more colourful." And for the second time that night, I'm shocked by my own gran. "She only had eyes for your dad, and he doesn't exactly light the world up with his fire, does he?"

"Gran, I think you need to stop now," I tell her. I mean, no one needs to know about their parents' love life, no one. If she starts again I might have to stick my fingers in my ears.

I'm saved by a buzzing in my pocket.

Relieved, I pull out my phone and my heart jumps a beat when I see it's a text from Darcy.

Darcy: What do you think about the forties?

As I have no idea what he's on about, I send him a flippant reply.

Nick: I might be two months older than you D, but it's a way off yet

Darcy: No, the 1940s

Nick: Now you're just being offensive. I wasn't around then. I don't think even my Gran was born then

I look up and ask her. "Gran, when were you born?"

"Nineteen thirty-nine," she replies without hesitation.

"What were the forties like?"

"Hard, dusty, and the food was terrible—they were the best years."

I laugh at her.

Nick: Gran says it was miserable

Darcy: Then why are people so nostalgic
about it?

Nick: I dunno

I wonder if he has a point.

Darcy: The classes are getting really popular,
so I was thinking of doing an event. Music
and food all themed around the forties

I sit up a bit straighter. It's not actually a bad idea.

Nick: Sounds like a great idea. Do you think
people will come?

Darcy: I do. I think people will like it

"Gran, would you go to a forties-themed day or evening?" I
test the water.

"Oh, that would be lovely, if I could get out more, of course. Reggie and I used to love a good dance." I didn't point out that she would have been eleven at the end of the forties, so wouldn't have met Grandpa by then, but I guess that people still cling to the old dances and ways.

Nick: Gran says it's a great idea

Darcy: You with her now?

Nick: Yes, so none of your dirty talk

I've never heard him say anything that I'd consider dirty talk, but I like to tease him and to show that it might be something for the future.

He sends a blushing face emoji followed by LMAO and I grin down at the phone, missing him, counting the hours until I can see him again.

Darcy: Will you help me?

Nick: With the dirty talk? Sure

Hmmm, that sounds promising.

I've always wanted to try West Coast Swing.

I smile, catching a bit of his enthusiasm.

We text for a few more minutes until I need to help my gran up the stairs. I can't wait to see him the next day.

Chapter 14

Darcy

"Will you get over here and stop cha-cha-chaing all over the place?" calls Nick, and I grin at him. He feigns tiredness and collapses on the floor, lying with his head propped on one elbow.

"What, have you run out of stamina, old man?" I tease, turning and giving him a look over my shoulder as I keep moving. He's a couple of months older, something I never let him forget.

We've been dancing for a couple of hours and it's getting late.

"I have plenty, thank you, but I've also done a full day's work," he whines. I do have a modicum of sympathy for him, but not enough to stop teasing.

"Yes, it must be tough, splashing a bit of paint around."

That goads him enough to get up, and he catches me as I move to dance past him.

"I'd like to see you spend a day up a ladder painting a ceiling—*that's* hard work."

"Well, you just rest up then, and I'll keep dancing."

He has me by the hips and isn't letting go, but he sways his in time with mine. I like it. I move closer.

"Mmm, maybe we should incorporate this into our dance," I say, giving my hips an extra sway.

We're trying to choreograph our routine for the regionals in a couple of weeks. We'll dance two numbers, a traditional and a Latin American, but so far we haven't agreed on much.

"If you dance like that with me in the regionals, honey, I'm not going to last the dance," he says, grinding himself closer and my cock twitches with the friction. This effect he can have on me is a new sensation, and I like it. Not that we've had much chance to explore further. We don't get a lot of privacy. I'm trying to work on it because now that Nick is causing these feelings, I want to experience a lot more.

Nick's holding me closer now and grinding a little harder against me. "But if you do want to dance like this, I know where we can go."

"Where?" I huff out in a breathless whisper, as I'm getting a little light-headed, all the blood having rushed to my groin.

"Come to Brazen with me. It's the best club around. We can dance like this all night."

"I thought you'd not last the dance," I counter, very pleased he asked.

"Tease." He presses kisses against my neck, and this time I slow my hips and snake my arms around his neck to kiss him fully. After a long moment I pull away and see the starry look in his eyes and the slow smile that spreads across his face.

"I want to go there with you, Nick."

"To the club?"

"Everywhere." That receives a chuckle and another kiss.

We pull apart again and I don't think I can plan anymore

tonight. Though we need to decide soon. For the traditional dance, I want to do the quickstep but Nick thinks we should do the waltz. I tell him it's better suited for male and female couples, but I think he just likes to sweep round the dance floor. For the Latin American, I want to do the cha-cha-cha but Nick wants to do the rumba. I am coming round to the idea of that as I think we can make it look really good with two guys dancing it, but I haven't told him that yet. I don't want him to get a big head from being right. But I'll tell him soon. If he agrees to the quickstep, of course.

Nick glances at his watch. I know he has to catch the bus home soon, and be up early for work. I was truly just teasing him about his work earlier. He works very hard.

I grab us some water from the kitchen while we change our shoes. Nick pulls on his hoodie and coat while I grab a jacket. I want to spend every moment I can with him, so I'm walking him to the bus stop.

"Goodbye, Mr and Mrs Franklin," he calls up the stairs to our apartment, and receives a reply in return.

We walk past the shops. Well, not past, as I don't think Nick can pass a shop without buying something to satisfy his sweet tooth. Then he laces his fingers through mine as we take the entrance to the park for a walk before his bus arrives. This has become a habit and the rightness of it feels like we have done this forever, and in a way, we have. While we've always headed up to the park to hang out, it's only the hand holding and the kisses that are new.

We take our usual path, but before we emerge from the trees and out onto the play park at the top where we can see the lights across the city, Nick pulls me into the shadow of a tree and manoeuvres me against it.

In dancing, I take the lead as the male partner, and even dancing with Nick, we've adopted those roles. We've decided that would be how it is in the competition as I have more experience. But when he takes charge and moves me into position, even though it's over in a second or two, a thrill spirals through my body. I surrender to him. He smiles at me as he leans close. I bite my lip and he groans softly.

"Do you know what that does to me, D?" he asks.

"No." I flick my eyes at him and he groans again.

"And you follow it with the lashes. For that . . ."

He gently takes my hand and places it against his cock so I can feel how hard it is through his trousers. "There, that's what you do to me."

I've not touched anyone else's cock before. I experimentally rub my palm up and down, feeling the solidness through the material of his trousers.

He utters a low moan. "Um, actually, you're going to have to stop that or we'll be in trouble."

But I don't want to stop now. I want to explore further, even though I agree with Nick that this is probably not the place and time. I wouldn't want a late night dog walker to suddenly come up the path and find us. However, I can't quite bring myself to stop and I play my fingers over the end.

"*Umm,* D honey." Nick is panting slightly, and I keep up the pressure, feeling my way up and down. I vaguely register that for the second time tonight he's used a nickname, and I like it. Now is not the time to ask him about it, though. I'll save it for another day.

"Well, you showed it to me. What's a guy supposed to do?" I tease, and his eyes lock onto mine.

In the dusk they look like bottomless, inky-black pools, and I can't tear my gaze away from them.

"No, you really need to stop now, D, please." He whines a little.

I enjoy seeing him like this, reacting to my touch.

"Are you telling me you're going to come just from me doing this?" I whisper, amazed but excited.

"Y-Yes." His eyes flutter and he leans his forehead against my shoulder.

"Then I'm not going to stop." I love the feel of his soft puffs of breath against my neck and I press harder. He grinds a little against my hand and I keep up the rhythm.

I want to do this properly. I want to be able to see him. Nick has always been the composed one, the strong one. To see him unravel before me makes me feel exhilarated just watching and feeling him. My own cock thickens and I can't help but put my other hand on it.

"Jesus, D. I want to watch you do that to yourself." Nick's voice is husky. I thought he had his eyes closed. "Can you imagine how sexy that would look? To watch you touching yourself?"

I don't have an answer for that, as I'm caught up in my own mental image.

"Oh fuck, D. I can't hold on any longer."

He shudders against me, and his mouth finds mine as I wrap an arm around him.

"Oh shit, that was unexpected." He giggles, and I catch the infection from him and start giggling, too. It becomes uncontrollable and tears of laughter run down my face as I double over, partly in shock, part relief, and part something else I can't define. But what I do know is that I want to do it again, do more than that. The thought surprises me. I've barely thought about sex until now, but I want to explore more.

"I'm sorry," I say, as I straighten up, trying to regain my composure and wiping the tears from my face.

"Hey." Nick catches me. "Please stop apologising. I led you on, but you do things to me, Darcy. Even a look from you can have me sporting a semi, and I've been close to the boiling point for so long. In truth, I used you."

"Oh, I think I was very willing to do that," I reply with a smile.

"Do you think the bus has gone?" I ask, and Nick looks at his watch, cursing slightly, but then he shrugs. "I'll walk home." He gives a little grimace as he adjusts himself in his trousers.

"Um, is that going to be uncomfortable?" I ask.

"A little." He gives a rueful smile. "But I'm thinking of it as keeping the memory for a bit longer. It was the effect of watching you touching yourself that sent me over the edge, D. I'd like to watch you properly. I want to see you. Would you do that for me?"

"I'd like that." I swallow. Yes, I could put on a show for him.

We eventually make our way back down to the road.

"Do you want to go out next weekend, Saturday night?" Nick asks before he leaves. It's a bank holiday so the dance school won't be open on Sunday or Monday. I reply that I'd love to, and after a quick kiss as we are in a very public space, even though there aren't many people about, he sets off down the street to walk home.

Chapter 15

Darcy

"So, can you help me?" I ask Claire as I dig my hand into the bowl of popcorn that sits between us. I want her help, and when I asked her earlier, she invited me over to her apartment to watch a movie. Not something that we've done for a while. Too long, really.

"Let me get this straight. You want my help to get Mum and Dad out of the house so you and Nick can—"

"Claire!"

"Well, why else would you need some private time?" She waggles her eyebrows.

"Will you help me or not?" I ask, resolutely ignoring her question.

"Not until you tell me what you and Nick will be getting up to."

Really, sisters are the worst.

"Urgh, please don't make me say it." I can hear the whine in my voice. "Please, just help your little brother."

For that, I get the expected eye roll. She smirks at me and reaches across to grab a handful of popcorn.

"I might let you off." She pops a kernel into her mouth. "If you admit I was right." She takes another piece. "Tell me you've been in love with Nick forever. Tell me all it needed was your big sister to nudge you in the right direction."

I scoff. "I was already halfway there myself."

"Nonsense. You needed me to show you the way."

"I was doing just fine," I protest.

"Rubbish. You were acting like a moody teenager who couldn't accept what was in front of his face."

"Was not."

"Admit it. Tell me you needed my help."

"Never!" I smirk back.

"Tell me or you won't get my help, unless you own up that you want Nick alone for se—"

I don't hear anymore as I jam my fingers in my ears, stick my head down and start singing very loudly, "*Lalalala.*"

Eventually I look up and she's just sitting, feeding popcorn into her mouth, grinning at me.

"Okay, you were right, and I couldn't see that I liked Nick," I concede.

"Liked?" She snorts with derision.

"You want some time alone with someone you just like? He's been your best friend forever, surely even that is worth more than *like*?" She won't let up at all.

I grit my teeth. "Will you just help me, please?"

"Sorry, I can't hear you." She cups her hand over her ear and leans in closer. "What was that? Yes, Claire, I needed your help because I love Nick *soooo* much."

I sigh in exasperation and throw a cushion at her.

"Fine, I more-than-like Nick." That's all she's going to get from me.

What was she asking, though? Yes, I fancy him and want

to be with him. Yes, as a friend I said I loved him, but this step is huge. Was I *in* love with him? I don't want to think about that right now.

She preens a little at my words and luckily doesn't ask me to say anything else.

"Actually, I do have a plan. I've already sorted it." She smirks at me again. "You can just chip in for it, if you want."

"What?" I whisper.

"I've booked a hotel in London for Mum and Dad's anniversary next week. I've also booked a show for Mum—an evening with Bruce de Silva—and I've booked them a meal at Bertoffs for Dad to enjoy."

I stare at her, well aware that my mouth is hanging open and I'm blinking like a newborn in the light. Bertoffs is a Michelin-starred restaurant my dad has wanted to visit for a long time, and I think my mum would enjoy seeing Bruce. She met him a long time ago when she still danced competitively, before he struck stardom on the dancing shows on television.

"You're welcome," she says, and pretends to ignore me by turning back to the movie.

I'm part shocked, part madly happy, and part mad. I decide to tackle the initial emotion first.

"You arranged all that, and you didn't tell me?"

She gives a casual shrug and I ask, "When were you going to tell me?"

"Tonight."

"But I . . ." I trail off as I know where this is going. I asked for her help first. Which brings the mad back to the surface. "You put me through all that and you'd done it, anyway."

She grins at me. "You're too easy, Darcy, always have been."

I rock back away from her. "You evil witch." I always resort to insults when I'm mad at her.

"You're so cute when you're mad. Does Nick think so, too?"

I launch at her with a cushion, piling on top of her, trying to smother her while she cackles helplessly. I end up laughing, too. I'm still mad at her, but I am also grateful to her. Immensely grateful. Eventually, we subside and sit side by side on the couch, panting. She grins at me again.

"Thank you." I manage to be gracious this time, but a thought suddenly occurs to me.

"How did you know?"

"Oh please, Darcy, why do you think I left home? You should try it sometime. It'll do wonders for your sex life." She gets up and pushes past me. She picks up the bowl and heads to the kitchen to microwave some more popcorn. I stare after her. My sister has never mentioned anyone else in her life, never brought anyone home or introduced them to us.

I follow her, too intrigued to stay in front of the movie; not that we've been watching it for a while, anyway.

"You have a sex life?" I sit at the breakfast bar while she sets the microwave and fetches us a drink from the fridge.

"Just because I don't tell you something doesn't mean it doesn't happen."

"How come we've never met any of your, er, many partners?"

She turns round and her eyes flash. "Not many, just some, and not any I'd want to bring home."

It's my turn to tease her.

"Bad boys, biker boys, ones our parents wouldn't approve of?" I grin, and her sly smile lets me know that I'm not too far off the mark.

"You sly one. Anyone I can meet?" I raise my eyebrows suggestively.

"I thought you had a boyfriend."

Before I could protest that that wasn't what I meant, my brain catches on the word.

Boyfriend.

It seems to have weight to it.

Friend.

Best friend.

Boyfriend—I haven't even defined us on those terms. We've always been best friends.

I roll the word around my mouth, trying to feel the shape of it.

Boyfriend.

I practise in my head. Hello, this is Nick, he's my boyfriend.

I've never considered what that could mean—to me, to my family, in society. I guess I've always lived in a heteronormative world. Hetero until proven otherwise. Do I now have to define myself with a label—gay, bi—what am I?

I don't consider myself into guys. I consider myself into Nick.

Nick seems to navigate the world as a gay man quite well. I think back to Mark and Justin, and they seem to be happy. Maybe it's something I could do. Would clients think of me any differently? Would it reflect badly on the school? Would we lose clients? The thoughts bubble up and choke my mind. I can't breathe and start gasping for breath.

I don't know if what I'm doing is right; it shouldn't feel like this, should it?

Soothing hands rub up and down my back.

"Hey, it's okay." Claire's hands are calming, and I eventually manage to draw in steady breaths. After a few more minutes, I can sit up again.

"What was all that about?" she asks, while I try to sort out my racing thoughts and the implications of giving in to my feelings for Nick.

"What if people hate me now?" I whisper "What if people don't come to dance anymore?"

"Oh, Darcy." She draws me into a big sisterly hug. "No one could ever hate you."

"But I don't know what to do? I don't know how to be gay."

"Umm, I'm not the right person to ask about that."

I manage a small chuckle, as that's not what I meant.

"Oh lord, I think Nick's got his work cut out. But I also think you'll be fine. You just need to be you."

"Thank you." I sigh and try to take on her advice.

"How are the tryouts going?" she asks, putting the fresh bowl of popcorn on the counter in front of us. I take a handful and stuff some in my mouth, to give myself time to think about how to answer.

"The tryouts are awful," I eventually answer. "But I'm going to dance with Nick instead." Just the memory of how good it feels when we dance together lifts my mood. "He's really good. We dance well together."

"That's fantastic," she starts, looking delighted, but then her face falls. "You won't win. You know that, don't you?"

"Why? It's not against the rules."

"Darcy, that might be true but no one has ever entered as a same-sex partnership. The dance federation aren't ready for that. They won't put you first, even if you're the best in the room. Surely you must know that."

Her words settle over me, each one piercing my confidence. I deflate as I realise she's telling the truth. There is no way they'll let us win. It's a goal that I've been planning for most of my life—the ultimate competition. I have always had my eye on the Nationals. But even though I know that, the thought of dancing with anyone other than Nick makes me feel nauseous, and I know that I'd rather not dance at all than dance with someone else.

"I don't care. I want to dance with Nick."

Claire nods as if she knew that was going to be my answer. "Have you told Mum?"

"Not yet. We're going to surprise her at the regionals next week."

"She's not going to like it." She levels her gaze at me to make sure I understand.

"I can do what I like. It's my life," I protest.

"Yes, sure it is." She gives me a sad smile and I turn away, ignoring her meaning, my previous elation now a muted shackle around my chest.

Chapter 16

Nick

I release Darcy's hand and hold out mine for him to place his other one in my palm. He does and I bend over it, running the brush over his nails. Applying nail polish is a bit like painting glosswork; both require a steady hand. We're getting ready to go out and I'm excited for him to meet my other friends. I offered to paint his nails, and he readily agreed, choosing a green that complements his eyes. Those beautiful eyes, which, when I glance up, are framed by a creased brow.

"What's bothering you?" I return to my task and hear him sigh.

"What if your friends don't like me?"

"They'll like you," I state simply, and give him a smile.

"How can you know that?"

"Because they're my friends and I know them," I reply. But I know Darcy well enough to know that this isn't the real question. He sighs again. I wait him out. He'll tell me what's really bothering him when he's ready. He doesn't keep me waiting long.

"I don't know how to act around them." I let go of his hand and he places it on his knee while I screw the top on the bottle and face him. We're sitting cross-legged on his bed, facing each other. I consider his statement for a moment. I can understand where his thoughts stem from. Darcy has a naturally serious disposition and has been taught from a young age to be on a stage, performing. He rarely gets to just be himself. I feel privileged that I see that side of him. The natural Darcy, who is so smart and funny. But I also know that I can cut through that worry and encourage him to not take himself quite so seriously.

"I wasn't going to tell you this yet, but I think the time might be right."

"What weren't you going to tell me?" His voice is an excited whisper.

I reach for the silver glitter nail polish, and drop my head to attend to my own nails so he can't see my face. There's no chance I would be able to keep a straight face.

"About the code."

"The code?" He gives the word reverence and I almost feel guilty—almost.

"Yes, we all have a code we have to abide by."

"Really?"

"Oh yes, if we break it we're excommunicated. Cast out from the gay community." I give him a quick glance as I swap hands. It's hard not to smirk at his glittering, wide eyes, waiting for me to drop my wisdom.

"First of all." I pause slightly and feel him lean in a little closer. "You have to wear pink, somewhere on your person, at all times."

When I finish my nails and cap the bottle, I risk a little

glance, and see him biting his lip, his face creased into an adorable frown as he digests what I've said.

"Then, you must always refer to yourself in the third person."

I put the bottle down and look at him as the line above his eyes deepens.

"But you don't—"

"And you must call everyone '*Duckie.*'" I can't resist a smirk, and watch as he fully realises that I'm pulling his leg.

"Oh, Nick!" he exclaims, and starts to launch himself at me, but I hold up a hand.

"Don't smudge your nails. They won't have dried enough yet."

He settles himself back down again and glowers at me, but I can see it's not in earnest.

"That wasn't fair." He pouts, which is very cute, but something I won't tell him as he could easily weaponise it against me.

"Darcy, I understand you're worried, but you have no need to be. You just need to be yourself—your beautiful, amazing self." I lean forward and press a brief kiss to his lips, receiving a small smile in the process.

"I am worried about other things though," he says, and the sadness I hear at the edges of his words is not something I'm going to make light of this time. He has my full attention.

"What things?"

"Will people view me differently? Will I lose friends? Clients?"

I take his hands and hold them between us, because I'm not going to sugarcoat this bit for him, and want to feel connected to him as I say it.

"Yes, to all of those things, D."

He looks at me sharply as if he expected me to tell him everything's going to be alright. But these are not my friends we're talking about; this is everyone else. I give his hands a gentle squeeze and continue.

"Yes, people will view you differently. You've changed their perception of you. That isn't the important part, though. What *is* important is what they do next. It shouldn't make a difference to them, considering it's none of their business, but sadly, the world is full of people who can't accept others just being who they want to be. So yes, you may lose friends and you may lose clients. But if that happens, D, then they are not worthy of your friendship and surely you don't need their business."

I stop speaking and watch him swallow, taking in what I've said. He closes his eyes and nods, exhaling a deep breath.

"And." I squeeze his hands again. "You have me, every step of the way, side by side."

He opens his eyes, and whilst I can't see his usual brightness in them, they're no longer tinged with melancholy.

"Thank you," he says, and this time I receive a kiss. I want to deepen it and am delighted when he opens in answer to my request to explore with my tongue. I put all the feeling I can into the kiss, to tell him it will be alright, we can do this together.

I don't want it to end, but we are definitely going out, so I pull back, and this time his eyes are sparkling and his smile is back.

"So, makeup or not?" I ask, as in my opinion you can never be too underdressed or overly made-up for Brazen.

I apply my usual eyeliner, a little colour, and glitter. Darcy opts for some eyeliner, which sets his eyes off so beautifully that I find it hard to look at him; his beauty catches my breath. I try to avoid staring at him, knowing that if I look too much there'll be no option of going out tonight and that even if his parents are in the house, I'll find a way to finally make him mine.

As we walk up to the entrance to Brazen, I catch Darcy's hand and lace our fingers together. I tell myself that it's easy to get separated in the busy club, and that I also want to give him some reassurance, but that's only part of the truth. I'm suddenly feeling very possessive and I want to send out a clear message that he's with me. As the door opens to let us in, the heat and the noise hit us like a wall. It can be startling if you're not used to it. Darcy grips my hand and I pull him with me into the melee. I wend my way through the throng and over to our usual corner. I've told Riley and Kieran about Darcy before. Not too much information, but I let them know he was coming with me tonight. I stand back and watch as Darcy takes in the size of Riley, who stands over six feet tall and is pure muscle. He also has an impressive beard that helps give him his bearlike appearance. But he is one of the kindest and gentlest guys I've ever met, and I know he and Darcy are going to get along really well. Kieran, by contrast, is almost a foot shorter and a ball of energy. He does his customary launch at me and I let him hug me, still keeping hold of Darcy's hand. I introduce them and he hurls himself at Darcy. I check if he's alright and receive a beaming grin in return. I don't think he was expecting such an exuberant welcome.

Once Kieran has released him and is back standing under Riley's arm, placed protectively round him, they ask Darcy a few questions. His grip on my hand eases and I sense him relax. I'm pleased they're getting on really well, and after a few more minutes, I let him go and take one of the drinks Riley has bought. A song starts and Kieran screams, grabbing

Darcy by the hand and dragging him to the dance floor. I catch Riley's amused look as we both follow them.

We spend the next few hours dancing and it's good to watch Darcy enjoy himself, not having to worry about poise and position. He has an instinctive ability to avoid anyone else on the dance floor, born from years of competitive dancing. In the mass of people, I relish the chance to hold him close, grinding my body against him, feeling him go with the moment and grind back.

After the club closes and we all walk to catch a late tram, Riley extends his invitation to head out to the Slippery Stones, suggesting the bank holiday on Monday. With that agreed, Darcy and I board the tram that takes us close enough to his house, then I'll walk the rest of the way home.

"How was it?" I ask, as he's a bit silent. "I told you my friends would love you."

"They're great. Thanks for bringing me. I had the best time."

"What's up then?" He's slipped into his serious mode. I reach for his hand and pull it into my lap, holding it between my palms.

"I'm not sure how to tell Mum and Dad."

"About us?" I guess that this is his current worry. His sigh is all the confirmation I need.

"Claire knows, right?" He nods his affirmation.

"Then no doubt she'll have told them by now." That gets a low chuckle-snort; he knows it's true.

"And I don't think there'll be any problems," I continue, turning enough so he can see me wink as I place my hand on my chest. "Because I know for a fact that your dad adores me."

He laughs and bumps his shoulder into me. I bump him back, pleased to have him smiling again.

Chapter 17

Darcy

I look round at the stunning vista before me. The Peak National Park is one of the most beautiful places in the country and I forget it's right on my doorstep.

Riley had picked us up from my house and driven us to the reservoir visitor's centre. As far as the road goes.

Nick is standing beside me, also looking out over the view from Derwent Dam, and I give him a small nudge with my arm, receiving one of his widest smiles in return.

"Isn't it amazing?" he says, and I have to agree. I inhale deeply, breathing in the clear air. The midday sun is warming, promising a perfect afternoon.

"Are you two going to stand there gawping or are you coming?" We turn so see Riley and Kieran further along the path.

"Come on, there's still a way to go," Nick says, and starts off in their direction. I take another look at the view down the valley and follow them. The path takes us round another reservoir and then we follow a small river. I'm not sure where we're going, but I am aware I haven't seen anyone else for a while.

"Where is this place?" I ask.

Riley, who's leading us, stops and turns round at my question. The path has been climbing steadily for a while and he's a little out of breath. Kieran is still bouncing around and Nick looks fine. I feel alright too, as dancing keeps me pretty fit.

"It's still about a mile away," Riley explains.

"Wow, that's so far." Still, I hadn't expected it to be such a long distance from the car park.

"Oh, wait until you see it," Kieran says excitedly. "It's totally worth the walk. Not only because it's lovely, but also because almost no one bothers to walk it, so we'll probably have it to ourselves."

Kieran wasn't exaggerating when, fifteen minutes later, after following what now looks like a large stream, we come to a crossing of large stones. Kieran points out the pool beyond. It's not large, probably ten metres in diameter, but it looks deep. The path next to it rises, creating an overhang.

"Made it." Riley unshoulders the rucksack he's been carrying and folds himself onto the ground, lying on his back, his knees bent. "Just give me a minute," he chuckles, panting.

Kieran throws himself down next to him. He grabs the bag and rummages around in it, pulling out four bottles of water and handing them round.

"Do you want a swim first, before some food?" Nick asks as he opens the water and drinks half of it down.

"Sure." I'm warm, so cooling down first would be welcome. Nick grins and strips down to his swim shorts. I drink in his broad back and slim legs, his beautiful ass. I've seen him shirtless before, when he's getting changed after dancing. I've touched most parts of him, in hugs and dancing holds. I've felt his lean, hard muscles beneath his shirt. But somehow, this is different. This time, I want to play my fingers across his strong chest. Let my fingers follow the fall and rise of definition in his perfect abs. It's like I'm seeing him for the first time. No, not the first—he's still "familiar Nick," but the angle has changed. I haven't moved, still staring at Nick. He catches me looking, gives me the widest grin possible, and opens his arms wide.

"Come on," he shouts, walking backwards towards the lip of the overhang. Then he spins round and leaps off the top. I rush to the edge, not knowing if he's alright. I thought it was just a shallow pool, but a few seconds later he bobs to the surface, laughing and shaking water from his long blond fringe. I can't get my own clothes off fast enough and follow him in.

The water is cold. I lose my breath with the shock of it, and rise out of the water, gasping. Nick is there, concern written on his face.

"I'm fine," I croak, still fighting to draw air into my lungs. He rubs my back and soon I'm able to take steady breaths.

"Sorry, that was, erm, much colder than I'd expected."

His hand gently pushes away the hair that got plastered to my face in the plunge. The gesture, so seemingly normal before, is now achingly intimate.

"You've never been wild swimming before?"

"Never," I admit.

"Not even in the sea?"

"We never had time." The only occasion I'd ever been to a seaside town was for a dance competition, and we didn't get time to enjoy the seaside as well. A cloud drifts across my memories, that maybe I'd missed out on a few things in my childhood. I realise I wouldn't be the dancer I am if I hadn't have worked hard, but I can't help feeling an ache at missing something I never had the chance to have. It would have been nice to have run barefoot in the sand—just once.

"We'll make time." Nick's promise pulls me to the present, and I barely get the chance to say "thank you, I'd like that," when we're caught in the spray of a form landing in the water next to us. I see Kieran's red hair before the rest of him emerges. He shakes his curls like a dog, flinging water over us both.

Laughing, Nick flicks water back at him, and I join in until I can barely see and there's water flying all over. Riley jumps in and we all receive another drenching. He swims over to rescue Kieran as we're still dousing him with water. Nick is the first to get a dunking, but I manage to swim out of his reach just in time, and I hide behind Nick, who has resurfaced.

We carry on playing like this for a while. Dunking and soaking each other. Taking it in turns, throwing each other up out of the water to perform backflips. Something in my chest eases. My thoughts of not being accepted by Nick's friends are blown away on a breeze.

Eventually, Riley calls time and climbs out of the pool. Now we've calmed down, hunger pangs edge in, and I climb out too. I grab a towel, handing one to Nick as he flops down onto the grass. Kieran joins us and once he's also partly dry, hands round sausage rolls, sandwiches, and packets of crisps. He fetches out a bottle of beer each too, and although the picnic is simple, I can't remember a time I've enjoyed myself so much.

After we've eaten and cleared the rubbish away, Nick stands and offers me his hand. I take it and he pulls me up.

"C'mon," he whispers with a smile. Nick has a hundred different smiles, and this one holds promises.

I glance back at Riley and Kieran, but they look to be dozing in the afternoon sun.

We walk to the top of the overhang and look over.

"On three?" Nick asks, and I nod.

We jump in, still holding hands, and this time because I've already acclimatised to the water—which isn't as cold when you get used to it—I stay breathing properly.

Nick tugs me to the edge of the pool so we're directly below the overhang. There's a rocky ledge where we can stand, the water at waist height. I'm surprised at how secluded it is. Even if anyone did walk along the path, they wouldn't be able to see down here. Nick's promise-filled smile is accentuated by his darkening eyes as he places a hand on my waist and cups my face with the other, drawing me in for a kiss. I raise my hands to the nape of his neck, pulling him down further and deeper into the kiss as his tongue finds mine. He pushes his hips forward, grinding slowly. I can feel his hard cock through the flimsy material of his swim shorts and my own thickens in response. I know he feels the effect he's having on me as he grins against my mouth and I nip his lip, earning me a soft groan in the process. That only serves to make my cock bounce slightly, and he chuckles gently. He pulls back from the kiss and looks at me. He runs his fingers across my chest and then traces lower, stopping just above the surface of the water.

"Can I?" he whispers. The request, given so respectfully, lodges somewhere in my ribcage, and I can only nod my assent because you need breath to speak and I don't have any left.

His eyes never leave mine as his fingers run along the

waistband of my shorts and dip inside. He grazes the tip of my cockhead and I jerk slightly from the sensitivity of it, despite being underwater. He eases my shorts down until my cock is freed. The water is surprisingly clear, and I watch as he runs his hand up its length. I've fantasised about what it would be like to have his hands on me, but whatever I imagined doesn't come close to the delicate touch he has. And yet still I want more.

"I want to see you," I whisper, suddenly wanting to see what his cock looks like.

"Oh yes, D," he says as he pulls his shorts down, too. I reach out and explore with my hand. It's long and thick, a bit more than mine, but not excessively.

"*Mmmm.*" Nick edges a little closer until his cock touches mine and I feel a frisson of excitement, and thrust a little at him, a move which catches me by surprise. I see delight dance across his face.

"Put your hands on my hips," he says, and I comply. My curiosity at his command is satisfied when he takes both of us together in one hand and starts languidly stroking up and down.

"Holy fuck, Nick!" The words slip out and he chuckles breathily. I can't keep my hands on his hips, because one wants to grab the perfect flesh of his ass, pulling us closer while the other clings to his shoulder. What I cannot do is tear my eyes away from the sight, even underwater, of his hand rhythmically sliding up and down. I'm mesmerised at the sight of our cockheads disappearing and reappearing through his fist. I'm aware of the friction of his hand on one side and the solidity of his cock on the other. It's all I can do to try to hold on, to allow this moment to go on forever, but I can't. A warmth blooms through my lower back and my balls tighten.

"Nick, I—" He doesn't let me finish as he captures my

mouth, kissing me hard while he increases the pressure with his hand. It's enough to push me over the edge and I jerk as my orgasm washes over me. He strokes a couple more times and I feel him shudder against me, his kisses lightening, and eventually he pulls away. He looks at me, and although he is smiling, he's gnawing slightly on his bottom lip. I know this to be a nervous trait, which doesn't happen very often, and I realise he's waiting for my reaction. My heart feels too big right now, like there is no longer any room for its expansion, though it could just be because it's pumping harder than normal. I swallow.

"I have no idea what that was, but when can we do it again?"

He releases a huge breath and gives me a smile, like I've just given him the world.

I look down between us, at the white strings floating on the water's surface, and wonder if we should have desecrated this beautiful spot in such a manner. Even worse is that they cling to us.

"Um, should we have done that?" I see some of them start floating across the pool, heading for the stream that runs towards the river.

"I don't know." Nick laughs. "But maybe we should get out for a bit."

I can't agree quickly enough.

Drowsily blinking in the light, I realise I must've dozed off in the sunshine. Nick is lying next to me, propped up on one elbow. I can't see Riley or Kieran, though all the bags, clothes, and towels are still strewn across the ground. I hear laughter and splashing, so assume they're in the pool. I stretch in the warmth, content and enjoying the feeling of not needing to be anywhere, not doing anything for a while.

Nick glances down at me.

"Hey sleepy," he says.

I yawn. "Well, someone drained the life out of me." And it earns me a giggle. I notice he is turning something over in his mouth.

"What have you got there?" I ask, knowing full well it'll be something sweet based.

"What's it say?" he asks, and flips it over between his teeth. It's a candy heart, with "Be Mine" written across it.

"It says, 'Be mine,'" I dutifully read out to him, and get the merest flash of his mischievous smile before his lips are on mine and he tongues the sweet into my mouth. I don't have a chance to resist, but I'm up for the game, and as he draws his mouth away, I follow him, wanting more kisses. He tastes of candy, and while I don't have quite the sweet tooth he does, I could develop a liking for him tasting of it. I push the sweet back into his mouth and halfway in he bites down, breaking it in two. Half each. It's silly, it's just a sweet, but when we break apart and I crunch on the rest of it, letting the pieces dissolve on my tongue, I can't help feeling that, once again, the prism has shifted and my life is now pre-sweet and post-sweet.

Chapter 18

Nick

I raise my glass and take a long drink of the cool beer.

Darcy and I have been practising hard over the last few days for the regionals, as well as what we plan to dance at the Nationals. We've also been discussing plans for the forties event, though that will happen after the competition. But today, Darcy is having a family dinner with his sister and his parents for their anniversary. And so it is that I find myself at a loose end on a Sunday afternoon and accept my dad's invitation to join him at the club.

It's been a long time since I've gone to the working men's club. It used to be a regular haunt when I was younger, being dragged along to bingo nights and cheesy discos. I don't think it's changed much since then. The bench-style seating is still covered in the same worn Draylon, and half the tables have beer mats wedged under one leg to counteract the wobble. If you sniff too deeply, not to be recommended, you can still smell the faint whiff of stale tobacco from when smoking was permitted. It's also been the event location for every imaginable personal occurrence in our community. From christenings, through birthday parties, weddings, and wakes, the club is a focal point for recording all the major events of life.

Mostly, though, it serves as a local pub—especially for the workers who have been, or still are part of the steel industry. Dad has been coming here to meet his friends every weekend since he started working. I can't remember a time when he's missed a Sunday. Even on Saturday match days, he would meet up with his friends prior to kick-off. Sundays were for game analysis, which was what was happening around me. My dad, Alan, and their other friend, Barry.

I let their discussion wash over me. I don't have any interest in football, so I'm completely oblivious when they ask a question.

"Is tha coming t'match next week?"

"Hmm?" I look up, a little dazed.

"T'match? Is tha coming?" It was Barry who asked.

"No, I can't. I'm dancing next weekend." It's the date of the regional competition, and my chance to prove I'm good enough to dance at the Nationals.

"Is tha still doing that?" They knew I danced, but I don't see my dad's friends very often.

"Yes, I am. Darcy and I have a competition next week."

There's a brief pause before Barry responds. "Darcy? She sounds summat posh for you."

I wince slightly, even though it's a natural enough assumption. Men dance with women, right? And it's not like Darcy is a masculine name. It can be used for any gender.

I catch my dad's eye. He's gone stock still, pint glass half-raised to his mouth. At this moment, I understand he'd never told his friends about me. I didn't think it was a secret, but I can't imagine him announcing to the world that he has a gay son. It's only been a couple of weeks since I knew he fully accepted me.

I don't have a problem with the world knowing who I am, but I'm here, in my dad's domain, and I don't want to make his life any harder. These aren't my friends, so I don't need them to know. I can just walk away. But these are my dad's only friends, and I think back to how I'd heard him with Alan when they were working together, the jocularity and how comfortable he was. I wouldn't ruin that for him.

As I watch him, he blinks very slowly, and then gives me a barely perceptible nod. Luckily I speak Dad, and I know he's saying, "It's up to you, son."

I'm pretty sure my dad knows his friends well enough to know they aren't homophobes, but he could be putting their friendships on the line here. A warmth spreads in my core and expands in my chest with pride, that he's willing to do that for me.

I give him a small smile to show that I understand.

It's my call.

He's known and worked with his friends for years. I know what working banter is like, especially in heavy industry, and to say it isn't politically correct would be an understatement. Even though they might not hold the prejudices behind their words, they are of a generation where racial and gender stereotyping were normal, especially on television. It's a hard habit to break, the sayings and catchphrases that have been beamed into your brain every evening for decades. I don't feel like taking on the role of educator for them. But at the same time, if I don't say anything now, I'll miss my chance.

It's my call.

I think back to Darcy's concerns that he felt he didn't know how to behave in society. His fears that he wouldn't be accepted. He wasn't even exposed to the same dour and unpretentious people I was through my dad and work, and he was still worried. But we can only make things easier for people like Darcy if we're willing to stand up for ourselves and normalise who we are. I could do this for him, I *would* do this for him.

It's my call . . .

And then it isn't.

My dad kicks it straight out of the park.

I watch as he turns to Alan and Barry.

"Darcy's a lad. He's Nick's boyfriend."

Time stretches. No one says a word. I receive a small, nervous smile from my dad and I fully understand what he's just done for me. He's been the one to stand up for us and I've never loved him more than I do right now.

I can see that, even though he was confident things would be alright, in this moment where everything hangs in the balance, a thousand possibilities are probably hurtling through his mind. The silence at the table warps, and sounds I haven't heard before create a jarring contrast. The clink of glasses at the bar. The door through to the toilets bangs. The clack as someone takes a shot at the pool table in the corner.

I reach for my glass, needing to ease the sandpaper lining my throat. As I take a gulp, Barry stands, and three sets of eyes follow him.

"Well, I hope he looks better in one of them fancy frocks than tha would. Tha's shoulders are too wide to carry it off." He slaps me on the back as he passes. I choke on my beer.

"Reyt, it's my round. Does tha want another?" He doesn't wait for an answer and toddles off to the bar. The world comes back into focus as I cough, trying to recover from my beer going down the wrong pipe. I snort to dispel the residue that's coming back down my nose.

My dad sits back, blowing out his cheeks in relief.

Alan glances between us and then fixes his gaze on my dad. "What, you didn't think we knew about Nick?" He jerks his head at me. I pick up my glass to take another swig. I'm very behind on finishing if Barry is fetching more.

My dad stares wide-eyed at him for a few seconds, a furrow across his brow.

"I mean, the lad doesn't like football," Alan pronounces.

I lose my beer again.

"You can't say that!" I cough, wearing more of my drink than I'd like, which is none.

"Well, it's true, isn't it?"

"Well, yes, I don't like football, but that isn't a prerequisite for being gay. There are loads of gay footballers, and fans."

Alan grunts at me. A noise that means he understands his argument doesn't hold up, but he's clinging to it anyway. I bite back a smile. My dad and his friends are cut from the same cloth. They'll believe what they want to believe and create a world around it.

Barry arrives back from the bar and, with a long-practised art, places three pint glasses down in one go, disappearing for a moment to fetch the fourth, and a few packets of crisps and pork scratchings which he plops down on the table. Beer snacks. This is unprecedented. It's almost a celebration. My dad, who still looks like he's in shock, turns to Barry.

"Did you know about Nick?"

Barry is busy opening a packet of pork scratchings. "Aye, suspected, for sure." Having extracted one, uses it for emphasis as he waves his hand in my direction. "He wears makeup, Frank."

Again, not an indication, but as I'm currently wearing a bit of eyeliner, I'm going to let that one pass for now. Looks like I got the educator role after all.

My dad runs his hand down his face like he can't take it all in, and I give him my most reassuring smile. He'll be alright.

I pick up the full pint glass in front of me and raise it slightly.

"Thanks Barry."

"Tha's welcome lad." Barry nods. "Now tell us 'bout this dance competition. Our Brenda loves that one on the telly. Is it owt like that?"

I spend the next few minutes explaining the similarities and the differences between official competitions and the celebrity versions that are broadcast. I tell them a bit about the regional and the national competitions.

They ask questions, some of them intelligent about the dances, and some of them for fun, like, *"Who gets to be t'girl?"* and, *"Dus thee have to wear a dress?"* I decide to take them all in good humour.

When I say that the Nationals are being held at the city hall this year, Alan pipes up. "Ooh, is that what our Maggie's been on about? She mentioned something the other day. I reckon I might get her some tickets, then."

"Aye, me too, for our Bren," Barry chimes in.

They both look at my dad, who's looking like someone has replaced his friends with aliens.

"You must have got some already, Frank."

That my dad would want to come along had never occurred to me. I wasn't sure he knew about it as I hadn't told him, though of course Mum knew. No doubt she would have found a way to make sure he came along in that subtle way she has with him. I see confusion cross his face, because if there's one thing my dad isn't, it's a liar. But I don't want him to have to uncomfortably own up to his friends that he doesn't have tickets.

"Of course he has," I reply for him, making a mental note to ask Claire if it's possible to get some really good tickets for my parents.

My dad smiles a look of thanks, and recovers enough to

join in the rest of the conversation. He looks more comfortable when talk returns to familiar ground, and we stay for a couple more rounds.

Later, we walk back up the hill towards home. I'm trying to process what just happened. I've spent a lot of my life feeling like I just existed in my dad's life. That he was fine with me as long as I didn't draw attention to being *different*. That he could ignore it, sweep it under the carpet.

I discovered he was more accepting the other week. But what he did tonight has blown me away; to own me in front of his friends is no small thing.

Dusk is settling around us, and I don't know if it's the effect of the afternoon drinking, or if it's that time of day—on the cusp between light and dark, when confidences seem able to slip more easily through the cracks—that prompts him to speak.

"I'm sorry, son." His voice is quiet and I'm not sure if I've heard him right. I don't answer.

"I'm sorry for not taking an interest. I didn't realise it meant so much to you."

He stops and I halt beside him. He's staring straight ahead and I want him to look at me. I want to know if he means it.

"Dad?" He turns to face me. "Thank you for doing that for me back in the pub."

"I'm proud of you, Nick. I might not always have shown it, but I am. I want you to know that."

He opens his arms and I step forward into them. I can't remember the last time my dad hugged me. I bury my face in the rough material of his jacket and hug him back. Eventually, he releases me and I step back. He gives me a couple of nods and I smile. He doesn't speak and I know why. If I can see the dampness I feel in the corners of my eyes mirrored in his, then the lump in my throat must be there, too. We silently resume our journey back home.

Chapter 19

Darcy

I pace the dance studio again, wiping my palms on my sweatpants for what feels like the twenty-fifth time. Nick will be arriving soon and for once, I don't know what to say to him, what to do. It isn't like I haven't planned the evening meticulously . . . Well, the first part I have. Dance practice and then dinner. After that is a big fog of trying not to think about it. My parents left an hour ago for their couple of days in London. I send a silent thanks to Claire for thinking of it and organising it. I'm excited about the chance to have Nick stay over, but that doesn't mean to say I'm not nervous about it.

Like I say, I've planned it all. My dad helped me make a chocolate torte for dessert—yes it's Nick, so I started with the sweet course—and I've planned pasta for the main course. Everything is prepped, I just need to cook it later. But it won't take long and it's something I can do—I've practised.

Dad gave me a hug before they left. Of course, they already knew about Nick. I'm not sure they even needed

Claire to tell them. At least my dad didn't, and despite Nick's arrogance about it—that I *will* call him out on at some point —yes, my dad does adore him. But the way I see it, who wouldn't? Not me, that's for sure.

My mum hasn't been pushing for more tryouts lately. Which is odd, as the regionals are only a few days away. But she did mention something about being excited, and mentioned a surprise, so maybe Claire had told her about my plans to dance with Nick. If so, that can only be a good thing. I wanted it to be a surprise for her, but perhaps that's what she's referring to and Claire had asked her to not let on that she knew.

After another couple of laps of the studio and some half-hearted warmups, I have a stern talk with myself about being a pro and that I can't let nerves get to me - but this is worse than any competition, big or small. I'd rather be standing, waiting to dance for the damn royal family right now, than suffer the nervous bubbles that are dancing some sort of jive in my stomach.

I put on some music, determined to concentrate properly on some warmup routines. I hear the door open and there he is. He looks so gorgeous, his cheeks a little pink from the walk from the bus stop and a rucksack hanging off one shoulder. He smiles and the bubbles settle to a low boil.

"I . . . er." My power of speech seems to have failed me, though. He walks over and cups my face with both his hands, following with a gentle kiss.

"You were saying?" he says as he pulls back.

"Um . . . hello?" Nope, speech is still beyond my capabilities right now.

He sniggers and says, "Hello to you, too." He plants a kiss on my forehead before releasing me and heading to the changing rooms to take off his jacket and change his shoes.

As he comes back out, I change the music to our dance song as I'm not sure I can go straight into a hold with him right now. As he hears the first bars, he gives me a grin and I know I've made a good choice. We dance it through a few times and I feel better able to function. It's loosened me up and I'm having fun. I push everything else to the back of my mind. I'll worry about that later. Right now, I want to dance.

A couple of hours later, we're both pretty tired, and quite a lot sweaty. We've been through our dances for the regionals several times, nailing the timings. Nick won on his choice of the waltz and I got my choice of the cha-cha-cha. We've also been through what we plan to dance at the Nationals. We'll do the two from the regionals, but we'll also dance the other eight dances. The Viennese waltz, the faster of the two waltzes, still needs some work and we still have to finalise the paso doble. Traditionally, in that dance, the man takes the role of the bullfighter and the woman dances the role of the cape. We have yet to work out how to make it look effective with two guys instead, but I'm sure we can figure it out in time.

I think it's about time to finish, but Nick suggests dancing the waltz one more time—for luck, he says.

The music starts, and the familiar notes of "Is it You" fill the room. Nick steps into my hold with a small smile and a gleam in his eye that I don't recognise. The music takes us through the start like we've practised hundreds of times. One-two-three, one-two-three. We reach the first turn and coming out of it, Nick moves a millisecond before me. My feet are doing the correct steps, and after years of dancing they're on automatic, but it takes a few seconds for my brain to kick in that I'm going backwards and Nick is now leading. He's in control. A fizzle travels up my spine and spreads across my chest.

We reach another turn and I step forward, taking the lead again. There's a small part of me that registers that I didn't actually take it, but that Nick moved first, allowing me to step into the space he'd created. My heart starts hammering on my ribcage. I glance at him, and his sexy smile flips my stomach, the effervescence returning. I lead us into the whisk and the chassé, following with the promenade, and then another turn. Nick moves quicker again and my traitorous feet follow. I can't think straight, and if I didn't know the moves so well, I'd probably end up in a heap. As my brain short circuits, all I know is that I don't want this to end. We turn and Nick leads me into another whisk and chassé, followed by a spin turn, and I realise that this is no longer our choreography. Nick is ad-libbing. The thrill of not knowing what will come next sets every nerve ending alight as he dances me around the floor. He leads into a reverse turn and I recognise that we've returned to our practised dance and are entering the final sequence. Our ending features us splitting apart, holding hands with one hand and the other outstretched, but as we reach it, Nick moves his hand to my hip and pulls me closer. As the music stops, we're pressed together. He ghosts a kiss across my lips, and I swallow, waiting to see what will happen next, hardly daring to breathe.

Another song begins. When the first sounds of the guitar intro starts, I recognise the soft sounds of "More Than Words," a perfect song for the rumba. I didn't know Nick had swapped the playlist, and his thoughtful planning causes my knees to lose their ability to hold me up. Nick changes his hands to a leading hold. He gives me his tiny sexy smile again, the one that sends my insides fluttering. He kisses me again and as he does, he steps forward and I follow. Kissing while dancing is not something I've tried before, or even thought about. But it feels so right and natural. After the first basic step, he pulls back slightly and lifts his arm for me to turn, and as I step under, he brushes a hand down my back, my skin tingling from his touch. We open out for the New York step, and I seductively sway my hips away and back, earning a lustful look that sets my body aflame. Then, as we come back together, it seems natural to kiss. After a couple more basic steps, my ability to count to four almost fails and brings our bodies closer, making me dizzy with desire. Next, he leads me into a fan and the Alemana turn, where I step under his arm again and he trails a hand across my ass, keeping it there as we come back into a closed hold and another kiss. I think it's at about this point that any steps that can be recognised as anything officially ballroom are abandoned and we make it up, moving in synchronous harmony.

The final bars of the song fade and we're standing close. He has his hands on my hips and he drops his head to kiss up my throat. I lean back slightly to let him. I can't think past wanting to be closer, and this doesn't seem nearly enough.

"What is it you want?" He breathes open mouth kisses along my neck.

"I . . . I . . ." Words are definitely not my strong point today, but what he's doing is very distracting and I can't marshal my thoughts. "I don't know," I gulp.

"It's like a dance, D. Someone needs to take control, someone needs to lead." He kisses across to the other side of my throat and I'm glad he has a tight grip on me, as I'm not sure I can stand on my own. My hands are gripping his biceps, his strong arms, which have just been spinning me round. Not a position I usually find myself in and I want more of it. I plan to say *I want you*, but my brain, somehow filtering through what has happened, translates this into something else.

"What about you?" I whisper.

I feel his breathy chuckle against my neck. "I learned both parts."

Chapter 20

Nick

"Teach me, please." Darcy's words make me want to scoop him up in my arms. What I do instead is grind my hips into his, knowing he'll feel how hard I am from dancing with him for the last few minutes. His sharp intake of breath makes my cock twitch, and I notice his own erection pushed up against me. I can't help but nip his throat, eliciting a small whine. I grab his hand, as if I don't move now, I'm going to be taking him in the middle of the studio floor. I pull him after me and up the stairs to his room.

Once inside, I claim his mouth with mine and walk him backwards to his bed, following as he lies down, and cover his body with mine. I want to explore every inch of him and if I don't slow down, I'm not going to get very far. I pull back and look down at him. His green eyes are shining. A slow smile spreads across his face.

"You okay?" I whisper, and he nods back.

It's then that I remember I've left my rucksack downstairs, which has supplies in it.

"Be right back." I roll off him, missing the warmth of his body already.

"Do you want a drink?" he asks, and I smile at his ingrained professionalism. It's one of the things I love about him. He's not wrong to ask, though. We've danced for hours and haven't hydrated. It would be a good idea.

"Yes, that'd be good, thanks."

When I return, he holds out a bottle of water and I take it, downing it in a couple of gulps, not realising how thirsty I am.

I reach for my phone and put on some music. It's a playlist I've spent a fair amount of time creating over the last couple of weeks, making sure it doesn't include any of the songs we're going to be dancing to. I don't want any interruptions about what would be a good step to include. I need no distractions from me extracting every ounce of pleasure I can from Darcy's lithe body.

I strip off my T-shirt, and head to where Darcy is sitting on the side of the bed. I hope the small break hasn't allowed any of his usual fears to crowd in, though if they do, I plan to kiss them all away again.

I crouch between his legs, resting my hands on his thighs. His hands reach out to explore my chest and I turn my head so I can kiss the back of one of his hands. He cups my face with it and directs it so he can kiss me. His tongue pushes against me and I open, giving his bottom lip a nibble in the process. After a few minutes, I stand and pull him up with me. I push his T-shirt up and he lifts his arms so I can pull it off over his head. I drop my head to kiss his shoulder while running my hands down his back and grasping his ass to pull him closer.

I want to feel more of him, so I slide my hands inside the

waistband of his sweatpants. He yields against me and moans softly. I love it. I've just discovered my favourite sound and I want to hear it over and over. Grabbing his perfect ass, I hoist him up and he wraps his legs round my waist and his arms lock round my neck. I walk him the couple of steps to the bed and lower him down onto it. He releases me and stretches his arms above his head. He looks so perfect, well nearly; he has far too many clothes on. I want to see him naked. I tug off his sweatpants and socks, leaving his briefs on, and kneel between his legs. I pick up his leg and plant a row of kisses from his ankle, past his knee, and up his thigh. Placing the gentlest kiss possible on his cock which bulges through his briefs, I smile at the involuntary shudder he gives and continue down his other leg until I reach his ankle.

"I want to taste you, D. See if you taste as good as you look."

"Yes." It's all the encouragement I need, and I carefully pull his briefs over his cock, sliding them off.

He looks utterly sexy, stretched out on his bed. I'm about to feast on him when he lifts a foot and pushes it against my thigh.

"Take these off."

Well, I suppose it's only fair. I climb off the bed and take off my own sweatpants.

"Um, Nick?"

I turn round to face Darcy.

"What are you wearing?"

"What, these?" I run my hands down my abs and over the lacy shorts I have on. Not all lace, as I didn't want to be uncomfortable while dancing, but these are soft and stretchy and silky and a lovely soft blue colour.

"*Fuuuuuck!*" Darcy scrambles off the bed and his hands are on me. It feels so good. "They're gorgeous." His voice is full of wonder. "I didn't even know this was a thing."

His hands are exploring, running over my ass and he plays his fingers up and down my cock, feeling it through the lace.

"*Fuuuuuck.*" His exclamation is softer this time, but no less potent to me and I see a dark mark of precum showing on the material.

"You'd like some?" I ask, wanting to kiss him, but he doesn't answer. He's looking down between us, one hand on me, his thumb teasing over the end of my cockhead through the fabric, which is giving me problems focussing. His other hand is fisting his own cock. I remember back to the park, and I can't tear my eyes away.

"Would you carry on? Doing that?" I indicate his hand and he raises his eyes to mine. They're luminous emeralds and I get lost in their beauty.

"To me or you?" He gives a small smile, and for a second, I forget what the question is.

"To you, I want to watch."

"Mmm, can you leave these on?" A part of me wants to rip them off and bring on my own release, because Darcy's fascination has my cock aching to be touched. But the thought of having his eyes on me while I watch him invokes some delicious edging and I can't refuse him.

"Sure I can, honey," I croak out. "Now on the bed."

He sits on the bed and scoots back so he's leaning against his pillows. I reach for my bag.

"I have lube," he says, and waves a hand towards the drawers by the side of his bed. I cross the room and fetch the bottle, handing it to him. He opens it and squeezes some into his hand. Then, with a coy smile, he goes back to stroking himself.

I'm captivated by the sight of him with his head thrown back, his eyes hooded as he watches me. His hand rhythmically skimming up and down his length. It's the sexiest scene I've ever witnessed. I kneel between his legs and lean over, capturing his mouth, meeting his tongue with mine, and not knowing which of us groans first when he runs a hand up my hard cock.

I rock back on my heels and reach for the lube.

"Bend your knees," I say softly and Darcy complies, half blissed out already.

"Oh, wow," he exhales, as I graze a finger across his hole.

"You like that?" I ask, doing it again.

"*Mmmmm.*" He wriggles down the bed a little, giving me more access. I play my finger across it a few more times and then withdraw it. The whine Darcy gives at the loss of contact is adorable.

"Just need more lube," I explain, and he sighs slightly.

This time when I press my finger, he thrusts against it slightly.

"You want more?"

"Uh-huh." His eyes flicker to mine briefly before dropping back into their languid state.

I breach his hole and he jerks.

"Too much?" I ask, concerned I'd hurt him.

"Fuck no, do it again." He pushes down onto my finger and I go a bit deeper.

"You're so tight, D." I love how he grips me, and I thrust my finger in a few more times before adding a second one.

He makes a low moan and the noise travels straight to my balls, sending a tingle shooting up my spine. I can't take it any longer, the vision of him jerking himself whilst practically impaling himself on my fingers.

"Damn, D. Honey, you're so beautiful." I kneel over him, and with my free hand, manage to tug my shorts down to release my cock. I *need* to touch it, the ache has become unbearable.

I grab the lube and hand it to Darcy.

"Can you help me out here?"

He flips the cap and squeezes some into my hand. Throwing the bottle back on the bed, I take hold of my cock, smearing the precum round the end and coating the shaft with lube. I'm not going to last very long.

I shift my fingers slightly, hitting Darcy's sweet spot, watching as his abs contract, and he throws his head back further.

"Nick, I'm going to come." His voice is barely a whisper.

"Yes, come for me, D. I want to see that." I hit his bundle of nerves again and his hand speeds up. His eyes flutter closed as he jerks, cum spilling over his chest. I withdraw my fingers, and with a few more strokes, my release joins his, mixing them together. I lean down and kiss up his beautiful neck as he sighs and stretches languorously against the pillows.

"D, honey?"

"Hmmm?" He blinks slowly at me, a gentle smile on his lips.

"I think we should get showered."

"I, um, I don't think I can move. I don't seem to have any bones left." He stretches again with feline grace.

I laugh at him and head to the bathroom to grab a washcloth instead. After I clean us up and then climb onto the bed and put my arms around him, he's already asleep.

Chapter 21

Darcy

I'm not sure if it's my rumbling stomach or my need to pee that wakes me, but both are making a bid for the number one spot. Nick is naked, sprawled out on my bed, which is way too narrow for us to be really comfortable, but it's only for a couple of nights.

I draw my knees up and hug them. I'm enjoying watching him. I've seen him asleep before, and he's fallen asleep on my bed many times. But this is different. I've never woken up next to him in the morning, naked. I watch his eyelids flutter as he stirs slightly, his blond eyelashes barely showing against his cheeks. He has a smattering of stubble across his chin, again, hardly detectable. My eyes track down his body, across his broad shoulders and chest, his impressive biceps, and strong arms. Certainly strong enough to lift me up. The memory of that swirls in my stomach along with a reminder of what we did yesterday. I look lower, following his narrow waist and the dusting of treasure trail to his cock, now soft, nestled in hair which is a darker blond. Would I like it filling me up? If what it felt like with his fingers is any indication, then the thought excites me—a lot. I can't believe how lucky I am to have my best friend and a boyfriend in one very handsome, sexy package.

I get to enjoy this for one more day—until my parents return. It seems ridiculous really, but I can't afford my own place. I know Nick is saving up for a house or flat, but I'm not sure how it's going.

I wonder if we could afford a place together. Is it too soon to think those thoughts? Probably, as this thing between us is so new, though it's not like we haven't known each other for years. But living in the same space permanently . . . That's a big step. So, yes, probably best to not have those thoughts yet, even though I feel a bone-deep surety of how right it is that we're together.

My bladder wins the race to force me to stop admiring Nick and actually move, so I head to the bathroom, grabbing some sweatpants on the way, as I intend to fix my hunger right after.

I'm just making two mugs of tea when Nick stumbles into the kitchen in sweatpants, his hair tousled, and rubbing sleep from his eyes. He comes over and puts his arms around me from behind, nuzzling into my neck.

"*Mmm*. I wish we could do this every day," he says against my neck, and I sigh a small *yes*. My heart catches at him having thoughts similar to mine.

I resolutely ignore it, as it's too soon to think about any of that. We'll just have to make do with things as they are.

"Can you get the milk from the fridge?"

"Do I have to?" His hand is gently caressing up and down my back, his mouth sucking little marks onto my shoulder. It's both beautiful and distracting and I'm finding it difficult to concentrate.

"Well, no, not if you don't want tea or any food."

Reluctantly he pulls away and I can think again, though a part of me wants to call him back and forget about food, forget about the hours of dance practice we have planned for today, and to drag him back to my bedroom. But we didn't eat last night after expending a lot of energy, and I can feel the beginnings of nausea from the effects of low blood sugar, so even if we were to spend the day in bed, we'd still need some energy.

"What do you want for breakfast?" I ask. "Cereal, toast . . . we have eggs, maybe some bacon?"

"I want this." He withdraws his head from the fridge and holds up the chocolate torte.

"Nick! You can't eat that for breakfast."

"Did you make this?" His smile lights up the drab morning light. "For me?"

"Yes, for dessert yesterday." I try not to get distracted by the thought of *why* we missed dessert, or any food. Which just serves to remind me we still haven't eaten. He puts the plate down on the countertop and stands in front of me, bracketing me with his arms.

"Thank you," he whispers, and presses a soft kiss to my lips. "It means a lot that you made this for me." He kisses me again. "You know that making me dessert is the way to my heart, don't you?"

I'm caught off guard by his words. Was he saying he loved me? I mean, we love each other as best friends, but as boyfriends? Are we declaring it? There is no question that I love Nick. I don't have a problem with that. But to admit it out loud feels like a step change, a non-returnable point. It seems far too big a declaration to whisper, half dressed, in a kitchen. So instead I deflect.

"Is it the way to your cock as well?" I hook a finger into

the waistband of his sweatpants and release it with a twang, as I can see very well what effect it has.

He gives me a look, like I've just served myself up for dessert, and pushes his hips forward, whilst at the same time sliding his hands inside the back of my sweatpants and catching hold of my naked ass, pulling me forward to grind into his erection.

"What do you think?" he murmurs, before kissing me again, this time long and deep.

The loud grumble from his stomach is what eventually causes us to stop, though I could have happily stayed in his arms forever. He pulls away and I'm filled with a warm glow from the thought that this is so easy. Us, being together, expressing ourselves—we've not had the opportunity before, as we've always been in someone else's space. I try not to choke on the reminder of how brief this time we have together is.

"You're still not having dessert for breakfast." I try to show my disapproval.

"I can," Nick protests, and reaches for a plate to serve some up for himself. "We can have dessert for breakfast. It's in the code."

I laugh at him. He's not getting me with that one again, but I can match him. "I'm sure it is. However, we've got a lot of practice to do today and just eating sugar isn't going to cut it. You need some carbs as well. I'm not having you crashing on your old ass later because you didn't eat properly."

"Old ass! Old ass?" he almost yells, clutching his hands to his chest like I've just delivered the most crushing insult. I have no sympathy.

"Well, it's older than mine." I grin at him. "Actually, I might start calling you that for your nickname. Meet Nick, he's my old ass."

I place two bowls on the kitchen island and the box of cereal. Nick rolls his eyes but reaches for the box.

"If you do that, then I'll call you my baby boy," he blurts, and we both stop still. *Ewwww.* I'm pretty sure his grimace is a mirror image of the way my face is scrunched up in the way it does when you realise that you might have gone too far.

"I prefer 'honey,'" I say softly, and his face relaxes.

He continues to pour cereal into the two bowls and drowns both of them in milk, as is the proper way.

"So why 'honey?'" I ask, as I finish making the tea and then start tucking into my own cereal.

"Honey is the sweetest thing I've tasted," he replies, waving his spoon for emphasis. "It has so many amazing properties and is made by the most hardworking of all creatures. It reminds me of you."

I concentrate on my breakfast, not trusting myself to look at him right now. No one has ever said anything so beautiful or personal to me before. I risk a glance at him from under my lashes and see his dark blue eyes watching me.

"Thank you," I croak out, and his mouth curls upwards slightly before he returns to finishing his cereal.

When he's done, I can't stop him from reaching for the torte, and I fetch a plate so I can have some too, suffering his smirk as he serves me up a slice.

We've finished breakfast and are clearing away when there's a loud noise from outside, so we head to the window to look out. A huge digger now occupies the development site past the end of the row of shops, its huge jaws scraping across the uneven ground, clawing at anything in its way.

"I guess it's going ahead, then." Nick stands shoulder to shoulder with me as we look out.

"Mum says it might bring more business to the school." I shrug. Every time I think about it, I think there's more to this than my parents are telling me. I know the lessons haven't been busy. But they agreed to my event, and I want to practise more for that today, as well as making sure Nick and I are foot-perfect for the competition in a few days' time.

"Maybe, but right now, we have things to do," Nick says, pulling me towards the bathroom. "And the first of those is having a shower."

I turn the water on and while I wait for it to run through hot, I strip off my sweatpants. Nick does the same and then gestures for me to enter, stepping in behind me and shutting the door. The proximity of him, hot and naked, watching the water cascade over his toned body, has what was a fairly decent semi turning fully hard in seconds.

He notices and sniggers softly.

"You can talk," I protest, using a finger to pull his own erection down, and releasing it so it bounces back against his stomach. For that I receive a low growl and him using his body to push me against the tiled wall while he kisses my breath away.

"Fuck, Darcy," he says as he pulls back a moment later, leaving me kiss-blissed and happy. "I want to—"

"Yes," I interrupt.

"Yes, what?" A tiny line appears between his eyes.

"Fuck Darcy." I grin at him. He laughs, but shakes his head a little, spraying me with water droplets from his hair.

He leans forward, his mouth very close to my ear, and whispers, "There is nothing more I'd like to do than bend you over and bury my dick so far in you that you'll still be feeling it next week."

I can't answer. I just stare at him, my blood pounding and

my body alive with desire. The thought of that scrambling my brain.

"But I'm not going to."

"Uh?" Okay, what just happened?

"I'm all wet now and there's no way I can get a condom on wet. And"—his eyes glitter—"I'd rather go without, feel you properly."

I hear a whine. Did I just whine?

"I'm already on PrEP, but we ought to make sure about any STIs. So we'll go get checked out, together, at the clinic first. Is that okay?" Again, he's checking in with me. The care he shows sliding through each of my breathless pants and taking root deep in my soul. I nod. It's all I can do right now.

"Good." His mouth is back at my ear, his breath sending electric signals down my neck and making my cock twitch. "Until then, we'll have to think of something else."

With that, he lowers himself to his knees and looks up at me, his eyes dark as he licks his lips before parting them and wrapping them around my cockhead.

I try to watch, fascinated at seeing my cock sliding in and out of his mouth, but I can't. The sensations of his swirling tongue, coupled with the warm pressure of his mouth, have me on the brink within a couple of minutes. He pulls almost all the way off and applies just his tongue to the head, dipping his tongue into my slit, and it's almost too much. I groan, arching my back and thrusting towards him. Trembling starts in my thighs and I have to force myself back against the wall to stay upright. He takes me wholly back into his mouth and, when I feel it hit the back of his throat, it tips me over the edge and my orgasm rushes through me. He keeps his mouth locked on me, taking every drop.

Then he stands and gently turns me around. He leans forwards and whispers in my ear. "I knew you'd taste like honey."

I can barely stand, but I rest against the tiles. He grabs the soap and lathers some over my ass and his hands before snaking one arm around my waist. I'm grateful for the support.

He takes his cock in his hand and I feel it glide against my crease. I stand there, still in too much of a euphoric state to do anything except enjoy the pleasurable feeling of his cock occasionally grazing across my hole, and the rhythmic slapping sound of his hand. My brain idly wonders if jerking off has a time signature and what it would be. I feel him thrust once more and he spills over my ass cheeks. He presses against me, wrapping his other arm around me and planting a kiss on my shoulder, before I feel him rest his forehead against me, panting heavily.

"Give me a minute," he laughs against my skin.

"I'm not going anywhere," I reply, equally drained.

After a few minutes, he straightens up and helps me to stand properly. I reach for the soap to clean us both up.

Chapter 22

Nick

"I'll see you later," I call out to my mum as I head towards the back door.

"Nick," she says, and I turn around as she catches up to me. "Good luck, love. I hope it all goes well."

"Thanks Mum." She draws me into a hug. I'm due to catch the bus in five minutes. I'm going to Darcy's and then we're all travelling to the regionals together. I can barely contain my excitement as we've practised so hard for this. I'd taken my clothes to Darcy's last night when we had a final run through of our two dances. A formal suit for the waltz, and for the cha-cha-cha, a black high-necked tunic and trousers. Darcy's is similar; he has a blue pattern running down the front of his tunic, which is continued down the side of my trousers, so they're complementary rather than being the same. It took a long time to choose something that would work. Hours spent sitting side by side on his bed searching online shops. Okay, it might have taken longer due to the amount of kissing and cuddling that went on as well.

I have an exciting piece of news to share with Darcy as well later. I've nearly saved enough money for a fairly decent deposit on a place. It won't be big, and it might be something that'll need doing up, but that would be fun to do.

My mum releases me and I give her a peck on her cheek.

"See you later," I call, as I jump the back steps down onto the yard. I've just enough time to say hello to Gran. She'll be upset if she doesn't get to wish me luck, too.

I take her steps two at a time and burst through the back door, striding through to the front room.

"Gran, I'm off—" I halt on the threshold. My heart stops.

"What the—Gran. Gran!" She's lying on the floor, just in front of her favourite chair. I throw myself down next to her, checking for a pulse. It's still there. My heart restarts with a racing beat. I'm up, pulling my phone out of my pocket, cursing as I fumble at the key-lock pattern.

"Mum, Dad," I holler out the back door towards our house as I dial nine-nine-nine.

My mum pokes her head out of our back door at my shout.

"Gran's had a fall. I'm calling an ambulance," I shout. Half the street can hear me, but I don't care; they'll know soon enough, anyway.

I see her hand fly to her mouth before she disappears inside and I hear her shouting, "*Frank*," calling my dad.

My call is answered and I go back inside to give the emergency services as much information as possible.

My mum and dad arrive and kneel by her side.

"Mum, Mum, can you hear me?" My mum's voice sounds broken, and I fight back my own tears. Instead, I fetch a blanket. We can't move her, but we're supposed to keep her warm. The lady on the end of the phone is still talking to me.

No, I don't know how long she's been like that. My mum looks up, whispering that she'd helped her get up and down the stairs only an hour ago. I relay that information. I can hear sirens in the distance and I unlock the front door, going out to direct them to the house and make it easier for them to enter.

The two paramedics are efficient and we draw back as a unit, watching them check a few vitals before loading her onto a stretcher.

I barely hear my dad ask which hospital they're taking her to. We lock up and pile into his van to follow the ambulance. It's only then that awareness of the dance competition comes back to me.

I pull out my phone and text Darcy. We aren't due to dance until this afternoon, so I tell him what's happened and that I'll catch the bus straight to the competition as soon as I know my gran's going to be alright. His answer, of course, is sweet and concerned, and allows me a small smile and respite from my worries. The journey feels like it takes forever and I find it hard to keep still in the van. I grab my mum's hand and she gives me a sad smile as she dabs at her eyes with a tissue.

"Will you stop pacing, love?" My mum's voice is strained and weary. I sigh, plonking myself down into the plastic chair next to her. It feels like we've been sitting in the corridor for hours. Dad has gone to fetch us more tea, as that seems to be the only thing keeping us going right now.

My mum squeezes my knee, trying to give some comfort, but we're all worried. The feeling of being useless and not being able to do anything is unbearable. We've taken it in turns to ask about progress, knowing that they can't tell us anything new and giving us the same answer every time: *she's stable, and the doctors are running tests, and we'll be told as soon as there's anything to know.* It doesn't stop us from asking, though, as it's the only thing we can do. The patience of the nurses is legendary.

The buzz in my pocket indicates another text from Darcy. The warm glow that he's checking in with me only slightly appeases the gnawing anxiety that if I can't get there in time, I'm letting him down. But I'm not going anywhere until I know Gran is going to be okay.

I pace the corridor again, the last cup of tea a nauseating layer over the impotency of our situation. It's while I'm at the other end of the corridor, giving the notices a tenth reading, that a doctor approaches my parents.

I race back, trying to work out if the expression on her face is an indication of good news, or is delivering bad. I guess after years of a job like this, she's managed to train it into a neutral state for these occasions.

"Mrs Turner is now conscious. She is stable, and there's nothing wrong with her vitals, which is quite extraordinary for her age. She has broken her leg, though. However, it is a clean break, so it will heal in time."

"Can I see her?" I cut in. I need to see with my own eyes that she really is okay.

The doctor gives me an amused smile, the first sign of emotion so far.

"I assume you must be Nicholas? She's been talking non-stop about her grandson since she woke up."

"What can I say? I'm her favourite." I give her my widest smile and she laughs. The relief and joy that Gran is going to be alright begins bursting out of me. The doctor doesn't need to know I'm her only grandchild.

"You can go in." With her head, she indicates towards the room behind her and turns back to talk with my parents.

The room is in semi-darkness, which lowers my mood again. I've always thought low light is bad news, but this might be from watching far too many hospital dramas with Gran. She looks so small in the large bed, not that she was big, anyway. She's always been a vital force in my life. The hospital bed, surrounded by softly beeping machines and her medicine drip, has stripped that away like it's a veneer. I see her fragility for the first time and it breaks my heart.

She looks reduced somewhat, lesser and translucent, and I don't want that. I don't want the cold realisation that she might not always be here. I blink back tears as I watch her quietly. She looks asleep.

Snatches of conversation reach me from the door. *"Discharged in a couple of days. We need to think about a care package for her. She won't be mobile for a while. I'll arrange for social services to talk to you."*

Then my mum's voice, strong and insistent. She might be quiet, but she's still my gran's daughter. "We take care of our own. We always have."

I can hear the long-practised patience, with a hint of exasperation in the doctor's response, and part of my brain thinks she might not be from Yorkshire herself. "I understand your care, Mrs Richardson, but you really need to consider . . ."

I tune it all out for now and approach the bed.

I reach for her hand, and while it's still the familiar, warm hand I know, the one that's cupped my cheek a thousand times, it feels smaller now.

Her eyes open, and she fixes me with her blue eyes—my eyes—my favourite colour.

"Nicholas." Her smile is strong at least, and I grin back.

"Thought you were leaving us, did you?" I try to make

light of the situation, but her fading smile shows that she, too, has been forced to face her own fragility.

She gives my hand a squeeze and I try again, softer this time

"We were worried about you. What happened?"

"I tripped, that's all. I got up to get a cup of tea and fell. Well, that's all I remember." Then she frowns at me. "Haven't you got a competition? You haven't missed it, have you?" She gives me a stern look. It's one I recognise and seems to dispel some of the shadows of mortality that have been circling us.

"I . . ." I actually don't know. I haven't thought of the competition once since I entered the room. I've only been concerned about her. "I wanted to make sure you were okay."

She grips my hand, and this time it's strong.

"I know how much it means to you, dear. You must go. I'm fine. I'm glad for the rest, to be honest." This feisty woman is the Gran I recognise.

My parents enter the room and come over.

"Now, go do your dancing. I want you to come back and tell me you won." It's a dismissal.

I grab my phone and look at the time, I can't hold back a grimace as I quickly calculate if I have time to get from the fourth floor of the hospital and across the vast car park to the main road in seven minutes, which is when the next bus is due.

I can try.

I lean over and give her a kiss on her cheek. "Love you, Gran," I whisper, and receive a twinkling smile in return.

I whirl round and make it to the door, planning to break all the "no running in the hospital" rules.

"Nick." I spin back at the sound of my dad's voice.

The retort that I don't have time dies on my lips as I see he's holding out some keys.

"Take the van son, it'll be quicker."

"But—"

"Your mum and I will be here for a while yet, and we can catch the bus back."

"Thanks Dad." I'm astonished as he pushes the keys into my hand. He gives my shoulder a squeeze. "Go make us proud."

I send a text off to Darcy as I ride the elevator down to the ground floor.

Nick: On my way. Save the last dance for me

Chapter 23

Darcy

I blow out a breath as I read Nick's text, letting the wave of relief wash over me and repair the jagged nerve endings of anxiety that have had me on edge all day.

The dread that he won't make it has been building all day. We've been here for hours, supporting some of our clients who have entered the lower levels. Encouraging some of the juniors, trying to calm their nerves, whilst all the time trying to keep a lid on my own.

I roll my shoulders, easing the tension in them, wishing for a moment that Nick was there to rub them. No time for thoughts like that or I won't be able to dance when he arrives. The thought of him, though, helps ease my nerves further. Soon I'll dance with Nick, my Nick, and we can finally show people how good we are together.

I manage the first genuine smile of the day and head to go get ready.

"Ah, Darcy, there you are. Are you ready?" My mum

marches up to me with someone in tow. When I look up, I see it's three-time ballroom champion, Krystal Shaw.

"I'm just about to get ready. Nick will be here soon."

"Nick?" she queries.

"Yes, Nick. I'm dancing with Nick. He was delayed because his gran had a fall, but he's on his way."

"Nick?" Her voice rises with incredulity.

"Yes, Nick. I thought you knew." Her surprise is genuine, and I begin to realise with unease that Claire might not have told her. "I thought Claire—"

"Look. I can see that you have someone already," Krystal says and starts to leave, but my mum grabs her by the wrist.

"You're dancing with Krystal. I've arranged it all," Mum announces. No wonder she had been quiet about the tryouts.

"I don't want to dance with Krystal—no offence Krystal," I direct towards her. A few months ago, I would have jumped at the opportunity, but that was before I wanted dancing to feel how it does when Nick and I dance. "I want to dance with Nick."

"You can't dance with Nick!" my mum whisper-shouts at me, almost baring her teeth.

"Why not?" I've definitely checked the rules ten times over.

"Because you won't win!"

"I don't want to win. I just want to dance my way," I say with more force than I intend, and she draws back as if I've slapped her.

We stand-off for a couple of seconds while she looks at me as if she doesn't know me, which is probably not far from the truth right now. I go to push past her, but she releases Krystal and grabs my wrist instead. "Wait here," She issues the instruction to Krystal and drags me through a door. The room is some sort of storage room for chairs and tables, but it's empty of people. She releases me, but stands close enough to the door that I'd have to physically move her out of the way to leave.

I know I'm about to get a tongue lashing. I'm going to stand firm, stand up for myself. I'm sick of her telling me what to do.

"Darcy Franklin." Her voice is low and I know the tone is her most deadly. "Everything I've done has been for you, to let your talents shine. You can be the next ballroom champion. It's been something you've wanted your whole life. All you've dreamed of for years. This is going to be your year, everyone says so. You are dancing better than ever. You can do this Darcy, you can make your dreams come true."

Her voice softens as she continues. "You know we all love Nick, but you can't win if you dance with him. The judges will never award it to you. Those things only happen in movies, not in real life. Surely you know that?"

I do know it. Claire had been right when she said it, and my mum is right now. Julia's words come back to me and I echo them now.

"Winning was always your dream, Mum, not mine."

She physically deflates, and I take the opportunity to make a break for the door. My hand is on the door handle.

"Darcy?"

Something in her voice halts me. I'm used to a lecture, I'm used to her hardness, but this is a tone she's never used before. It's forlorn, with an undercurrent of desperation.

I wait to hear what else she has to say.

"Your dad and I didn't want to tell you this, but the school is in trouble. Real trouble. Lesson numbers have been dropping, you've seen that. We're finding it harder to attract new clients. Our debts are just going up."

My stomach drops, and I can't quite believe what I'm hearing. I'd suspected that things weren't good, but they'd always brushed it off.

"The forties event—" I turn around, trying to say something, anything to help.

"—is a good idea, Darcy, but it's a drop in the ocean. We've been approached by the developers. They've made us an offer."

"For the school?" My life as I know it is pulled out from under me and I fall on the ruckle of its passing. I have no future without the school. I have no other qualifications.

"For the building, yes." My mum nods. "But we don't have to accept it, not if we can make the school successful again. If you win the Nationals, people will want to come and learn to dance with us. You'll be famous. We need you to win it, Darcy. We're counting on you. You can see that, can't you?"

Everything adds up in my head—the worried looks and hushed discussions. The conversations that have stopped when I've entered a room. I guess that me being wrapped up with Nick has blinded me to what's been going on around us. I feel like I've been selfish, neglecting my family.

My mum comes closer and with a sad smile on her face. "There'll be other years."

My heart feels too heavy to hold right now. But I know what I must do. She's right, we'll have other years to dance together. But first, I need to save my family and my future.

"Why isn't Krystal dancing with Andrew?" I hadn't given any thought to why she might be available. Andrew is her husband, and together they're one of the greatest dance couples on the circuit.

"He had an accident and has broken his arm. He'll be out of action for at least six months. It is a misfortune, but can you see how it's even more of an indication that this is your year?"

It's extremely insensitive of her to say so, but her logic that one of the top contenders to the title is out of action and I can dance with the other is sound.

"Okay, I'll do it." The words are as thick as sawdust, and I open the door. My dad is standing outside as well.

"It's alright Dad, Mum told me about the school."

"Son—" he starts, but I don't listen. I don't want to know any more. My future as I know it hangs teetering on the edge, and I need to make it a solid vision again.

I turn to Krystal and hold out a hand.

"Shall we dance?"

Chapter 24

Nick

I'm grateful for the use of the van, but traffic is worse than ever on the journey. I'm in a hurry, which makes me impatient, and I curse a few other drivers with language that would make my mum blush. Probably not my gran, though. I can barely describe the relief I feel that she'll be alright, though some of the words I heard when my parents were talking with the doctor carve out little pockets of worry in me. I'll talk to my parents later. I'm with my mum—we take care of our family.

I emit another barrage of curses as I come to yet another roundabout— who designed this road?— but I can see the crooked spire of the town in the distance and know I'll be there soon.

It takes longer than I expect to find a parking space, but I eventually manage to squeeze into one and sprint to the Assembly rooms.

As I near the doors, my heart drops. I can hear the

familiar three-four time of the waltz and know that I'm too late. I've let Darcy down. Our chance has gone.

I slip in through the large double doors, and the music is being drowned out by the blood pounding in my ears from the sprint and the disappointment that I feel . . . That Darcy must also be feeling. I need to find him and apologise. He must be here somewhere. I wonder if he can bear to watch. I spy his mum to my right and, thinking he must be close, I make my way through the other spectators to her.

She gives me a smile as I approach.

"Oh Nick, isn't it exciting? I said this year was going to be it for him." She turns back to the dance floor and I follow her line of sight.

All feeling drains from my body as I see Darcy dancing with a woman. Not just any woman, but Krystal Shaw. How did that happen? I can't believe it. My chest constricts and I feel dizzy. I want to go hide somewhere and pretend this day never happened. Instead, I force myself to watch because, well, as painful as it is to me, Darcy is magnificent. Dancing with him is the most amazing feeling in the world, but I also love watching him. Krystal isn't the three-time national champion for nothing, and they look so majestic together. They might not have the flourishes that come with a choreographed and practised routine, but they're easily the best dancers in the room. Even though I'm breaking inside, I can't help but watch them. I can hear the *awws* and *ahhs* from the crowds as they sweep round the room together.

I don't know what I was thinking, believing that we could pull it off as a male couple. There's something elegant about watching a male and female dance. It might be the dress, I don't know, but it just looks different. I realise that I've just been hampering Darcy's chances of winning, and if anyone deserves to win, then it's him. He's worked so hard for years. He's talked about it for as long as I can remember, his eyes lighting up at the thought of competing in them. As much as it's cutting me up to see them out there, I feel proud of him. The music ends and they turn. Darcy looks straight at me, his face going ashen grey. I back away, needing some air. I push through the crowd, who all have their eyes trained on Darcy and Krystal, applauding loudly.

I can't get out of the main doors and down the steps fast enough. I lean over the handrail, gasping for breath.

"Nick?" Darcy's voice is quiet.

I turn to face him. He looks distraught, and I don't want to see him like that.

"I'm sorry I was late. I'm glad you got to dance," I say, and his face crumples in on itself.

"I'm sorry . . ." He trails off and I continue, as I don't want to see him trying to explain himself.

"You looked magnificent together. It was a joy to watch you."

"Nick, it's not like that—"

"Are you going to dance together at the Nationals? You should, you'll win."

"I don't want—"

"Yes, you do. We could never win. We know that."

He comes and stands in front of me. I'm just numb. I have to remind myself that this was just a dream, a stupid one on my part, thinking we could dance together in a competition.

"I want to explain."

"Shush," I whisper, and capture his lips in a brief kiss, because I want to taste him, and after the dream of the last few weeks, I want to make sure that part is still real. It's bittersweet.

"I understand," I say. "This is for the best, and after the day I've had, I can't take any more right now."

"Oh shit, Nick. I'm sorry." His face creases, but he still

looks cute, and I have to close my eyes briefly to defend myself from it. "Your gran, is she okay?"

"She's broken her leg. She'll be fine, but we have a few things to sort out and I need to go see if my parents are alright."

"I hope she'll be okay," he says, and I nod in affirmation. I see his mum coming down the steps, no doubt coming to look for him to go finish the competition. I don't feel like staying around to watch them, it's too raw for me at the moment.

"Bye Darcy."

"Is it goodbye?" he says, biting his lip hard, as if he needs to feel something. I know that feeling.

"Dancing with Krystal is the right thing to do, but I need a couple of days to get used to it."

His mum has nearly reached us, and as much as I want to kiss him, kiss his hurt away, hoping it will work on mine, too, I don't.

Instead, I give him a quick smile and walk away, wishing this day was already over.

Chapter 25

Darcy

Watching Nick walk away was one of the hardest things I've ever had to do. In movies, no one stands there hopping from one foot to the other in indecision over whether to make the grand gesture. They just run after the guy, declare their undying love, and everything works out alright.

But I can't make it alright. I could go after him, but the outcome would still be the same. I'll still be dancing with Krystal at the Nationals. But we are still *us*, aren't we? He *did* just kiss me. But then why did it feel like goodbye?

My mum tugs on my arm. She's saying something, but I don't hear her. I just watch Nick's form getting smaller and smaller as he walks down the street.

When I can't see him anymore, I allow myself to be led inside, hardly aware of changing into my outfit for the Latin dance. He said a couple of days. He gets forty-eight hours, and that's all. After that, I'm going to explain it all and make him love me again.

We win the competition, but the victory feels hollow as it wasn't Nick and I who won it. I don't even want to look at the trophy. My mum is delighted, my dad is pensive, and I can't rouse up any enthusiasm for anything. The car ride back is full of my mum's plans for when Krystal and I should practise and what routines we should dance for the Nationals. I let it wash over me, none of it penetrating the hard shell I've constructed round me. I'm no longer interested. I'll dance to save our school, but I don't want a future unless it has Nick in it, too.

"Hello love." Nick's mum opens the door to my knock, and I fight the rising anxiety enough to be able to answer her.

"Hello Mrs Richardson. Is, err, Nick in?"

"He's next door at his gran's." I nod and turn to leave, wondering which next door in the long line of terraces is her house. Left or right?

"Come through the house, love," she says. "We don't use our front doors round here. Remember that for next time, eh?"

So, she mentioned a next time. Maybe things aren't too bad if she believes there might be a next time. Or, even worse, Nick hasn't even spoken about me.

"Thanks Mrs Richardson."

"It's Doreen, please," she says. She's lovely, but then this is no surprise as I know Nick and you only need to have met him for a few minutes to know he was raised well. "How are your mum and dad? Are they keeping well?"

She hasn't seen them for many years, not really since Nick started catching the bus on his own to the dance school, but she still asks after them like it was only last week.

"They're fine Mrs Rich—Doreen." She beams at me as I stumble over her name, and I see where Nick gets his smile from.

"There you go, love, just up the steps there." She ushers me down the steps into their cheerful backyard, which is alive with plant pots cascading with colour.

With trepidation I walk up the steps to the house next door. Should I knock? The back door is open, so I just stand on the threshold of the back door and kitchen and call out. "Nick?"

Nick comes through from the front room, surprise written all over his face.

"Darcy! What are you doing here?" Surprise, not elation. I'm going to have to earn that back.

"You said a couple of days." I check my watch. "It's been forty-nine hours and thirteen minutes."

I catch the slight hint of a curl at the corner of his mouth. "Not forty-eight hours?"

"Buses," I sigh, with an exaggerated shrug, and he chuckles at me. It's not going too bad. It feels familiar and I'm hoping our old habits will carry us through this.

"I came to see how you are, how your gran is, and to explain what happened."

He accepts my reasons for being there with a non-committal, "Okay." It could be worse. "I'm just making us some tea, do you want some?" he asks. I agree, and he sends me through to talk to his gran while he puts the kettle on. I don't know if this is him stalling for time for me to explain, or what reason he has, but I accept it for now.

"Hello Mrs Parker," I say, as I enter the room and see that a bed has been brought in for her. I haven't seen her for a number of years and I'm surprised at how much she's aged.

"Hello Darcy, dear," she says. "How are your parents? Nick says they enjoyed a few days in London recently."

"Yes, they did." I'm a bit taken aback that anyone would think my parents are interesting enough to know anything about.

"That's good dear," she continues. "You'll give them my regards, won't you?" I assured her I would, but it was unlikely that my parents would remember her from when she used to bring Nick dancing.

"How are you doing, Mrs Parker? Nick said you had a fall."

"Aye, and I got a pot on my leg and a two-night stay in hospital for my troubles," she grumbles goodnaturedly. "I only came home this morning. Nick and Frank sorted this bed out for me, but it's not the best solution. I think I should go into a home, but they won't hear of it."

"No, we won't," Nick adds to the conversation as he places a tray on a nearby table. "We can look after you."

"Stubborn," Nick's gran says to me in a conspiratorial side whisper. "The lot of them. Though, I suppose I'm to blame, they get it from me." She giggles, and I glance at Nick as he hands her a china cup and saucer. He gives me an eye roll and I understand that this is an old argument. I feel a small sense of hope that he feels able to make jokes with me.

We sit for a few more minutes drinking tea while Nick and his gran work through the argument that proves they are just as stubborn as each other.

When Nick has taken the tea tray back through to the kitchen, she beckons me a little closer, and a small sliver of dread slides down my spine as I catch the steel in her eye.

"Nick says you're not dancing together at the Nationals." Oh no, am I going to be told off by his gran? She looks almost as scary as my mum.

"I've come to explain it all to him. I need to save the dance school. I can't do that if I don't win. I need to help my family."

She gives me an appraising stare. "You're a good boy. You'll do the right thing." I don't know what she means. I have to do it this way.

"Now, go through and talk to him. He misses you and I'm fed up with seeing him moping about. I want to see him smile again." I rise and she points to the television. "Just turn that on for me, lad. I think there's a *Poirot* on soon."

I comply and then go through to the kitchen.

"Nick, I want to explain."

"Okay," he says with a tentative smile. "I'm baking some cookies. Do you want to help?"

"I'd love to," I say, and he directs me to get the ingredients, telling me it's his gran's chocolate chip and oat cookie recipe, but he likes to add honey to make them extra soft and chewy.

As he has me weighing out the flour and oatmeal, I tell him what my mum had said about the school. That I could save it and we could turn the fortunes around if I could win the Nationals. While I rub in the butter, I tell him my fears for my future, that I only know how to teach dancing, and I don't have any skills for anything else.

He adds an egg, vanilla extract, and honey, and mixes them together while I tell him how sorry I am. How much I wish I could dance with him instead.

We keep working on the cookies, but he doesn't say anything, except to give me directions. I run out of words as he pours the chocolate chips in. I help him spoon the mixture out onto the baking trays. When they're in the oven, I can't stand it any longer.

"Please say something. You're just standing there silently. Just be mad at me, yell at me or something!"

He still doesn't speak, and it starts irritating me. It isn't like him not to have something to contribute.

I've apologised, I've explained, I don't know what else I can say.

"I've told you everything."

"Have you?" he asks quietly. He looks at me from under the shock of blond hair that's fallen over his eyes. My head scrambles around the words, looking back at what I've been saying for the last half an hour, pretty certain I haven't left anything out. Then my heart feels the tug that his eyes give, the same one they always have. The one that beckons me to come closer, that encourages me to be a better version of myself, the one that I never want to be parted from.

I take a deep breath.

"I'm so scared of the future, Nick. I'm worried about what will happen to my family if I can't do this. But the thing I'm most afraid of is not having you in my life."

The smile he gives me is painful, but with two strides, he crosses the room and encircles me with his arms.

"There you are." He presses a soft kiss to my forehead. "Everything you've said up to that point sounded like it came from your mum. They sound like the same lines you've been spouting most of your life, and I wanted to know what was really in here." He lays a hand on my chest, over my heart.

"I'd rather give up everything than lose you, Nick. I love you." I hug him close, believing that if I hold him tight everything will be okay.

He squeezes me in return.

"So, are we going to dance together at the Nationals?" I ask when his grip softens.

"No, we're not."

I'm confused. I just poured my heart out to him. Is he rejecting me? "But—"

"Darcy, you've been my best friend for a very long time. Along the way, that developed into something much deeper. That you feel the same way has made me the happiest person alive. That doesn't come with conditions. It doesn't happen only if you promise to dance with me. I'm here to help you celebrate your successes and to hold you when things aren't so good. I know you want to give saving the school your best shot. I see how hard you work to keep it going. We both know that if we dance together we wouldn't have a chance of winning. I would never stand in your way of achieving that success—you deserve it. Dancing with Krystal is the best chance you have. I've seen you together. You really can win and I'll support you every step of the way."

He leans a little closer and nuzzles into my neck, his hands gently kneading my ass. "As long as you save some special dances for me."

I nod and gulp, his touch having a potent effect on me. "Of course."

A beeping sound breaks the spell, and Nick disengages himself from me to turn the oven timer off and take the cookies out. They smell delicious, and look even better.

I turn to the sink to start washing the dishes. I look out of the window at the beautiful view across the valley. I can see the row of roofs leading down to the valley floor, but across the other side is woodland and then moors and hills in the distance. I'm reminded of the time we went to Slippery Stones . . . Was it really only a few weeks ago? It feels like a lifetime. I'm so caught up in my thoughts that I nearly jump out of my skin when arms snake around my waist.

"Mmm, I missed you." Nick kisses into my neck and I tilt my head, leaning it back onto his shoulder and enjoying his mouth on me. His hands trail lower as he plays his fingers over my jeans, and my cock swells to his touch.

"I see you've missed me, too," he murmurs, unbuckling my belt.

"Nick," I whisper. "We can't."

"Why not?" He unbuttons my fly and slips a hand inside,

the other one gripping my hip. He wraps his hand around my length and hums at its hardness. I find it almost impossible to recall what I was about to say.

"Your gran." I have enough presence of mind left to remember that we are not alone in the house.

"She can't come in here." He starts moving his hand up and down. He wipes his thumb through the precum leaking out of the tip and smears it round the head. My knees nearly buckle.

"She might hear us." It's my last line of defence.

"You'd better be quiet then," he purrs, his mouth still connected to my throat.

As he picks up speed, I involuntarily wince; it's too much. He withdraws his hand and I gasp at its loss, my cock aching, needing his hand back even though it was painful.

"Sorry, honey," he murmurs. "I don't have any lube, so you're going to have to help me out here." He holds his hand out and I lick it, pooling some spit in his palm. I almost sigh in relief as he grasps my cock again, my back arching to chase the movement of his hand.

"You like to fuck my hand, do you?" His voice is a low rumble on my shoulder, that vibrates down my back and tightens my balls.

I press my lips together tightly, preventing any sound from escaping, and try to breathe through my nose. My breathing is choppy as the pressure builds in waves, and I have to clamp my jaw together and try to swallow down the moan that's desperate to get out.

"That's it, D, fuck my hand. Fuck it hard." His voice is soft, a whisper against my neck, but all the more potent for it.

I grip the edge of the sink. As much as his name is on my lips, I am not going to scream it in his gran's house and give the game away, and he knows it. I'm barely holding it together when he goes in for the kill.

"What you're doing to my hand, I'm going to do to your tight little hole." I feel disoriented and lightheaded. I want all his dirty words. I can't hold off any longer and with a jerk, I come, spilling over Nick's hand. I gasp for breath and my heart rate starts to slow its staccato beat. When I can stand upright again, he releases his hold on my hip. I turn my head enough to capture his mouth in a long, lazy kiss. When we break apart, he smiles, and I see the light reflecting the stars in his eyes. Then he glances down into the sink, at the plate I'm holding, then back at me and, with a smirk, says, "You missed a bit."

Chapter 26

Nick

"Again," Darcy says, as the samba music ends.

Krystal stands with her hands on her hips and is panting slightly. "Darcy, it's fine."

I hide a small smile, knowing Darcy well enough to be fairly confident what his next words will be. From my vantage point, sitting cross-legged on the studio floor, it looked pretty good to me.

"I don't want fine, I want perfect," he replies.

"Then it's perfect." She throws one hand in the air with a whatever expression as she walks over to her bag and lifts out a bottle of water. He glowers after her.

"It can't be just fine and perfect. It doesn't feel perfect to me." Darcy is in full-on focus mode. He has been since the regional competition. He's staking everything on winning this competition, and I understand how important it is for him, but he has a habit of driving himself too hard. Julia knew him well enough to call him out on it. Krystal looks like she might rub him the wrong way instead.

"It's good enough," she replies, taking a swig. Yes, she definitely said the wrong thing.

"Good enough doesn't win," he says with some passion. "Good enough is mid-range, lower placings, third—if you're lucky. I *need* to win this."

"I'm surprised you've never won with that attitude."

Darcy deflates a little. "I've never had the chance to go; either Julia or I was sick or injured each year."

"Well, that's my luck then, as I'm sure Andrew and I wouldn't have won against you."

I don't need to see his green eyes right now to know that they'll be burning brightly. I see his jaw tighten and he clenches his fists. I debate whether to intervene. Whilst this is all extremely entertaining, Darcy could say something that jeopardises them dancing together. He looks on the edge, throwing a retort out, then he seems to realise this and turns away.

Krystal puts her jacket on, clear that she's done for the evening. I can't say I blame her. She works in the daytime and can only practise in the evening. She has to travel over to practice, which is anything up to an hour depending on traffic. She's done that almost every day since regionals two weeks ago. But the Nationals are only a few days away, so I understand why Darcy is pushing to get in as much practice as possible.

"I'll be back tomorrow," she says, picking up her bag.

"Okay, and thank you." Darcy seems to have recovered enough from what she said to not want to bite back any longer.

"Look Darcy, we'll be fine," she says. "The waltz is foot perfect, as are the quickstep and foxtrot. The samba, jive, rumba, and cha-cha-cha are really good. We just need another run through on the pasa doble, tango, and Viennese waltz and they'll be just as good. We still have a couple more days to practise."

"You're right. I'll see you tomorrow."

"Okay then." She turns my way. "Bye Nick." I raise a hand in a wave before she's through the door and gone.

Darcy settles down on the floor next to me with a sigh, then draws his knees up and folds his arms on top of them, resting his chin and looking glum.

"Don't let it eat you up." I nudge him gently with my shoulder. He closes his eyes and I stay silent, knowing he'll speak when he's ready. After a moment he opens them and lifts his head to rest it on the wall behind him.

"How can she be so blasé about it all? It's like she isn't even bothered. And to say that, about if I had competed. To say they probably won because I wasn't there . . ." He trails off and I know he's thinking that life is unfair and that success seems to come easily to people who don't appear to want it or work hard for it. It's a dangerous thought for him to brood on at any time, especially not a few days out from the most important competition of his life.

"You know, she really paid you a massive compliment."

He tilts his head to me and gives me his best "please explain this shit you're telling me" look. So cute.

"Despite what you think, we know Krystal does work hard, and she's a really good dancer. You can't say for sure that if you'd danced in the Nationals before, you would've won. It very much depends on what happens on the day. But the three-time national ballroom champion has just said you could have beaten them. I think that's a huge fucking compliment, D."

His face softens a little, and he allows a small smile to escape. I stand and hold out my hand to pull him up.

"Now, come and dance some swing with me. I want to

give Mrs Herringsworth the dance of her life on our forties day." We have it planned for two weeks after the Nationals. I've taken over the advertising, and so far there's been a lot of interest.

He allows me to tug him up and lead him to the middle of the floor. I leave him briefly to put on some suitable music and then return. I hold out my hand for him to place his in it and then, before we start, I trail my other hand down his body. I graze his hip, and cupping his ass, pull him towards me for a kiss.

"Well, Mrs Herringsworth is going to have the dance of her life if you're going to start like that." He grins at me, and I'm pleased I've managed to get him to set aside his demons for now.

"Cheeky." I nip his lip and he looks at me from under his lashes. It gets me every time. "Dance. It'll loosen you up, and if you're really lucky, I'll blow you later to relax you some more." I try not to think about that, as dancing is going to be uncomfortable if I'm sporting a boner.

"Maybe I'll blow you." He smiles seductively, and yeah, that's not helping the boner situation.

"No way! With a jaw as tense as yours, you'll bite it off, and I happen to be quite attached to my dick thank you."

"I'm quite attached to your dick, too." He gives me a smirk and then steps back out of my embrace so we can dance.

"I have something to tell you," I announce a while later. We're laid on Darcy's bed and I'm curled into his side, trying to summon up the energy to go home. We never asked if I could stay over, and with it this close to the competition,

Darcy needs all the rest he can get—and not much of that would be happening if I shared his bed. Which is what I wanted to talk to him about.

"Oh." He tenses, and it saddens me that his first instinct is for this to be bad news.

"I'm going to start looking for houses next week."

"What!" Darcy sits up, disturbing my position and making me sit up, too. "That's fucking amazing, Nick. I didn't think you had enough saved yet."

"The last couple of jobs with my dad have been hard work, but the pay has been good. I have enough if I'm careful."

"Awesome. Can I help you look?" He looks as excited as I feel.

"I was hoping you'd say that." I can't keep the smile from my face. We haven't talked about the future. I don't think Darcy wants to think past the weekend, really, and who can blame him? I would like to live with Darcy, share space with him, and share a bed. That couple of days we had when his parents were away gave me a glimpse of how we could be, and I'd love that.

"I . . ." I falter over asking him the next question, not sure how he will react. I'm normally confident about difficult subjects. I could have brought it up as a joke, almost. But this is so important to me, and is such a big step, that I find my mouth going dry and my hands shaking a little. I reach for his hand and interlace our fingers, as I need to feel connected to ask. I trace patterns on the back of his hand. "When I have a place, would you like to stay over?"

"Stay over?" he echoes, and I swallow.

"I mean, would you live with me?" I give his hand a squeeze.

"Oh, Nick." He squeezes my hand back, the silent gesture meaning more to me than a thousand words can, but he tells me anyway. "There is nothing I'd love more, but are you sure? Financially, I'm pretty poor. I could contribute a bit, but not much, so it would feel wrong. I don't want to be a burden."

"You could never be a burden," I say, and then add, "Well, maybe . . ." I wiggle my eyebrows at him and I get a laugh, but then he's serious again.

"I don't have much to offer—sorry."

"Darcy, *you* are *more* than enough." I lift our joined hands and kiss the back of his, and he falls back on the bed in a mock swoon, and I can't help laughing at him.

"Is that a yes, then?"

He smiles up at me from where he's lying on the bed and nods enthusiastically. I cover him with my body, and kiss him until we're both breathless and I'm in danger of missing the last bus home.

Chapter 27

Darcy

"We'd like you to have this." Justin hands me an envelope when I finish his latest dance lesson with Mark. Equal measures of surprise and pleasure rush through me as I see the very elegant handwriting addressed to both Nick and me.

I open it carefully, not wanting to rip it so I can show it to Nick later. The card inside is beautifully decorated and I unfold it. It's an invitation to their wedding. I whistle when I see the venue, Wortley Hall. That's an impressive, former stately home turned hotel just outside the city.

"It's, it's . . ." I'm speechless. "Are you sure?"

Justin laughs, and Mark comes over and puts an arm across his shoulder. "Of course we're sure. We hope you can both come."

Mark joins in. "Justin thinks that having you there will ensure he doesn't forget any of the steps to our dance."

"Oh, you're going to be just fine," I reassure them. They've improved a lot and I am sure they're practising a lot on their own. "But thank you. Can I get back to you when I've shown this to Nick?" Our first invite anywhere as a couple. It's thrilling, but apart from going to Brazen, which is a gay club, and spending time with Riley and Kieran, I haven't been anywhere else with Nick as his boyfriend. But I remind myself that this is Justin and Mark's wedding, so of course it's going to be fine.

"Sure, just text us on the number on the invite as soon as you know. We'll see you next week," Mark says.

"You don't have to keep coming for lessons. You already know what you're doing—you just need to practise." I'll hate to see them go, but I don't want to take their money needlessly.

"Do you know, that whilst we have enjoyed planning this wedding—since our mothers wouldn't let us run off to Gretna Green, and vetoed a quiet ceremony at the registry office—it's turned into a behemoth of a thing to organise. Coming here once a week is a lovely respite from that. We can enjoy ourselves and not feel guilty that we aren't doing something wedding related. It relaxes us to be here."

Justin continues. "We've been talking, and after the wedding, we'd like to come and join some classes, if you'll have us. We want to learn the dances properly."

"Of course. You're welcome to join any of our classes. It doesn't take long to get the bug, does it?" I ask, and see their wide smiles in answer.

The same smile that I wear for Nick as he walks into the studio half an hour later. I show him the invite and he's as thrilled as I am.

"Shall we go?" I ask, and once I receive his yes, I send a text off to Justin, receiving a thumbs-up emoji in return. A few minutes later, Nick's initial excitement at the invitation has faded, and he's slumped in one of the chairs bordering a side of the studio, his head bowed.

"What's up, babe?" I say, hunkering down between his knees to stare up at his face. The endearment slips out easily, surprising us both. He notices and flashes me a brilliant smile before his face drops again. That he hasn't picked up on it and thrown me some saucy banter indicates that something is wrong.

He sighs. "It's just a little hard right now. We've been looking at retirement villages for my gran. I know she wants to go somewhere that has better access and she says there will be company for her, but it feels like we've failed her, and I'm going to miss her. I don't think there's been a day in my life when I haven't been around to say hello and make her a cup of tea."

I put my hands on his thighs and give them a comforting rub. He places his hands on top of mine and gives me a little smile.

"Sorry, Krystal will be here soon. I'm not good company, I'll go."

"Stay Nick, please?" I don't want to see him like this. "You look beat. Why don't you go up to my room for a bit and I'll find you later?"

He nods and I stand, helping him up, too. I give him a hug and, for a few seconds, he rests his head on my shoulder.

"I like *babe*," he whispers, and then pulls away to disappear upstairs. I try to ignore the desire to run after him and hold him again. Instead, I put on some music and do some warmups until Krystal arrives, getting my brain in gear. I still have my school to save.

After Krystal and I have been through all of our planned dances several times, there's nothing more we can do. If we're not ready now, we never will be. We'll rest tomorrow and then the competition begins on Saturday. I do feel sorry for her, that Andrew is injured and he can't compete, even if that does give me a chance this year.

When I pass through the kitchen, my dad calls to me.

"Darcy, you know you don't have to dance—" I don't want to hear what he has to say right now, mostly because there's nothing he *can* say, and I'm eager to see Nick.

"It's alright, Dad. I'm ready, and I want to win this—for us." I keep on walking to my room.

Nick is sprawled out on my bed; he must have fallen asleep. I sit down gently, taking in his tousled hair and his face, soft in slumber. I feel incredibly lucky to have him in my life. I don't want to wake him, but I also can't resist the overwhelming urge to touch him. I lay down next to him, pressing myself along his side, wanting to connect at as many points as possible. He makes a low hum and turns towards me, flinging his arm across me. He doesn't give any other indication that he's awake. Still, I can't prevent myself from reaching out and running a hand down his side and over his hip, moving my hand over his firm, round ass.

"If you're going to turn me on, then you'd better be prepared to do something about it," he murmurs sleepily, his eyes blinking awake, mouth curving into a smile.

"Sorry, I didn't mean to wake you." I smirk slightly, and he rolls onto his back, pulling me on top of him.

"Yes, you did," he says, and grabbing my ass with both hands, he grinds his hips upwards leaving me in no doubt that he's rock hard.

"That wasn't my touch," I tease. "You must have been dreaming about me in your sleep."

"Either way, it's your fault." He grinds a bit more, which is making my cock take notice. I raise myself up so I can sit astride his thighs.

I peel off my T-shirt, and get an appreciative, "Very nice, keep going," as he stretches back on the bed.

I jump off and make sure my bedroom door is locked. Since the thrill of him jerking me off while his gran was just in the next room, we've become more daring. We haven't had penetrative sex yet, partly because of waiting for the results from the clinic—which came through negative a few days ago —and partly from a lack of opportunity. I want to wait until we have the house to ourselves again, and Nick agrees. But we have become very adept at using what time we do have and being quiet about it.

I turn Bearlero round on the dresser so he's facing the wall.

"Why'd you do that?" Nick snorts.

"His innocent eyes don't need to see this." Another snort.

I strip down to my briefs and go to sit beside him again. He pouts a little. "I want to see your pretty cock." I take them off as well and he hums in agreement. "Beautiful."

I tug on his T-shirt and he sits up enough for me to pull it up over his head, and I feast my eyes on his perfect abs as he lowers himself back down again.

I unbuckle his jeans and peel them off, catching sight of the lace underneath. He's wearing a black pair of lace shorts and the contrast between the dark lace and his pale skin is tantalising. I have no idea why it looks so good, but I can barely take my eyes off him. I run my fingers up and down his cock, which is stretching the front of the shorts and making the lace work hard to contain him. I climb back onto the bed and settle between his thighs. I lean forward and kiss him deeply, his hands on my ass the whole time, and whilst that feels fantastic, I have other plans. I abandon his mouth and kiss down his neck to his chest. I take one nipple in my mouth, first sucking, then taking it between my teeth and tugging slightly, watching as he arches off the bed with a groan. I apply my mouth to his other nipple before working my way across those amazing abs to the treasure trail that leads to lace.

I slowly lick up his hard cock, feeling the texture of the lace on my tongue, pushing the tip through the holes to the skin beneath.

"Yes, D," he moans softly, and I add a bit more pressure. I place my mouth round his cockhead, drawing as much as I can into my mouth, moving the lace with my tongue and feeling him jerk at the friction. I need to taste him properly. Taking hold of the top of the shorts with my teeth, I pull them down, releasing his cock with a bounce. I swirl my tongue through his precum before stretching my lips round the end and sucking him in. I slide my mouth slowly up and down, tonguing round the head and playing it along the vein running up the underside. He makes the most delightful groan, but I want to tease him a bit longer, so I withdraw until I just have my lips round the tip, adding more pressure to his cockhead. I hum in pleasure as Nick lifts his hips, trying to chase my mouth, and I tongue his slit. I can't resist a smile of satisfaction, hearing him whispering *please, please, please* under his breath, but I leave him a second longer before plunging down, taking all of him in one go. My own cock is aching painfully, but I don't want to get distracted from what I'm doing, so I try to ignore the desperation to touch it.

"*Fuucck, D.*" His hips crash into the bed and I allow him to hit the back of my throat, forcing myself to relax and breathe round the gag reflex. I hollow my cheeks and suck him in and out, watching his thighs tremble and his hands fist the sheets until he shudders and jerks, his release filling my mouth. I slowly let his deflating cock slide out of my mouth, and swallow it all. I sit back and see his cheeks are flushed a pretty shade of pink, accentuating his blue eyes as he smiles at me.

He beckons me forward and I move up the bed. When I reach his chest, he clasps my ass and pulls me forward until I'm kneeling over his face.

"My turn." He grins before he engulfs the whole of my cock in his mouth. The relief of having pressure on it is indescribable. I rest my arms on the wall, but I cannot keep my hips from moving and they thrust in time with his mouth as he makes slurping noises round me.

I know I'm not going to last long and I make the mistake of looking down at him, seeing his eyes locked onto mine, his glistening lips holding all of me.

"Oh fucking hell, babe," I exclaim, as he flicks his magic tongue up and down while still taking every one of my thrusts. He moves one of his hands so his fingers play up and down my crease, causing my spine to tingle and my balls to tighten, and I thrust harder. He grazes across my hole, just once, and that's all it takes to push me over the edge, my orgasm washing through me. Nick takes every single drop and releases me from his grip, but it's a few minutes before I feel able to push off from the wall and lie down on the bed, curling into his waiting arms.

Chapter 28

Nick

I look round at the packed city hall. The seating has been cleared from the central stalls area to make room for the dance floor, with the judges and an orchestra on the stage. There is further seating on the upper floors. The domed ceiling, with its stunning art deco laylight, adds elegance to the event.

"I still don't see why tha's not dancing." I wince slightly as Barry's voice cuts across the hubbub, and don't need to see my parents' expressions to know they've done the same. I've explained everything to my parents and they understand, but my dad gave Barry and Alan a very abridged version of why I was sitting with them, and not out there with Darcy on the dance floor.

Claire had arranged for good seats for all of us, saying it was not a problem when I explained that Alan and Barry wanted to bring their wives. Now I'm not sure it was such a good idea.

"I'm sure you're just as good. We wanna see thee dance, lad." His wife, Maggie, shushes him, murmuring something in his ear. He sits back in his seat and she smiles at me when I shoot her a grateful look. I appreciate his indignation on my behalf, but it doesn't help. Nothing helps, except knowing that this is the best way to support Darcy—and I would go to the ends of the earth for him. So I squash down my own disappointment that it isn't me out there, and think about how there will always be a next time. I want to be with him now, telling him how well he's going to do, calming his nerves. But he has his family and Krystal, and I'd just be in the way. And so I give him some space and sit with my family instead, in some of the best seats in the hall where we can see everything perfectly.

Maggie and Brenda are talking about who were their favourites on the TV show that pairs celebrities with dancers. I don't get the chance to watch it much, and don't really care for which soap star is dancing, but the show has done a lot for the popularity of ballroom dancing in recent years.

My phone buzzes with a text, and I pull it out, smiling when I see it's a text from Darcy. Not able to see him this morning, I've been texting my support along with very suggestive messages about what I'm going to do to him later.

I open it and am greeted with a picture of his ass—a reply to my last text. It takes me far too long to realise that I'm sitting so close to my mum that she could just look over and . . .

"What's that love?" she asks. I hit the power button, almost dropping my phone in the process.

"Just a text from Darcy," I squeak, feeling my face burn. I fumble for my phone so I don't have to meet her eyes.

"What'd he say?" she asks, which makes me think she didn't actually see the screen. I allow a small breath to escape. He didn't *say* anything.

"He says, thank you all for coming and he's looking forward to seeing you all later." I try to make it sound convincing.

"He's such a sweet boy," she says, and turns back to say something to my dad. I suppress a snigger. He *was* sweet . . . until I got my hands on him, and my mouth. Oh yes, he's *sweet* alright. I lift my phone closer to my face so no one can see my screen and take another peek at the picture. I can't wait to get my hands on those ass cheeks later; more than my hands if we can get a minute alone. I send a cheeky reply.

Nick: My mum says very nice ass, but she prefers dick pics. :) Lick you later

Chapter 29

Darcy

I laugh at the reply from Nick and throw my phone into my bag. It was too tempting not to send him a picture while I was getting changed, knowing he would enjoy it. I've been grateful for his texts all morning, keeping me distracted with his banter and flirting, along with his support. But now I'm ready, and since they'll be starting soon, calling us for the first dance, I need to find Krystal.

I'm still looking for her when I see Claire backstage, coming from the production room where she's been coordinating with the camera crew.

"I can't find Krystal anywhere," I say, and she frowns.

"Have you tried in the warmup area?" she asks, pointing towards the memorial hall which is behind the main hall and has been set up for practice and warmup.

I shake my head as I haven't yet.

"Well, I'm sure she'll be there, but I'll keep my eye out for her. I just need to head to the press room to make sure they're all fine before I round up the judges."

I go in the direction she points. I need to warm myself up, or rather calm down a little, as the nerves are fizzing under my skin. This is my first shot at the Nationals and it has so much riding on it, I don't want to buckle under the pressure.

I can't find Krystal in the warmup area, but I know she's here as I saw her earlier, along with her husband Andrew, his arm still in plaster. He's not a bad guy, and he gave me a rueful little smile and thanked me, as if *I* was doing *him* a favour.

I warm up a little, practising some basic moves, the familiar steps and patterns serving to bring my body and brain back into some sort of harmony with each other.

Claire appears at my elbow. "I think you should see this," she says cryptically, and starts walking away. I almost lose my footing as I scramble to catch up with her. She leads me along a corridor to a breakout room, and opens the door for me to enter before following me in.

My mum is in the room, along with Krystal and Andrew and another man I don't recognise.

"I want to move the date up to the end of the month." I hear him saying to my mum.

"That wasn't part of the deal," she spits out.

What deal? I look between them, but no one has noticed us standing there. I look over to Claire and she shrugs. She has no idea either.

"Well, it is now, or my daughter doesn't dance." The guy gestures towards Krystal, who places a hand on his arm.

"Daddy, not now. We're due to start soon. I will—"

"You're not going anywhere until I have this sorted." She takes a step back and I look over at Andrew to see his reaction, but his face is neutral, too bland, like he's learned to stay out of whatever this is.

"Do I have a deal?" He turns back to my mum, who looks furious.

"We can't move out by the end of the month. We haven't even told Darcy yet."

I've had enough.

"Told me what?" I step forward, Claire at my side, and they pivot as one to look at us. I register the shock on my mum's face.

"You haven't told him?" The mystery man sports a supercilious smirk.

"What's going on?" I look at my mum, the man, and Krystal—who avoids my eyes.

My mum extends her hand to me, and I jump out of her reach.

"Mum?" An icy finger of dread runs down my spine.

"We were going to tell you after the competition," she protests.

"Tell me what?" I'm still not getting anywhere.

"Doug Gregory." The man introduces himself and holds out a hand. Gregory? Gregory? Where have I heard that name before? No, I haven't *heard* it; I've *seen* it, every day as I walk past the hoardings near my house, the same name as the developer. Things start to click into place. I ignore his hand and turn back to my mum.

"We've sold the school." She deflates into a chair. "We had to. I told you it wasn't making any money."

"But you said if I danced, if I won, I could save it." I can't believe that she'd do this. I certainly can't believe my dad would.

"Dad—"

"Thinks you already know," she says, sagging further. A flash of guilt punctures my thoughts, that I have so focussed on this, this fool's errand by the look of it, that I haven't spoken to Dad much recently, and he did try to say something to me the other night.

The enormity of what they're saying has all my fears from the last few weeks crashing into my head with dreadful clarity. I'm homeless, jobless, with no prospects—or I will be very soon. I take a shuddering breath, refusing to bow down and let this happen. Fury spurs me on.

"Where do you fit into this?" I turn on Krystal as she'd clearly known all of this.

"My dad sweetened the deal if I would dance with you," she says matter-of-factly. I hate them all.

"I didn't think you were so cheap," I say, and something painful flares briefly in her eyes before it fades again. I don't want to know about their family dynamics, that's their concern. I have my own problems to deal with.

"But why didn't *you* tell me?" I direct at my mum, grinding out every word.

"I needed you to want to win. I wanted you to win. To have you win the Nationals, just once, would have been fantastic—an achievement. It's a competition I never won myself. But you wanted to do your own thing, one that threw away your chances of winning. I did it for you." I can't believe I'm hearing this.

"Do you know," I start, as calmly as I can manage right now. "If you had come to me, told me all this, asked me to dance to win—for *you*—I might have listened? But Julia was right: this was always your dream, not mine. You just sold it better to me. You disgust me."

I turn away. I can't look at her right now. I'm done with her. Finished.

I leave the room, and Claire follows me. She looks sad, but wisely doesn't say anything. I don't think she knew, but she doesn't look surprised. Then again, it doesn't affect her as much, if at all.

I'm furious with my dad too, but I know how persuasive my mum can be. She's taken everything I thought I had and sold it. What they're going to do with the money for the school, frankly, I don't care. It was my job, my home, my future—it was *everything* to me.

No, not quite everything.

I turn to Claire. "Can you find Nick for me?"

Chapter 30

Nick

"What's up, D?" I can see something is seriously wrong from the look on Darcy's face.

Claire hadn't been very forthcoming when she appeared at our seats a couple of minutes ago and said Darcy needed me. She looked grave, and I asked her if Darcy was ill or there had been an accident, but she wouldn't tell me anything, which did nothing to quell the disquiet that roiled in my stomach. She managed to get me backstage and pointed to where I'd find him, saying she had work to do before leaving me to make my own way.

"There's no time to explain now, but do you still want to dance?" he asks quickly.

Of all the things I was expecting, it definitely wasn't that, and it knocks me sideways.

"What? Why?" I scramble to work out what's going on.

"No time. Yes or no?" Darcy says again.

"I—" Was he really asking me this? I've given up on that

dream and I struggle now to get my head round the shape of it remanifesting. At my stumbling, his already serious face starts settling into a hurt frown. Did he think I would refuse? It's more the impossibility of the question that has me tongue-tied. But if I believe the question, then there's only one answer. "Of course I do."

He gives me a dazzling smile before his mask is back on and he grabs my arm to pull me along to the dressing rooms.

"But I can't wear jeans," I protest, suddenly aware that this is real, and I don't have the right clothes.

We enter the dressing room, and he leads me over to his stuff.

"Well, I might have been distracted after the regionals." He doesn't need to remind me of that day. "And forgot to take your suit out of the garment bag."

I look at the suit bag hanging up and smile. Never has his untidiness been so welcome, but I had a thought. "My Latin stuff?"

"Also there." He looks a tiny bit sheepish, and it's the first crack I can see in his armour, but it fades again. I start changing into the formal suit first as the traditional dances are danced before the Latin American ones.

Darcy sinks onto the dressing room bench as I strip off my jeans and pull on the loose black trousers. He's worrying the side of his nail with his teeth and doesn't say anything as I pull my T-shirt and hoodie off in one, pulling on my shirt and jacket.

"Can you tell me what's going on?" I ask. When he looks up at me, his usually bright green eyes are dull and bleak. It breaks my heart to see him, on what should be an exciting day—one he's been training for, for most of his life—looking like he's barely holding it together. I'm finally ready and he stands.

"I can't. If I do, I'll break."

Well, shit.

I have no idea what could be so bad, for him to be like this. Maybe dancing isn't such a good idea, but I know pushing him to talk isn't either.

"Okay, but if you'd rather not dance—"

"No." His voice is vehement, and I pull back slightly. He notices and lets out a sigh. "Please, I *have* to do this. I *need* to do this."

"Alright." I draw him into a hug because I need to connect with him, to hold him. He relaxes slightly and hugs me back. "Promise me you'll tell me all afterwards?" I say into his hair, and feel him nod in response.

Competitions always start with the waltz, which I'm grateful for today. The close hold and the beautiful sweeping movements are a good way for Darcy to relax and, I hope, enjoy himself, despite whatever's happened. I haven't had the time to get excited or nervous in the short time since Darcy asked me to dance, but the enormity of it sinks in when we both step onto the dance floor, hand in hand. The first same-sex couple at this level of competition.

We both hear a collective noise from the crowd, half gasp, half surprise. We walk to our starting positions, followed by a whoop, which I'm more than sure came from the direction of where my family and their friends are sitting. Barry is no doubt the caller. I can't quite believe I'm here. That we're here —together. And there is nowhere I'd rather be. I squeeze Darcy's hand and he squeezes back. In the brief second we have while waiting for the music to start, I whisper, "I love you."

It doesn't start perfectly, as we haven't practised these dances together for a few weeks, but soon we slip into the familiarity of it and Darcy loses some of the tension he's holding. Even though he's leading, I do my best to support him as we glide round the dance floor, elegantly avoiding the other dancers. As the music ends, we part the hold and take collective bows to the audience, receiving a huge cheer. I guess we've attracted some attention. Darcy's smile is dazzling, and whilst it soon fades and the burden of what he's carrying slips over his face again, his eyes don't look quite as dull as they did previously.

We have a few minutes to catch our breath, while the juniors are on the floor for their first dance. Then we're back out on the floor for the tango. It's one of my favourites, and I know Darcy feels the same, confessing to me that one day he'd like to go to Buenos Aires to dance the Argentine tango in the clubs there. The ballroom version isn't quite so risqué, but it's still sensuous and I put everything I have into it, thrilled that Darcy responds. For a few seconds, I almost forget that we're in the middle of a major competition, and feel like we're back in the studio; it's just us. Again, we're greeted with cheers and whoops as we finish, and this time, Darcy's smile stays longer and doesn't fade as much.

We dance our way through the quiet beauty of the foxtrot, the whirling excitement of the Viennese waltz, and the intricate steps, flicks, and hops of the quickstep. At the end of each one, I feel the excitement of what we're doing building, and even Darcy is looking relaxed and happier. There is an interval where we have time to rest and change into our clothes for the Latin American dances.

When we're back in the dressing room, I keep the conversation light, not wanting Darcy to sink back into his head again. Claire finds us there.

"You guys certainly have the popular vote," she says as she

breezes into the room, not caring if anyone was half-dressed or not. "I've been monitoring social media and you're trending."

"As a novelty, no doubt," Darcy huffs from his seat on the bench.

"Don't put yourself down bro," she says. "I think there's a huge number of people who've been waiting for something like this to happen in this sport."

Then she drops her next bit of news. "They've just announced the results from the first half. You're lying third right now." Darcy looks as surprised as I am. I hadn't expected anything close to being placed.

"I guess we can't disappoint them, then." Darcy stands with a bit more of the spirit and professionalism that have been his trademarks for getting to the top levels of competition.

Claire hugs him, and I hear her say, "So proud of you for going out there. Have you told Nick yet?"

I can see his frown form as he replies with, "Not yet."

She releases him and gives me a small, sad smile. I'm burning with curiosity to know what's happened, but I know now is not the time. I push down the worry I feel and concentrate on what we need to do next. It doesn't occur to me until we're walking back to the main hall for the second half that I haven't seen Darcy's parents at all.

The starting dance, the cha-cha-cha, is perfect for us to loosen up and get back into the right mindset for the competition. The following hour passes in a whirlwind. We dance our way through the energetic samba. The rumba is not called the dance of love for nothing, and I add in all the sensual hip sways I can to show it. As we near the end, I see the question in Darcy's eyes and nod my response. The rumba drop is dramatic, and while we've practised it, we haven't included it in our routine as it can go badly wrong. Darcy would be completely holding me with one arm—and I'm not light—while I'm draped backwards over it with one leg in the air and my fingertips grazing the floor. He changes the planned moves slightly to set it up and we go for it.

It's exhilarating, and I catch an upside down glimpse of the audience as they go wild. Darcy doesn't let me fall and, at that moment, doing the thing I love the most, with Darcy, I feel so full of love that I know we can conquer anything together. He pulls me out of it and the elation on his face mirrors mine.

The penultimate dance is the paso doble, a dramatic dance which requires a perfect strong posture from Darcy and flexibility from me. Whilst I love it, it's always the one I worry about the most, dancing as an all guy couple, as the sweeping dress of the ladies is a good visual aspect for the dance. I do everything I can to show fluidity even when on the floor as part of one of the most expressive moves.

There's a slightly longer break before the final dance and we grab a drink of water. It's the last dance of the senior age group competition. Darcy leans forward, resting his arms on the barriers circling the dance floor. I place my hand on his lower back and give it a slight rub as I lean forward and whisper, "That'll be us at that age."

He grins back at me and my heart catches at how he seems so much more cheerful than he did earlier. "What, creaking around the dance floor?" He straightens and turns to face me, the mirth dancing in his eyes. "I'll probably have two new hips by then."

"True, and I'll be needing new knees." I snort slightly and he smiles.

"Thank you," he says. Two simple words, but his eyes are loaded with the weight of what he's carrying right now. He looks so vulnerable, and there's nothing I'd like more than to press a soft kiss to his lips and whisper against his mouth that

I'm always here for him. But this is a very public place, so instead, I interlace our fingers and lift our hands to kiss his knuckles.

My hand is still threaded with his when we walk onto the dance floor for the last time. We take our places for the jive, and Darcy looks around the grand hall as if he's only just realised all the people are out there. He finally looks as if he's enjoying the experience.

"Let's do this," he says as the music starts up. The jive is a lively and exuberant dance, and I'm glad they leave it until the end as we chassé and spin our way through it. As the last notes of the music die away, we're both left breathless. We both take a bow and are greeted with a crescendo of cheers and whistles. I look over to where my parents and their friends are seated and see them on their feet along with half the audience. I wonder if we've done enough.

We sit and wait, close to the dance floor, as the judges tally up the final results. Darcy is leaning with his elbows on his knees, worrying his thumb again. I lay my arm across his back and idly caress his hip. He leans into my touch as if he takes comfort from it, and I continue it for the long moments until we're finally called up onto the stage with the rest of the dancers.

We're called in second, to a huge cheer, and I almost feel sorry for the couple who did win it. They danced brilliantly, and it was well deserved. That we had been placed so highly is pretty amazing, and I can barely contain my happiness. I look over at Darcy with a stab of concern as I know how much winning meant to him, but joy is written all over his face.

Chapter 31

Nick

It takes us a while to get off the stage and back to the dressing room with all the people who want to wish us well.

Once inside, it's busy with others who are also getting changed. Darcy sinks down onto a bench and sighs. He gives me a small smile and then rests his head against the wall, closing his eyes. I resist the temptation to try to find out what happened, but he'll tell me when he's ready. It's still busy, so I guess he's waiting until we're alone. So instead, I concentrate on getting changed back into my jeans and hoodie. When I'm done, Darcy hasn't moved, so I sit down next to him and take hold of his hand. He turns his head towards me and opens his eyes.

I'm not going to ask if he's alright as I can already see the answer to that question. Instead, I say, "Tell me what I can do."

"Can I stay with you, please?" His question surprises me,

as it's the last thing I expect, and it increases my curiosity and concern.

"Yes, of course you can." There is no other answer if that's what he needs. I just need to talk to my parents, as there isn't room for us all in the van.

I leave him to get changed, promising I'll only be a few minutes. It takes me a bit longer to find my parents and tell them what I know so far. My mum arranges a lift home with Alan and Brenda, and my dad goes to bring the van to the stage-door entrance.

Next, I find Claire, and tell her that Darcy is coming home with me. She looks relieved and thanks me, even though she still doesn't enlighten me with any more details. But she promises to call him later.

When I return to the dressing room, Darcy has changed and is just zipping up the bag. I grab it and check he's okay to grab the garment hanger, then he follows me out to the van.

"Do you need to go home at all? Get some things?" I ask as we settle into the van.

He looks bone weary and shakes his head slightly. "I can't do that today." His voice cracks and I pull his hand into mine, rubbing my fingers over the back of his hand.

When we get home, my mum is there and already has a pot of tea brewing—the national drink of healing, recovery, and condolence. Darcy accepts a cup, and she gives him her best soothing smile. It's a magical smile that I know well, and I see Darcy manage a little one back before I herd him upstairs to my room.

Once he's drunk his tea, because that's important, he sighs and presses his fingers to his eyes.

Usually when we talk, we sit cross-legged, facing each other, but I want to hold him, and I think it might be easier if he doesn't have to look at me. So I shift backwards until I'm leaning against the wall, and invite him to sit between my legs, his back resting against my chest. I rest my hands on his thighs, waiting for him to take whatever time he needs.

When he tells me how he feels like his life has been ripped out from under him, I can't help but move my hands until they're wrapped around him. He's always brought out some sort of protective instinct in me and I can't help it. It goes way back, years, to when we first met. It's probably why we became best friends—my need to look out for the dark-haired boy with the shining green eyes.

As he recounts what he found out, I'm glad he waited to tell me. If I'd known this and his parents were around, his mum especially, I might not have been able to hold back. I'm so angry with what they've done.

"Nick." It isn't a question, it's a statement.

"Hmmm." My mind is still whirring with what I'd like to say to them.

"Can you let go of me?" I've balled my hands into fists, clutching his T-shirt.

"I'm sorry." I unclench my hands and smooth down his T-shirt.

"I don't know what I'm going to do," he says. I can hear the desolation in his voice and it shatters me.

He turns sideways in my lap and puts his arms around me. I wrap my arms round him and hold him while he breaks.

I have no answers for him but to let him sob it out, and even when he stops, I keep him enclosed in my embrace. Eventually, he falls asleep and still I can't let him go.

Chapter 32

Darcy

"Here's another one." Doreen places a newspaper on the breakfast table and I glance at the headline. In the two days since the Nationals there's been a barrage of publicity. This is the third newspaper, in the last two days, she's presented me with.

"It's almost as if you had won." Doreen looks pleased that Nick and I are getting a lot of attention. I'm not so sure. It was the publicity we needed if the school was going to stay open. Now it just seems empty.

Yesterday, Nick borrowed his dad's van and took me back home to collect some things I needed.

My parents were home and I told them the two decisions I'd come to, but I still need to figure out all other aspects of what I'm going to do with my life.

"Darcy, there you are. We've been worried about you," my mum said when I walked into the living room. So worried they didn't try calling me. They knew where I was, as Claire

—who *did* bother to see how I was—said she'd told them. I ignore her and head towards my room.

"We're sorry. Can we explain?" I stop at their words and turn to them.

"No, you lost that privilege when you chose not to tell me what your plans were." I direct this mostly at my mum. My dad's not off the hook, but I know the subterfuge was orchestrated by her.

"I'm not coming home. I'm staying with Nick until I can sort something else out," I tell them. "I'll come back only for the lessons we have arranged for as long as I'm needed. I will not let our clients down. Nick and I will still hold our forties event in a couple of weeks because, again, *I* will not let those people down."

Having delivered my speech, I spin round and continue to my room. Packing up as many clothes as I can fit into all the bags I can find, I also pack in toiletries, books, chargers, my laptop, and of course, Bearlero.

Now, a day later, I'm trying to come up with ideas for a new career. I reach for some more cereal. After not eating Saturday evening and very little yesterday, I woke up hungry, so I'm taking it as a good sign.

My phone rings and I pull it out of my pocket. It's Claire.

After asking how I am—really, what can I say?—she states her reason for ringing.

"Would you and Nick be up for an interview with local radio?"

"What about the people who actually won the competition?"

"They aren't local, and well, frankly, they aren't news. You guys are hot property right now."

I don't really know what to say to that, so I ask Nick, who's stuffing his face with toast.

"If you want to, then I'm happy to be there." He shrugs,

seemingly unaffected by the thought of appearing on the radio. He also seems quite content to stay in the shadows, and I'm not prepared to let him do that. He was as much a part of the competition as I was. I couldn't have done it without him.

I tell him as much later when we're back in his room.

"It was never my dream . . . well, not as much as yours," he tries to explain. "It was something you'd planned and trained for. It's not right for me to take away from that."

"It doesn't matter that I've trained for longer. You've put in plenty of hours, too," I insist. "We're a partnership, Nick. I'm nothing without you."

I capture his smile with my mouth, and kiss him long and deep, trying to imprint my words and their meaning onto him. His face is flushed when I pull back and look at his kiss-bruised lips.

"Well, *that's* a partnership I could definitely get on board with," he says, then drags me towards him for another kiss.

When we resurface, I remember the problems kissing him has banished from my consciousness for a while, and that Nick hasn't gone to work. It's Monday, so surely he should be working. I pace the room . . . Well, try to, as the room isn't very large.

"It's fine," he reassures me. "My dad has taken Alan with him today. I'm not needed."

"You're losing money because of me!" It doesn't make me feel any better.

"And it's okay Darcy. I promise you," he says, and I sit back down. "I was thinking we could go look at a house this afternoon." He adds, "I think the need to find somewhere has become a bit more urgent."

I look around his room at the space all my stuff takes up and I can't disagree, even though my chances of being able to contribute anything to the costs are practically zero. At some time I'll remind him of that, but the set of his jaw tells me that this is not the time. Instead, I answer that I'd love to.

Chapter 33

Nick

"Hi Gran, how are you?" I call, when I enter the kitchen and walk through to the front room.

"Hello dear," she answers, then seeing I'm alone follows it with, "Where's that lovely boyfriend of yours?"

I can't stop the grin—which probably looks really sappy—from spreading across my face when she uses the word "boyfriend." As Darcy has been a part of my life for nearly half of it, I can't imagine life without him. But it still catches me unawares to hear the evidence that our relationship has changed, said out loud. I haven't had many people in my life that could use that title, so it feels really special and causes a warmth to flood through me.

"He'll be around later," I reply.

I've left Darcy having a shower and I would've loved to join him, but not in my parents' house. There's not a lot we can do either, the walls are far too thin and we're never alone in the house. But I have a plan so we can spend some time together.

"How was the house you went to look at yesterday?" she asks.

"Urgh, it was awful. There was rising damp in every room. Now I know why it was so cheap."

"You'll find something, love." I'm glad she's optimistic, but I'm not so sure. They're all either too expensive, falling down, or in an area I don't want to live in.

"Are you ready for your appointment today?" I ask, to change the subject. She's due to have the cast removed from her leg which means she'll be able to move around a lot easier. She reminds me we're also going to see a retirement village later.

"It's not a home, dear." She must have seen my face at the mention of it. "It's still independent living, just with some assistance. I don't like that you all have to do so much for me. I can do some of it myself, but you know I can't manage those stairs."

"Can't you move into a bungalow?" I ask peevishly, still reluctant to think that anyone else should be helping with my gran.

"It's more than that, Nicholas." She fixes me with her steely glare. "I enjoy seeing you every day. There's nothing I like more. But if I'm honest, since I lost Reggie, I've been lonely. I'd like some company my own age. Plus, I have to ask your mum, your dad, or you if I want to go anywhere or get anything. This place has a shop, a hairdresser's, a cinema, and even a spa. I'd like to be able to enjoy those things while I still can."

I sigh. She has a point, of course, and it's not like she'll be far away. She *does* deserve to be able to enjoy life, and I hadn't thought how confining it must be for her here. But still, I will miss her a lot.

"Well, you won't be able to stop me from visiting you every spare moment I get," I say, trying to lighten my mood a little.

"I can't wait to show off my handsome grandson to everyone." She beams at me and I rise, kissing her cheek, telling her that Dad will be around soon to take her to the hospital.

I want to catch Darcy before he has to leave. He has a couple of lessons today, including Justin and Mark's final rehearsal.

"Mmm, are you sure you have to go out?" I put my arms round him as he's looking in the mirror, running his fingers through his damp hair. He looks gorgeous, and his hair is wonderfully tousled. I can't help but nuzzle into his neck, one of my favourite things to do, pressing soft kisses where his neck meets his shoulder. I inhale the clean citrus scent from his shower gel. I want to keep kissing him, undressing him as I go, rather than letting him out of my grasp right now. In fact, we haven't done much apart from kissing and cuddling in the few days he's been here. He needed comfort after the shock and emotion of the last few days, and I didn't want to pressure him. But I know I have a higher libido than Darcy and I'm already struggling, ready to blow half the time. Maybe when he's gone out, I'll take matters into my own hands.

His reflection smiles back at me. "I won't let my clients down, not even as tempting as you are."

I show him my best pout and then pull back, reluctantly releasing him.

"Are you sure you don't want me to come with you?" I ask, even though I know the answer as I'd asked him several times already. But the protective instinct is strong.

"I'm fine, babe. It'll be okay."

I know it will. His speech to his parents a few days ago proved that. Showed me he was stronger than I thought he was, and I feel bad for underestimating him. It doesn't stop me wanting to help, though.

"Alright, and I hope it goes well for Justin and Mark. I can't wait to see them on Saturday." I'm looking forward to their wedding and a surprise I have planned for Darcy. Just thinking about it makes me want to throw him down on the bed and not let him out of the room, not until he's come, screaming my name. But well, parents. And now I can't stop thinking about it, and the semi I'm sporting just from kissing him a minute ago is thickening. I adjust myself in my jeans.

"What's got you all hot and bothered?" Darcy asks with a smirk, looking pointedly at my crotch.

"As if you need to ask that," I say, trying not to look at him as it's making matters worse.

"Do you need help?" He steps closer and places his hand over mine, which is ineffectually attempting to make it more comfortable.

I glance at him and see him nibble his bottom lip, with a question in his dark verdant eyes. I'm doomed.

I swallow.

"Er, that isn't helping, D." My voice is thick and I'm on a hair trigger. But a huge part of me doesn't want him to stop at all, delighted that he seems to know what I need.

He gives me a sly smile and bats my hand away, unbuttoning my jeans before I can stop him. He pulls my trousers and boxer briefs down, allowing my cock to bounce free of its constraints.

"Um, D. Honey?" No, this isn't really helping, and I utter a curse under my breath as he wraps his hand round my length.

He presses his lips to mine, questing with his tongue while he starts slow strokes with his hand, his thumb brushing over the tip. Then he walks me backwards until I'm up against the wall.

"Shhh now," he whispers, before he drops to his knees.

I have to tip my head back and squeeze my eyes shut, as the sight of his lips engulfing my cock is too much, and I'm going to be coming within a few seconds. Instead, I give myself over to the feeling of his tongue swirling around my end and the exquisite sensation of his mouth. I try to steady my breathing and keep quiet, letting out a series of *fucks* under my breath. I feel rather than hear him chuckling round me at my struggle to hold on, and it's enough to push me over the edge. I let the wall support me when my knees almost give way as I shoot straight to the back of his throat. He slowly slides his mouth off me and stands in one deft movement, always elegant.

I'm still recovering, unable to stand unaided and staring at him with a mixture of love and wonder.

"That was amazing, D," I say, eventually managing to pull my jeans back on. "Thank you."

"You looked like you needed that," he says bluntly, and I mock-frown at him.

"That obvious, huh?"

"I can read you like a book." His eyes are full of mirth. "But I need to go or I'll miss the bus." He presses a quick kiss to my lips and then he's gone, and I'm still leaning against the wall trying to get my breath back.

When I've recovered, I go down to the kitchen, seeking out my parents. My dad is just off to take Gran to her appointment. He isn't working today, either. I've asked for the rest of the week off to be with Darcy. Alan is still helping my dad as the job he wanted at the steelworks didn't go his way, so taking time off isn't difficult. But there is a big job planned for next week that will need all three of us. Until then, there's something else I need to do, especially after what just happened. I need to double my efforts to find somewhere for Darcy and I to live.

Chapter 34

Darcy

Thankfully, my parents aren't home when I enter the apartment above the studio. I have a short while before Justin and Mark are due to arrive, and then there are a couple of lessons after them.

I'm glad I don't have to face my parents today—despite telling Nick I'd be fine, I'd rather not have another confrontation right now. It feels eerie walking through the empty house, as if it's already been abandoned. In a way, it has. The family unit we had no longer exists, and the more I examine it, the more I wonder if it truly existed as I thought it did. Was I just a puppet for my mum's dreams? The thought doesn't diminish my love of dancing, but it does apply a tainted patina to what my childhood really was. Or rather, what it wasn't. I had none of the experiences and friends that regular children have. It was full of practice and competitions and helping in the school. I didn't have many friends at school either, not enough to bring them home. If it hadn't been for Nick, I would have been an extremely sad and lonely boy. His friendship was solid and unconditional, and he's always allowed me to be myself, supporting rather than pushing, and I am full of gratitude for him. I have no idea what he saw in me back then that made him want to be my friend, or what he sees in me now, but he's more than family—he's the other half of my soul.

As I stand in the quiet kitchen, I idly wonder where my parents are and then push the thought straight back out of my head. It's clear their plans didn't include me, so mine won't include them. Not that I have any plans right now. That reminder flattens my mood, which had been quite buoyant after leaving Nick in his room, flushed and breathless. I smile to myself that I can do that to him, affecting his calm confidence that way.

I collect some more clothes from my room, but I can't keep filling Nick's room up. That situation isn't ideal, and a layer of guilt that I'm being a burden further dulls how I'm feeling right now. Nick, with his starry blue eyes and a million smiles, is the only bright point in my life right now.

I go downstairs to open up the studio. I refuse to wallow in self-pity. I can at least help make someone else's life better instead.

"Congratulations!" Justin says, as soon as he enters the studio. "You were amazing on Saturday."

"You were there?" I ask, a little confused.

"We weren't, but then Mark caught a newsreel reporting that you'd changed partners and were dancing with Nick, and then we just had to find everything we could about it."

"Oh." I didn't know what to say to that.

"Do you know how wonderful it was to see someone from our community dancing?" Mark chimes in. "We've not had that before."

"I guess I didn't," I say hesitantly. I hadn't thought about it, that it might be something others would want to see. I just wanted to dance with the person I wanted to.

"It's validating for us. It normalises it. Every time someone has the courage to go out there and show everyone what can be done, it makes it easier for us."

I'm suddenly drawn into a group hug by both Mark and Justin and it overwhelms me—their emotion, their words. I drop my head, not wanting them to see the effect it's having on me.

"Oh, sorry," Mark says, hurriedly dropping his arms. "We didn't ask if you'd be okay with a hug."

"It's fine, I was just . . ." I didn't know how to explain it. I hadn't thought about the wider community. It's one I don't actively feel part of outside of Nick and a couple of his friends. I feel I ought to own up to that. "To be honest, I wasn't doing it as a way of being seen. I just wanted to dance with Nick. I'd been told I couldn't, but that changed, and so I did what I wanted."

"For love?" Mark almost squeals and swoons with a hand over his heart. Justin rolls his eyes at him and I laugh.

"Something like that."

"Well, whatever the reason, it's inspirational," Justin says "We said we wanted to continue lessons and now we're thinking we could try a competition, the beginners' level, someday. If you'll teach us." Mark nods his head in enthusiastic agreement.

I sigh, and their eagerness makes what I have to tell them even harder.

"I'm really sorry, but I can't continue the lessons. The school is closing."

"What!" Mark's exclamation is a piercing contrast to his earlier swooning.

"My parents have decided to close the school," I reply, not willing to be drawn into any further discussion on the whys or wherefores.

Both Justin and Mark look ready to ask a million questions, but I direct them instead to their lesson, and make sure they're confident they'll be able to remember it on Saturday.

They dance well and, whilst they might not be foot perfect, they make up for it with enthusiasm and the love for each other that oozes out of them. It's joyful to watch, and I find I'm looking forward to seeing them perform it for real on Saturday. I'm also looking forward to their wedding because I've never been to a wedding before. Is that normal? We have no other family outside of my mum, dad, and sister. Claire isn't likely to be getting married soon, and without a network of friends, I've never been close enough to anyone to be invited. It just serves to remind me of another thing I've missed out on, along with birthday parties and holidays.

As people are arriving for the next class, the beginners, which will be followed by the improvers, the phone rings. I answer it and it's someone enquiring about lessons. I explain the situation to them and return to the studio to start the lesson. The phone rings again and it's the same enquiry, but from someone else. I tell them the same, too. After it rings for a third time, this occasion five minutes after I've started the lesson, I take the phone off the hook. That's more enquiries than we'd received in a week before. For the next couple of hours, I concentrate on the classes, enjoying myself and noting with a sense of sad pride those who are improving, knowing I can't help them continue. They're all full of congratulations, the same as Mark and Justin were, and it's also very difficult to tell them that there won't be any classes after the end of the month. Their disappointment is unanimous, but I tell them there is nothing they can do.

After the same question has been directed at me for the dozenth time, my patience starts wearing thin and I answer more sharply than I had intended.

"Even if I could continue the lessons, there'll be nowhere to dance. This building will be demolished to make way for the new housing development."

"Years ago, we just used to learn in the village hall." One of the clients pipes up, with agreement from the others.

"Yes, we used a church hall; dancing on Tuesdays and Sunday school on Sundays," says another.

"Couldn't you rent a hall for lessons?" someone else asks. "It doesn't matter where it is for me. I just want to keep dancing."

"I don't know," I respond, because I need to give them some answers. I don't elaborate, as I need to think. Was it something I could do? More importantly, was it something I now *wanted* to do?

Nick arrives as I'm about to lock up the studio, and I remember belatedly that we're catching the bus into the city centre for the radio interview.

"Hi," he says with a smile, and then looks round the place with a frown. "It feels different somehow."

"You notice it, too." It isn't a question.

"It feels sad," he says, wrinkling his nose slightly, and I know what he means as I feel it as well.

"Shall we?" I gesture to the door so we can go.

"Your—"

"Are not in," I reply, as I know exactly what he's going to ask and I don't want to talk about it. He just nods, and I'm grateful he doesn't push.

We get settled in at the radio station for the interview. I try to give general answers about my upbringing, not wanting to go into too much detail. They ask about my dreams, and I reply that the opportunity to dance at the Nationals had always been a dream that had eluded me for many years. I get caught up in my own words, words that come naturally without overthinking. I said to dance; I didn't say to win. I've always said to win before, and it's with the clarity of distance that I fully comprehend how much I've been shackled by my mum's vision. And just like that, they fall away. A lightness expands in my chest that is both freeing and terrifying. I miss the next question.

"Sorry, what was that?"

The presenter frowns at me.

"Right now I'm playing a song, as we can't have dead air." I must have spaced out in my head for too long. "The question I asked was, *What made you want to dance with Nick?*" You have . . ." The presenter looks at the display in front of him.

"One minute and twenty-three seconds until the end of the song, then I'll ask you again. So be ready this time."

I nod in understanding and look across at Nick, who's looking back at me with an amused expression on his face.

The presenter, with ultra smooth professionalism, recaps for the listeners who he's interviewing, and cleverly disguises the fact that I fluffed it—for which I'm grateful. And this time, when he asks his question, I'm ready.

"When you're dancing in top-level competitions in ballroom dancing, you need the right partner. Someone who's in sync with you. It has to be someone you trust implicitly. But even then, there has to be that extra connection, so you can dance with a harmony and fluidity that feels and looks like you're dancing as one. Sometimes you click straight away with a dancing partner, and sometimes it takes a while to develop. Nick has all of that and is a very special person to me. I can't imagine not dancing with him. I'd rather not dance at all than not dance with Nick."

There are a few seconds of silence which, this time, I think the presenter deliberately leaves in and then hits me with another question.

"Is it true that you're also in a relationship with Nick?"

"Yes," I answer, without even thinking. There are a few more questions for the both of us, some about the future, which I avoid answering other than to say that I'm considering my options. Then we're finished and allowed to leave. It's getting late, and we walk back to the bus station. Nick shops for sweets, as he says that was intense and he needs some sugar to cope. He offers me one and I suck on a Love Heart while we walk.

"What you said was beautiful," he says softly. "Thank you."

"Every word was true." I meant every word of it.

"Do you know you just came out on air?" He drops in casually.

"What? Wait! Did I? I just thought everyone knew anyway." I stop and look at him and his expression is a little painful. It tugs on my heart and I get the feeling I've done something wrong.

"Even if others know, there is an expectation that people need to announce it."

"Urgh, that sucks." I grimace and his expression softens.

"I just want you to know that now you've confirmed it, you are more likely to get asked about it."

I hadn't thought about the consequences. I was just answering the question truthfully.

"It just feels so natural that I don't think of it being a thing I need to tell people about. I can't define myself as being whatever label people have for me, for us. I'm yours. I feel you fused into my being in a way that is much deeper than the harmony we have when dancing. It's everything. I think it's been that way for a long time, but I just didn't recognise it."

"You're incredible. Do you know that?"

My answer to his question is left unsaid as he claims my mouth like he's claimed my soul.

Chapter 35

Nick

"How do I look?" Darcy asks for the umpteenth time, and receives the same answer.

"Absolutely gorgeous."

He flashes his bright green eyes at me and I take a step closer, talking low into his ear. "If you ask me one more time, I'll show you *how* gorgeous, and neither of us will be going to this wedding."

I watch the adorable flush of red spread from under the collar of his shirt, up his neck, and across his face. I have to step away as I'm in danger of acting on my words and I want to go to this wedding, I want to show Darcy the surprise I've planned for later.

"That wasn't fair," he protests.

"Neither is seeing your handsome face on display twenty-four seven, but some of us just have to bear the burden of that."

He laughs, and is about to say something no doubt sassy

in return, when my mum walks into the front room where we've been waiting.

"I think the taxi's here," she says, a second before I hear the beep of the horn announcing its arrival.

"You boys have fun then." She hugs me and then holds out her arms for Darcy, and he allows himself a hug from her, too. I roll my eyes at the wink she gives me over his shoulder and pick up the small bag I have ready.

"What's that?" Darcy asks as he spots it.

"A surprise. I'll tell you later." I keep my face deadpan and receive a frown in return. Too bad. He'll have to wait.

Darcy is dumbstruck as the taxi drops us off at the entrance to Wortley Hall. He stands there staring at the elegant stone façade of the former stately home. I'm not far behind him. I think it's stunning as well. Justin and Mark picked a beautiful place to hold their wedding.

I take hold of his hand, and we walk up the steps. Inside the foyer, a big sign directs wedding guests to a spacious room with several tables and a large dance floor. Beyond, I can see several foldback doors opening out into the gardens. There are a couple of dozen people milling about, but I pull Darcy past all of that and over to the front desk.

I try not to look at his face as I check us in, but I can feel him bubbling beside me. I ignore his attempts at questions as I drag him up the stairs to the room I've booked for us. I wait until we're in the room and have put down my bag.

"Surprise, honey," I say, and stalk my way towards him, grasping his hips and pulling him close, planting a soft kiss to his lips.

"For us?" He looks around the room.

"For us." I punctuate my words with kisses. "No parents." *Kiss.* "No small bed." *Kiss.* "No one to disturb us."

"It's perfect." He gives me his sassiest smile and puts his arms round my neck, kissing me back. I move my hands to cup his ass, lifting him up, and he wraps his legs around my waist. I walk him to the bed and place him on it, following him down so I'm covering his body.

"Shouldn't we be attending a wedding?" he asks, when we briefly pause our kissing a short time later.

"We have a few minutes," I reply, fusing my lips to his once more and seeking his tongue.

We make it down to the wedding in time, even if our suits do look slightly crumpled and our lips are reddened from kissing. Luckily, no one is paying us any attention and we slip into the garden, finding a space towards the back of the chairs that are arranged in lines. A carpeted aisle runs between the two sets of chairs, leading to an archway that's bowing under the weight of the roses growing up it.

We only have a few minutes to wait before I see Justin stand at the end of the aisle, looking smart in a white suit and pink shirt. The whole decor is pink and white. I hadn't noticed the cellist seated to one side, until they start playing, and we all rise as the opening notes of "Perfect" drift over the garden, mixing with the heady scent of the roses. Darcy seeks my hand and I interlace our fingers.

The first thing I notice of Mark's arrival is the joy and love that lights up Justin's face. I don't know if Darcy sees it too, but he gives my hand a squeeze and I return it. We turn to see

Mark in a pink suit, which looks fabulous on him, being accompanied down the aisle by an older gentleman who I assume could be his father.

Two young boys and a girl, also dressed in pink and white, follow them, each carrying a small posy of flowers. There's an array of very proud looking parents watching them, calling them to their sides as they reach the end of the aisle.

The celebrant makes her introductions and opening speech, and we're instructed to sit. I pull Darcy's hand into my lap, wrapping my other hand round it as we watch Justin and Mark declare their love and commitment to each other, each having written their own vows.

I have attended a few weddings before, mostly of cousins and other distant relatives, and each one has been unique in its own way, but this one seems more special to me. It might be because I feel it's more relevant to me, being a same-sex couple. Or it could be because I now have someone in my life who I would make that commitment to. The thought hits me out of the blue, and now it's taken hold in my head and my heart. I know it's true. I would like to be married to Darcy one day. I look at him, and he's watching Mark and Justin with a rapt expression on his face. He must have sensed I was watching him, and he turns to look at me. His smile is soft, and I feel the need to taste it with a gentle kiss.

After the ceremony, we congratulate Justin and Mark and are hugged within an inch of our lives, then we're shown to our seats at a table, along with some of their other friends. Food is brought, wine flows, and the conversation is cheerful. We talk easily with the people we're seated with and I enjoy myself. We're treated to an array of speeches from the best man, Justin's brother, and from the family on both sides, all of whom seem very accepting of Justin and Mark, though I suspect anyone who isn't wouldn't have been invited. The speeches make us laugh with the obligatory embarrassments, and make us *ooh* and *ahh* with the incredible love shown. Then champagne is handed round, and the family takes turns toasting them and we all join in. Then Justin stands, pulling Mark up with him.

"When Mark agreed to marry me, he made one condition."

He pauses to the heckles of *"only one?"* and a few other shouts, including several rude words. He waits for the laughter to die down.

"The condition was that he wanted a proper first dance. So we've been taking lessons."

A few whoops and cheers along with some laughs that they take good-naturedly. Justin again waits for quiet before continuing.

"Some of you might have noticed that our city hosted the national ballroom championships last weekend. Some of you might have seen the news reports that for the first time a same-sex couple danced at the top level in the competition. We're pleased to tell you that it was our dance teacher, and we're happy to have him and his partner here today."

Justin gestures over to our table and then starts clapping. "Darcy, stand up," he shouts, and Darcy, looking slightly embarrassed, stands and drags me up with him. We sit again, and are met with a round of questions from our table occupants along the lines of:

"Why didn't you tell us?"

"How exciting."

"I've always wanted to dance."

The hubbub dies down again and Justin says, "Of course,

if we fall on our faces, it's all his fault." The room erupts again, and Justin leads Mark onto the dance floor. Everyone rises and follows them, ringing the area and leaving enough room for them to dance.

They wait for the room to go quiet before the music begins. The familiar sounds of "Love is in the Air" ring through the room and they start. They look fantastic together and the applause they receive is well deserved. Then they ask for the song to be played through again so we can all join in.

We don't leave the dance floor for another few hours, except for water or a bit more champagne. We dance with Justin and Mark, various members of their families, and friends. But mostly we dance with each other. Just enjoying ourselves, playing with some of the swing moves we've been practising.

The reception will be going on for a good while yet, as everyone is still going strong. When they bring out the buffet later, I turn to Darcy.

"Do you want to go upstairs?"

His enthusiastic nod is all the encouragement I need.

Inside the room I kiss him slowly. As much as I've been waiting for this moment, I want to take my time. I want to savour every minute.

I unbutton his jacket and slip it off his shoulders. He goes to unbutton his shirt, but I put my hands on his.

"No, honey," I say softly. "I want to undress you."

I take off my jacket, and my shoes and socks, and reach for my phone to play some music. Of course, I've created a playlist for the occasion.

I kneel in front of him and ask him to lift each foot in turn so I can remove his shoes and socks. Then I rise and lead him over to stand near the bed.

I slowly unbutton his shirt, pulling it free from his trousers. I run my fingers up his chest and cup my hands round his jaw, tasting his lips, biting them gently before sliding my mouth down to place a row of kisses down his throat, humming my approval as he tips his head back to expose it more for me. I withdraw slightly, keeping my eyes on him as I undo my own shirt and take it off.

I return to studiously sucking marks on his neck, pulling his shirt down and trapping his arms as I kiss my way along his shoulder. I notice the way his breath hitches when I have him held fast and I file that information away for the future. My cock is certainly on board with that idea and responds with a twitch.

"Do you like that?" I ask, looking back at him, seeing the answer in his heavy, lust-filled eyes. I have a sudden image of him spread out and restrained for me and it's all I can do not to rip the rest of his clothes off and take him. I take a few breaths, mostly to stop the rush of blood that is making my dick want to act independently of what I have planned. I almost hear him whine when I pull his shirt all the way off.

I delicately cage my arms round him, wanting to feel his skin against mine, and I caress my hands up and down his spine. He wraps his arms around me as I sway my hips to the rhythm of the music, and he mirrors me, slow-dancing for the rest of the song.

As it finishes, I lead him back to the bed, trailing my hands down his skin, and tracing across his abs. I unbutton his trousers and slide them with his briefs down over his hips, asking for him to step out of them.

"Fuck. Honey, you look good." I feast my eyes on his erection. "Now get on the bed for me."

He sits down and moves backwards until he's laying back on the pillows.

I take off my trousers, giving Darcy a flash of my latest pair of lace shorts, before they join the rest of our clothes on the floor.

I crawl up the bed towards him, pecking kisses on his thighs, and sucking a mark on his hip. I continue up his body, applying my mouth to his chest, seeking out a nipple with my tongue. Darcy moans and stretches languidly beneath me. I transfer my tongue to his other nipple, feeling it harden at my touch, and his moans grow louder as I flick it with my tongue, nibbling it gently.

"Mmmm, that's good, babe." He stretches again, and his erection bounces against my chest, reminding me of its presence.

I work my way down his torso, following his faint treasure trail until I can hold the base of his cock and lap at the precum leaking from the end, savouring the taste.

"Tell me what you want," I say huskily, sitting back. "Tell me what you need."

"I want you," he says lazily.

"How do you want me?"

"I want you to fill me up." His voice deepens.

"That's it, honey. Keep talking." After weeks of hushed hand jobs and muffled blow jobs, I want to hear his voice.

"I want to feel you."

"*Mmm,* sounds good." I bend each of his legs in turn, placing a kiss to the inside of each knee. "Hold your knees, honey."

He brings his legs up to his chest, exposing himself to me. He looks perfect and wanton and I want to hear more. I reach for the lube, flipping the lid and coating my fingers.

"Where do you want to feel me?" I ask.

"In my hole."

"This hole?" I tap it with my finger, watching it contract as he jumps.

"Yes." He lets out a breathy whisper.

"I can't hear you." I rub my finger round his perfect pucker, feeling it respond to my touch, watching his struggle to voice anything.

"Y-yes. T-that hole." He pushes against my finger.

"It's a needy little hole, isn't it?" I tease his rim a bit more before breaching it with one finger, feeling it grip me as he almost sighs in relief. I start sliding my finger in and out.

"It needs more," he responds again.

"Does it? It's a greedy hole as well." I add a second finger, working them in and out, scissoring them to prep him slowly.

"Yes, it's a needy, greedy hole." His breaths come in short pants, and I work my fingers a little faster, in time to the thrusts he's pushing back on me. My cock is rock hard and aching at the sight of him thrusting back on my fingers. Precum stringing between the end and my stomach as it twitches every time he opens his mouth.

"What does it need?" I add a third finger, watching his abs contract with the feel of it.

"It needs dick, babe. It needs your dick." The last word said between clenched teeth as I hit his sweet spot.

"Can it take my dick?" I fucking hope so, as if I don't get in there soon, I'm going to come just watching him. It's as if something in him, some internal restraint, finally snaps and loosens his tongue.

"It can take your dick. I need it. My needy, greedy hole wants your dick. I want you to fill me, fill me so full. I want to still feel you next week. Please, babe, fuck me. *Pleeease*."

Seeing him spread, ready and begging for me, is almost more than I can take. I withdraw my fingers, enjoying one last glimpse of his hole opening and closing, grasping for something.

I flip the lube cap once more and smear some along my length and line up with his hole.

"You ready?" I ask as I nudge at his entrance.

"*Pleeeease.*" He jerks his hips for emphasis. I push in slowly, checking that he's okay and I'm not hurting him, but his breathy whispers of *"more, more, more"* are my undoing. I thrust in deep.

"*Ungh,*" he groans, and for a second I think I've hurt him, but then I see the smile on his face and the pretty flush of his cheeks.

I start moving rhythmically, unable to stop my hips. My need to speak takes over.

"Fuck, honey. I knew you'd feel good. You're the perfect fit. Your ass is just right. It's like your pretty little hole was made just for me. *You* were made for me."

I know I'm not going to last much longer, it's too exquisite and I've been waiting too long.

He arches off the bed, changing the angle slightly. "Oh, fuck babe, I'm going to come." His voice coming in short breaths, his eyes fluttering closed.

"Yes, do it, honey." I can't stop relentlessly pounding, the slap of my balls against him sending tingles down my spine. I'm close to the edge, holding on for as long as I can.

"Oh fuck! *Nick*!" He shouts as his body jerks once more and his release spurts across his chest, his hole tightening around me even more, gripping me as his orgasm shudders through him. That's all it takes to tip me over the precipice I'd been clinging to, and my own orgasm rips through me with an intensity that leaves me speechless.

It takes a few minutes for me to regain enough awareness to slide my deflating cock out of him.

I know we need to clean up, but for now I just want to crawl up the bed to lie by his side. His eyes are closed and he isn't moving and I think that something is wrong.

"D, honey?" I say softly, trying not to show the concern that starts bubbling up in me, thinking that I'd hurt him or that he thinks what we did was wrong.

"I was just checking I was still alive." He blinks his eyes open and turns his head towards me, his smile easing the constriction that has been tightening around my chest. "I wouldn't have believed I could take that much pleasure, happiness, and love all in one go."

He turns onto his side to face me. "Unless I have died and you're, like, some fucking glorious angel." He reaches out his hand and traces his fingers down my face, so tenderly that my heart swells and threatens to burst through the confines of my ribs.

"Kiss me angel," he whispers, and I do.

Chapter 36

Darcy

"The event on Saturday is still going ahead." I try to reassure the seniors in their Monday afternoon class. They haven't taken the news that the school is closing very well, and have been grumbling about it for the last few minutes until someone asks about the forties event.

"We're still having everything as we've already planned."

They return their complaints back to the lessons.

"What are we going to do?" and, *"You can still teach us, though, can't you?"* being the main ones. I've given some thought to the suggestions from the other classes, that I rent a hall somewhere so I can still teach them. I haven't done anything about it, though. I'm not sure I want to either. I'm not sure what I want right now. I feel rudderless, just drifting aimlessly downstream, unable to weigh anchor just yet. I suppose I must or I could get swept out into the ocean and swallowed up by the waves. That was how it felt straight after the competition, that I'd been tossed off the edge of a cliff into

the stormy sea. The waters are calmer, but I still have no direction.

I ought to talk to Nick about it. The thought of Nick brings warmth and excitement to my core. He's gone back to work with his dad and Alan today after taking the week off for me. There's a large project they're working on, some sort of sports pavilion. He says he needs to work so he can buy a house. I've suggested renting, but he's set against it, saying that renting is so expensive he won't be able to afford to save up any more money. I understand that, but I can see his stubbornness in there, too. I'm all for getting a place of our own after the night away at the weekend. It was incredible, and I swear I can still feel the effects of being so gloriously filled by him even today. Maybe I should be looking for work, any work, rather than worrying about what I want to do right now. That way I can contribute and we can move out even faster.

The thought of that, of doing something useful, helps keep me in good spirits as I lock up the studio. I still haven't seen my parents. I didn't bother going upstairs to our house today. There's nothing up there for me now. I don't think my parents are at home, though. They know when the lessons are, and I think they're avoiding me, which suits me just fine.

Even the sight of the new development doesn't bother me anymore. I feel hungry, having missed lunch, so I pop into the shop for some much-needed chocolate. I pick up some gummy sweets and Love Hearts for Nick, too. I think it's cute that he likes them so much. I hear the shop is due to close at the end of the month too, and that the whole lot will be demolished. I should've realised that the school wasn't going to be spared in all of this. Maybe I was blinkered to what was going on around me. No, I refuse to accept the blame. My mum deliberately lied to me about it. I look at the empty chocolate wrapper in my hand and realise I've eaten it subconsciously while being angry at my mum. I didn't even get to enjoy it. Just another thing to be annoyed at her for.

By contrast, Doreen is welcoming when I get to Nick's parents' house. She makes me a cup of tea and I offer to help with dinner for when Nick and his dad get home. I still want to learn to cook better, and she readily accepts my help. After dinner I lend a hand, helping them pack up some of Nick's gran's things as she's moving into the retirement village tomorrow. She has a small suite of rooms, so she isn't taking much. We finish, and sit amongst the boxes, drinking tea and eating biscuits. The mood is partly melancholy, but there's also a hopeful air, as his gran seems excited about her new start.

It's quite late before Nick and I are in his room and I get a chance to talk to him. We sit cross-legged on the bed facing each other.

"I'm thinking of looking for a job," I open with.

"Doing what?" he asks, his face neutral.

"Anything. I just want to be useful. I want to help with costs so we can move out. I really want us to have our own place." He doesn't say anything, so I carry on, my mouth running away with me. "I mean, I don't have any skills, but surely I could work in a shop."

"Do you want to work in a shop?" he asks eventually.

"Well, no, but does anyone want to? It doesn't have to be a shop, though. It could be anything?"

I can see his frown forming. "What is it you really want to do?"

At first, I don't answer as I don't have a ready reply. Well, not a useful one, as my only answer is to keep dancing.

"Darcy." He takes a breath. "You're in a unique position. You are one of the best dancers in the country. You have no ties, and you could do anything you want to, go anywhere you want."

"What do you mean? I can't leave you. Is that what you want?" I whisper in horror, his words cutting me.

He reaches for my hand and I love his need to be physically connected. "No. No, of course not, but I would never hold you back from your dreams, D. You're free of the influence of your family. You can make your own choices now. You could dance in shows, on cruises, even on the television if you wanted. I know you want to dance and I would never want you to settle for anything less. You would never be happy and it would kill me thinking you were doing it for me. I want us to be together, but not at that cost."

I think on his words. Fame doesn't hold any appeal for me. I've never craved anything like that, now that I can look back on my childhood—what there was of it. It was never the winning that kept me competing; that was my mum's dream. I loved the opportunity to improve, better myself, and just keep dancing. What I also like doing is helping people find joy in dancing, helping them improve, be something they look forward to each week, and I think that's why the school closing has hit me so hard. I really enjoy my work.

"I'd like to keep teaching," I say, and tell him about the ideas that the clients had given me about renting a village hall to hold lessons in.

"Then I'll help you find somewhere," Nick promises, pulling me forward into a hug.

Two days later, I watch as Nick paces the room. I dragged him upstairs after dinner after he went out the back door twice before coming back, looking forlorn, as he remembered his gran was no longer next door.

"She'll be okay," I say, trying to offer him some comfort. He stops and sighs slightly.

"It's not that, it's just that things are different. I either spent my evenings with Gran or visiting you and dancing. But you're here and she's not."

I hadn't realised that Nick doesn't have anywhere to dance, and I know how much he loves it, too. He spent a lot of time either helping me, dancing with me, or just using the space, and I feel bad that he doesn't have that outlet. I know my plan of teaching dancing is good for me, but it doesn't help Nick much. He's been affected by my mum as well. I need to come up with something better.

My phone starts ringing, which is a rarity, and I grab hold of it, seeing that it's Claire.

"Are you watching the news?" she calls hurriedly down the phone when I answer it.

"No, why?" I say. It's not something we watch often.

"Well, switch it on, quick." she almost shouts. "Look North." She clarifies what programme and I follow Nick as he clatters down the stairs and into the front room, snatching up the remote and switching channels.

What I'm greeted with takes all the breath from my lungs.

There's a news piece about our competition dance and a video of us dancing plays in the background, but what hits me first is that they're interviewing my mum.

I stand there appalled, seeing her basking in the glory of what we achieved. I watch her take credit for me dancing with Nick, as if it was her idea. She acts the proud mum, as if our success was hers alone.

I can't take it anymore.

"Please turn it off," I whisper, and Nick complies.

"I'm sorry, love," Doreen says, standing and offering a hug. I welcome her embrace, but once she releases me I start pacing, the movement keeping a lid on my anger—barely. If I stop, I might allow the screaming that's reverberating through my head to start. Nausea rises, forcing bile into my mouth. I clench my jaw shut and try to swallow the bitterness that burns my throat. Of all the things she's done, this is the most despicable, and I need to stop her. I turn to Nick.

"I can't let her get away with that. Will you help me?"

"Are you sure, D?"

"Yes." I start pacing again.

"What do you want me to do?"

"Come with me?"

"Now?" He seems surprised, but I have to do it now. I have to confront her now or there's a chance I'll lose my nerve.

I tell him that, and he agrees. I start towards the door and Frank calls us back.

"Take the van," he offers. I marvel at how lucky Nick is to have such a wonderful family.

While Nick drives, I call Claire back.

"Did you know anything about it?" I demand, probably a bit harshly, but I'm fuelled by fury right now.

"No I didn't. I swear, Darcy. I only found out when I switched the television on. I haven't spoken to them since last week."

I tell her I'll call her later and ring off. I can see lights on when we pull up outside the school, so I know they're inside. I have no idea what I'm going to say, but I need to say something. Maybe I'll feel better when I have.

I take the back stairs to the balcony that leads to the kitchen. When I burst in, they're on the couch watching something on television.

"Oh, Darcy," my mum says with a smile. "Did you see the news? Isn't it fantastic?" I'm not totally sure what she's on about, but I'm still furious.

"You've got a nerve, haven't you? Telling everyone that it was your idea for me to dance with Nick. Taking the credit."

"Well, I had to do something. If you'd danced with Krystal like I wanted you to, you would've won. But no, you wanted to throw away your chances. Dancing with a guy! Who does that? It's not right."

I'm genuinely shocked by her words.

"He's my boyfriend," I spit.

"I don't care if he's the fucking pope. On the dance floor, you should dance with women."

I feel my mouth drop open as I'm rendered incapable of forming words. It allows her to continue.

"But I've worked hard to turn around the mess you made of it. I made it look like a publicity stunt. And I got you a contract. A shot at the big time on television. They're looking for new dancers for Strictly Come Dancing."

I stare at her.

"When were you going to tell me this?"

"Well, I only got the call from Bruce earlier, and then I had to go to the interview so—"

"You said it on air?" That's what she meant about fantastic news. "Before you told me?"

"Well, I was just so excited, and it just came out. But it's great and you're going to be a star, Darcy. It's the big time."

"You're unbelievable." I didn't even think she was capable of something like that. "I don't want to be on television."

"After all I've done for you, guided and taught you through childhood to want this, and you throw it back at me?"

"I never had a childhood," I yell back at her. "I never got to play with other children. I never got invited to other children's birthday parties. I've never even been on holiday."

"You had Nick." She gestures over to where he's standing,

looking like he's about to say a few things of his own. With my eyes, I tell him I've got this.

"Nick is the one good thing in my life." I lower my voice. "But you. I'm finished with you. Stay away from me. I never want to see you again." I turn and head towards the kitchen door. Nick follows behind. When I'm outside, I lean on the balcony rail, drawing in breath and the blood pounds in my ears. I hear the door go behind me and I spin round, expecting my mum to want the last word. But it's my dad looking bereft.

"I'm sorry, son," he says dejectedly. I sigh. I'm mad at my dad, but mostly for his inaction.

"You could have told me, Dad. You could have told me everything."

He shrugs a little and looks back inside, and I understand him well enough. I don't want to cut him out of my life, but I can't accept him right now either.

"You're a coward, Dad. You're gutless. I pity you for that. If you can find some courage from somewhere, maybe there's hope for you yet."

I don't wait to see the expression on his face as I take the stairs two at a time, just wanting to be as far away as possible.

Chapter 37

Nick

It's been two days since my gran moved and I still have to stop myself from calling in to say hello, checking up on her before I leave for work, when I get back, and well, anytime really. She's been such a large presence in my life that I'm struggling to not have her here. She's always ready with the advice, the support, as well as the usually well-deserved admonishments. I know she's not far away, but still it's not the same as having her next door.

I will still see her later though, after work, the same as I did last night. It's going to be a while before I'm going to let a day go by that I don't call in. She seems to have settled in well and is making friends already, so I'm pleased that she's getting what she wants.

I finish masking the room and put on some overalls and a mask. It's a large space, so I'm spray painting it. For the next half an hour, I apply myself to covering the walls. It's a manual job, and like most of those, it gives my brain space to think. Or to worry. I try not to worry about Darcy, but he's been strangely quiet since we got back from his parents' last night. His courage was amazing, and whilst I was struggling to not jump in and protect him, I saw he didn't need it and it was better for him to do it alone. His whole life has been controlled by other people. He doesn't need me adding to it. But to cut himself off from his parents, that's harsh. Not that I can blame him. He called Claire whilst I drove him home, but he did nothing except tell her what he'd done and then hung up. She sent me a message later, but other than confirming that, of course, I'd make sure he was alright, I didn't elaborate. That's for Darcy to talk to her about. All he did when we got home was to climb into bed and hug Bearlero. I hugged them both.

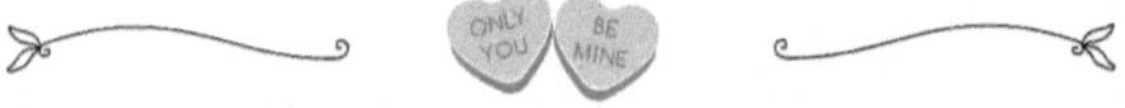

I felt awful leaving him this morning, but he got up and had breakfast, which I took as a good sign. He still looked sad, but said he was researching places to rent so he could continue lessons. I think he feels he wants to prove himself more.

I finish the room and need some fresh air after the stuffiness of the mask, so head outside. We're helping to refurbish a sports pavilion. It used to be owned by one of the local foundries as a sports and social club, one of the dozens that were attached to various steelworks or breweries in the city. Since the foundry closed, it's been closed too, but a local community group wants to take it on as a community sports space, and they've set up men's and women's Sunday league teams, as well as juniors. There'll also be a gym for the local community to use. I walk around the football pitch, taking a bit of time before I have to return and start in another room. My dad and Alan are painting and decorating in the bar area. We hope to have it completed within a couple of weeks. At the far side of the football pitch, I see another building with a grassed area outside. It looks like it might have been used for playing bowls at one point, but like the main pavilion, it's in need of some refurbishment. I'm curious though, and take a closer look.

I can't see much through the windows and the grounds are a bit overgrown, but a nub of an idea takes root.

"What's the old building across the pitch?" I ask, after tracking down the manager, Jasmine, in her office when I get back to the pavilion.

"That's the old bowling club. No one seems to want to play bowls nowadays, and it's too far from this building to be useful. It even has its own car park. Under our conditions of guardianship of this building, we can't dispose of it, but as yet we don't know what to do with it. Something will have to be done soon, though, so it doesn't become too derelict."

"Would you rent it out?" I ask tentatively, and she looks at me with more interest.

"We'd be delighted to. What do you have in mind?"

"Would you mind if I have a proper look before I answer that?" I ask, and she gets up and heads to a key cabinet.

"C'mon, let me give you the grand tour," she says brightly.

I blow out a breath as she unlocks the main door, and we enter the foyer. It does need some work, a bit more than I thought, but not impossible. There's a kitchen, changing rooms, and a store room to one side, but what I really want to see is the room where they used to play indoor bowls. I stand in the centre of the room and turn around completely. It's perfect . . . Well, it could be, with some work. All I need to do now is see if it's viable and sell the idea to Darcy. I walk to the window and look out on the bowling green. It needs mowing, but you can see it was well maintained in the past. I try not to let my imagination run away with me. There's still a long way to go, but I feel excitement pushing its way up. I contain it, as I need to be serious.

As we walk back to the pavilion Jasmine asks, "Well now you've seen it, what do you think?"

I shrug a little, keeping my face as neutral as possible. "It needs a lot of work."

"It's in about the same condition this place was," she says, gesturing to the main building as we reach the doors and head back to her office.

"What's the rent?" I ask. There's no point going any further if it's not feasible.

She names a figure, followed by, "Five-year fixed term." My heart sinks. That's a lot of money. Just one year's rent would take half my savings. There's no way I can commit to that. I think for a minute before I reply.

"Two years with a possible extension to five, the first year half price due to it needing so much work." I hold my breath. Even this was a big gamble, but it would be worth it.

She sits back in her chair and regards me for what seems like a lifetime, then a small smile spreads across her face.

"Where did you learn to negotiate like that?"

"I'm a Yorkshireman," I say in a deadpan voice, and she tips back her head and laughs.

"Well, you have yourself a deal."

"I need to talk it through, but I'll be in touch," I say, and walk back to where I need to get back to work, only now allowing a grin to show through.

Chapter 38

Darcy

"What do you think?" Nick asks, as he stops his dad's van in the car park of what looks to be a derelict building. Not that I can see much from the jungle of weeds that obscure the view. But Nick seems excited, so I try to sound positive. I fail.

"Um, okay, I guess." I'm not sure what I'm looking at. He said it was a surprise. Last time he told me there was a surprise he'd booked us into a hotel for a night. This definitely wasn't a hotel. He doesn't look too downcast by my less than lukewarm response.

"Wait until you see inside." He clambers out of the van and I follow. With the entire site now visible, I can see that, whilst overgrown, it doesn't look as bad as I first thought.

He leads the way to a door in the centre of the building. It opens into a space, but Nick is already bounding forward.

"Kitchen," he announces, gesturing towards a door to his right. "Changing rooms." Another door, and I try to keep up with him, attempting to take it all in. "Storeroom." A final door, but then he makes a sudden left turn and opens some double doors into a large space. He throws his arms wide and turns around in a complete circle.

"Now, what do you think?" His blue eyes are shining.

I look around the space. Well, it could work as a dance studio. In fact, it could be a really good one. It already has a great wooden floor, but the building needs a lot of work. Even I can see it's not usable as it is, and an entire building must be expensive and . . .

"I can see you're overthinking." Nick drops his arms and comes over to stand in front of me.

"I have just one question," he says. I look at him and nod my head.

"Okay." He can ask his question.

"Could you see this as a dance studio?"

I look round the room again and I know the answer. Still, the enormity of something like this is too much. I was thinking of renting somewhere for a couple of hours a week. I look back at his hopeful expression and answer.

"Yes, but—"

"No buts," he cuts in. "Hear me out, please?"

Again, I nod. He takes my hand and holds it between us, slowly tracing a finger over the back of it, focussing on that rather than looking at me.

"Do you know I used to be envious of you?" he starts, his voice poignant. I can't imagine anyone being envious of my joke of a life.

"I used to dream that I'd been born into a dancing family. That I had the opportunity to dance all day and go to competitions."

"You know that's not what it's cracked up to be," I say, and he looks at me with a sad smile.

"Yes, but what I'm trying to say is that I always had a dream to dance, perhaps to teach like you. This place needs a lot of work, but it's work we can do. This could be our place. We could run it—together. You saw how many of Justin and Mark's friends wanted lessons as well. We could make it an inclusive place, for people like us."

I look at the hope brimming in his blue eyes.

There's a lot of potential, I just don't have the means to do anything about it.

"Since the competition, I've had a load of emails in the school's inbox, most of them enquiring about lessons. I haven't had the heart to answer them," I reply, and his smile broadens, thinking of the possibilities. But I don't know what it will cost him. I need to know that.

"How much?" I ask.

"Nothing we can't manage."

"No, Nick. You are *not* going to dismiss this question. All my life people have fobbed me off with half the information and kept things from me. I want to know how much, and I always want to know the truth. Okay?"

His shoulders sag as he realises he's acted the same as everyone around me. He apologises, then tells me a figure and the terms he'd negotiated. Even then it seems huge to me. I'm struck by the gesture, so grateful that it hurts in my chest, but I can't have him do that for me.

"I can't let you do that," I say.

"I'm not asking you to," he flashes back. "I'm doing it for us, for our future, for something we can do together, D. I thought you might want that."

He drops my hand and walks over to some windowed doors that look like they would fold back, opening the space up. I follow him and see the flat but overgrown lawn outside.

"I do want that Nick," I say, and I feel him take a breath next to me waiting for the but—which he knows is coming. It breaks my heart to do it to him, but I have to anyway because I really need to make sure. "That money was for you to buy a house, and that can't happen now. I don't want to be the reason for you not being able to have a place of your own."

"*Our* own," he says. "It was always going to be ours, D. Do you think I haven't thought of that? So it'll take a bit longer to save up again, but we'll manage. We can make it work, I know we can. It'll be hard at first. We have to fix this place up before we can do anything, but I can always do some work for my dad to keep us going. I think he'll be happy to have Alan helping him instead of me. I think he feels a bit guilty that he can't offer him more work. But now he can, and I can help when needed for extra money."

"You've worked this all out, haven't you?" I look at him and he turns from staring out of the window.

"Of course I have." His smile is so sweet. I don't deserve him, I know that, but I love him. I can't think of anyone else I'd rather go through this with and it *would* be fun to do it together. I swing my gaze back to look out the window.

"That lawn would make a great space to hold events, wouldn't it?"

He doesn't reply, he just reaches for my hand and holds it tight.

"Twinkle Toes," I suggest.

"Really? How old are you? Twelve?" Nick snorts and I throw Bearlero at him, which he deftly catches, but to my mild annoyance, doesn't hand him back. I think better when I have something to do with my hands and without him, I don't know what to do with them.

"Still younger than you," I retort. We're sitting on the bed, trying to come up with a name for the new dance studio.

We've spent hours going through it all. Through all the start-up costs we can think of, what clients we know we could already have, and a marketing plan for finding more. We've worked out roughly what needs doing to the building, and have the start of a project plan for that. Nick's dad has roped Alan and Barry in to help, and Doreen said she had some friends willing to lend a hand. All we need to do now is register a business, and for that, we need a name.

"Two Men and a Dance Floor," Nick says and I let out a groan.

"Accurate, but hardly catchy."

"Still better than it sounding like you're a ballerina. When are you going to treat us to the 'Dance of the Sugar Plum Fairy?'" He smirks and I launch myself at him, smothering him with a pillow and wrestling Bearlero off him. No one gets to insult me and hold my bear at the same time, not even him.

"Dancing Feet," I offer, and Nick mulls it over. It's better than any of our suggestions so far.

"Who would've thought this would be so hard?" he grumbles, and I can't disagree.

We're both silent for a few moments and I try to come up with something else.

"Cool Shoes," Nick throws in.

"Roll over Fred Astaire," I reply and he laughs, but it's not that bad. "We'll add it into the mix."

We lapse into silence again.

"Step by Step," Nick offers again. He's good at this.

"Since when were you a New Kids' fan?" I giggle, and he holds his hand to his chest and says solemnly.

"Once a Blockhead, always a Blockhead."

"Really? How did I miss that?" Then I catch his smirk and almost throw something at him again.

"You're such a dick," I mutter.

"What was that? You want my dick?" His smile turns

predatory, and he moves fast. Before I can stop him, he has me pressed to the bed, sitting astride my hips, and my hands pinned to either side of my head. I make a half-hearted attempt to struggle out of his grasp, but he holds me down, a grin on his face.

He looks at me for a few seconds, as if he's deciding what to do. Then he spots that my T-shirt has ridden up, exposing part of my stomach, and from the look in his eyes, I know exactly what he's going to do. He grabs the edge of my shirt with his teeth and pulls it up further to gain more access, then licks a stripe right across my abs.

"*Eww*, that's disgusting," I protest, making a greater effort to throw him off. He laughs and lies down next to me while I use my T-shirt to wipe his saliva off my skin.

He props himself up on his elbow.

"Still a dick," I say, giving him a look.

"Careful, I might not be so lenient next time." He laughs.

"So, where were we before you started misbehaving?" He laughs again. "Oh, yes. Which one did you have a crush on then?" That gets me a glare and I figure I've got my own back.

"Step by Step isn't bad as a name, though," I say.

Nick stares off for a minute before speaking. "What about New Steps?"

"New Steps?" I like it. It works.

"It's new for us, and we will be fully inclusive, so it kind of fits."

"Yes, I like it." I grin at him. "You're a genius."

"I thought I was a dick."

"A genius dick," I answer, and kiss him because, well, he's both those things, and I love him for it.

Chapter 39

Darcy

I look around the studio and at the throng of people enjoying themselves, getting into the nostalgic spirit of the forties. I catch Nick's eye from where he's standing by the door and he flashes me one of his most brilliant smiles. I match it.

I'm amazed at how many people have turned out to our first event. I'm calling this our first because we are planning many more. As soon as the new studio is open.

The last couple of days have been extremely busy. Along with the last few things that needed organising for today, Nick and I have been setting up New Steps. Registering the business was perhaps the most exciting, but daunting, part of it. Even though we applied online, there was a moment when my finger hovered over the final "submit" button and I turned to Nick, whispering, "Are you sure?"

"I've never been more sure in my life," he replied, and put his finger over mine to click the button. Then we met with Jasmine about the contract, returning the next day to sign it.

We've filled in an application for a bank account and have an appointment next week. All of this in between pinning up bunting, setting out all the tables and chairs, and arranging the refreshments for today. Doreen and a few of her friends have been helpful, and made some sandwiches and baked cakes, which they're now serving from the kitchen with tea and coffee.

I feel a warm hand on the small of my back and my heart jumps. I love how Nick can do that to me. His hand stays in place, a comforting presence, while I finish talking to the group of people who've been asking questions.

"Are you ready to start?" he leans in and says quietly, and I tell the group I'll be back later. Now we have to get this event officially started.

We're going to dance a medley of different dance styles that were popular in the forties and then we'll invite people to have a go, aided by the seniors class who've been practising for weeks. For anyone who's new and doesn't feel confident joining in, we've opened up the other studio where we can give some instruction.

But before all of that, I want to say a few words.

Just as we head to the centre of the room the door opens and half a dozen people enter, older than our seniors. A couple of them are using walking sticks. They don't look like they're about to foxtrot round the room. I spot Nick's gran in the group at the same time he does.

He jogs over to them, and I see him hug her before he herds the group to a nearby table and waits until they're seated.

"Were you expecting that?" I whisper when he returns.

"No, I wasn't." He looks like he's about to bubble over with excitement.

I turn to the room.

"Welcome, everyone, to our first themed event." There's a

chorus of cheers, and I wait until they die down before continuing.

"We want to thank our lovely seniors' group who, because of their enthusiasm for the period, inspired this event, and who can blame them with all the great dances that were popular at the time? Shortly, I'll be showing you a selection, with the assistance of Nick." I gesture towards where he's standing next to me and receive a few more cheers, and I feel a glow from their acceptance of us. "Then we'll be on hand to teach you some of the basics so you can join in and have fun. Also, enjoy the refreshments supplied by Mrs Richardson and her friends."

Nick starts the music and takes my hand. We dance our way through the Charleston, the lindy hop, the jitterbug, and of course, swing. Almost immediately after we finish, we have a group of people wanting to join in, and the next couple of hours are spent teaching and showing them enough to enjoy the dancing.

I look round for Nick and see he's talking to his gran. I wander over to join them and she looks up at me when I reach their table.

"Hello, Darcy. This is a great event."

"Hello Mrs Parker. I didn't realise you were coming to join us."

"I commandeered the minibus," she says with a gleam in her eye. "I loaded in some friends and talked young Clem into driving us." She points to a man wearing a polo shirt displaying the name of the retirement village, who is dancing with one of the residents. "We like an adventure." She makes it sound like they've broken out of prison for the day rather than an outing, and I laugh.

"Well, it's great to have you here," I say.

"Don't underestimate how much people like a social dance, as well as their lessons. Being able to show off the steps they spent hours practising is also important." She's right, and I file that information away for what we can plan in the future for the new studio.

"Thanks Mrs Parker," I say.

"I was just asking Nicholas if you would be interested in coming to teach us at the village. There are a few of us who can still move our hips enough to dance, and I think everyone would enjoy the music."

I look at Nick, who's nodding enthusiastically. It would help bring in some money until the studio is ready, and I think I'd enjoy it too.

"I'm sure that we can sort something out," I reply, and she looks delighted. I leave her talking to Nick and head off to thank some of our regulars for helping us out.

"Do you want a cup of tea, love?" Doreen appears at my elbow with a cup in her hand and a plate. "And when did you last eat?"

When I admit I haven't had anything since breakfast, she gives me a look that says she knew before she asked me.

"Thank you, Doreen," I say, gratefully taking the cup, gulping down the tea, and eating half the cake in one go. "I don't know what I'd do without you," I say when I've finished.

She cups my cheek in her hand like I've seen her do to Nick a thousand times. It's her gesture of love and caring, and my heart that was ripped apart by my own mother heals a little from her touch.

"You're family Darcy, love."

Chapter 40

Nick

"Where's tha want this?" Barry asks, holding up a sign. I hurry over from where I've been putting the final coat of paint on the walls in the foyer.

The sign displays the New Steps logo that Darcy designed a couple of weeks ago. A silhouette of two guys dancing with a rainbow-heart background. It looks amazing, made real and two feet tall. I call Darcy, who's cleaning the kitchen.

"Wow!" he exclaims when he sees it. "I didn't imagine that it would look so good."

He ushers Barry outside the front door and shows him the place where the sign will go. Barry's offer to make the sign has been gratefully received, but it's not the only assistance we've had. We've been overwhelmed by how many people wanted to come and help. My dad and Alan have helped with the renovations, along with Barry, on the weekends. Mum has been incredible, and marshalled Maggie and Brenda into helping. Justin and Mark, freshly back from their honeymoon, got in touch with us and lent their help, mostly clearing the jungle outside, mowing the old bowling green, trimming the hedges, and weeding the car park. Mr Hamilton came forward as he's a knowledgeable gardener and took ownership of the flower beds, directing Justin and Mark in what can be saved and what needs replacing. Claire has helped with the marketing, offering some great advice and useful contacts. We'd given ourselves a month before opening, thinking that as long as the studio room is ready, we can start, and work on the rest as we go. With everyone's help, the studio is almost completely ready when Barry brings us the sign two days before we're due to open.

When it's hung, we gather everyone together to have a look.

"I'm proud of you, son." My dad puts his arm around my shoulders and draws me into a side hug. I turn and hug him properly.

"Thanks Dad. We couldn't have done it without your help."

I release him, and I see him go over to Darcy. I don't know what Darcy says to him, but I see a rare smile blossom on my dad's face and then he hugs Darcy, too. A warmth spreads in my core, watching them together. I think I've come to understand my dad more in the last few weeks than I've ever done in my life. I feel a lot closer to him. Seeing him and Darcy together makes me really happy, especially when Darcy's relationship with his own parents is so broken.

Before we leave for the day, we stand and stare at the sign again.

"I feel like a phoenix rising from the ashes," he says, and I can understand that from what he's been through.

"Greek?" I ask, as I have no idea about mythology.

"Egyptian," Darcy replies, giving it a final look.

"Are you nervous?" I ask Darcy, the morning of our grand opening.

"Yes. Well no, but yes." He stops speaking and laughs. "I'm excited about what we're about to do, but nervous in case no one wants to come and dance with us."

I understand him, and I feel it too. But I also know that we're fully booked for the first two months. Darcy created a website with an online booking system. We booked in all those clients who wanted to join us from his parents' school, and then Darcy had sent the information to all the people in his inbox. The response has been phenomenal and we haven't even advertised yet, simply relying on word of mouth and the publicity from the competition.

I put my arms round him and nuzzle into his neck, inhaling his warm citrus and honey scent.

"Are we crazy?" he asks.

"Probably." I chuckle. "But I can't think of anyone I would rather be crazy with."

"Do you want to drive?" I ask, as I reluctantly release him.

"Oh no, not today. I'm far too nervous for that," Darcy laughs. Once we'd finalised the contract for the studio, I bought a car. Just a cheap runabout, but it was clear we were going to need one to get to the new studio, fetch supplies for renovating it, and to get to the lessons we're giving at Gran's retirement village. Darcy is learning to drive as well and making good progress.

We're just about ready when people start arriving. It's a beautiful summer's day, and we can open up the studio doors and use the garden as well.

My parents arrive, along with Barry, Maggie, Alan, and Brenda. They soon apply themselves to helping and making refreshments. Justin and Mark are not far behind them, bringing some of their friends that we met at their wedding. Claire came straight over and hugged us, saying she was a very proud big sister. All our clients from the forties event bring their support, as well as many people we've never even seen before.

I feel a burst of pride when my gran arrives with some of her new friends who we've been teaching lessons to. I go over to greet them.

I see Darcy talking to someone and it takes me a moment to realise that it's Julia.

"Hi Nick." She greets me as I walk over. "I'm back for a few weeks, between sailings, and I heard what had happened. I wanted to check in on you and give you some support. I'm so happy for you both and I'm glad you're alright Darcy." She gives us both a hug.

"Thanks Julia. I guess you were the one who saw my mum for what she really is. I wish I'd seen it sooner," he replies, his face darkening.

"Don't beat yourself up about it, she could be really persuasive. But let's not let her influence darken your day any longer. How about you show me around and a dance for old times' sake?"

"Of course." Darcy's smile returns and he leads her off for a dance.

We take turns giving tours round the small building, and explain some of the plans we have for classes and events. We end up taking even more bookings, so we're going to be busy for a long while. At this rate, we'll have covered the first year's rent within the first few months, as well as being able to pay ourselves enough to live on. We've agreed that we'll be frugal and make sure we have all foreseeable expenses covered before we give ourselves a raise. We're hoping that people don't tail off after the first rush of interest. We've installed a sound system that we can Bluetooth to our phones and I play some music. As usual, Darcy and I start with a dance together. It's one we've been practising for some of the competitions we're planning to enter, hoping we have a shot at the Nationals again next year. Then we encourage others to dance and we both dance with different partners.

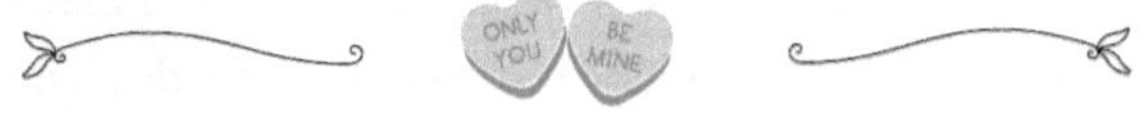

Taking a short break, I collect two cups of tea and take them over to where Gran is sitting.

"It's going well," she says, and I agree with her.

She takes an envelope out of her bag and hands it to me.

"What's this?" I frown. It looks very official.

"It won't open itself," she replies with a smile. I give her my best "not funny" look and open it, withdrawing the papers from inside. The first thing I notice is a solicitor's name across the top. I shoot her a worried glance, but she's just giving me one of her best enigmatic smiles. I quickly read through the first page and sink down onto a chair before my knees give way—they feel very wobbly right now. I read through it again and then look at her.

"You can't." My voice is nothing more than a papery whisper.

"I think you'll find that I can do what I like," she says primly.

"It's too much," I croak, as speech is difficult and everything feels difficult, like I'm moving through treacle. My brain feels the same way.

"What's wrong?" Darcy appears by my side, concern tingeing his voice. I don't take my eyes off Gran, but hand him the paper. All is silent for a moment while he reads it through.

"*Oh,*" he says, handing the papers back.

Gran reaches across the table and places her hand on top of mine, giving it a squeeze.

"Nicholas, seeing you grow up from a young boy with potential into the kind, thoughtful young man you are now has been one of the greatest joys of my life. I can't thank you enough for the joy you've given me—and are *still* giving me with what you and Darcy are going to achieve here.

"I was always going to leave it for you in my will, but I don't need it anymore. I don't see why it has to stay empty or why you should wait. I know you were saving up for a place of your own, and how you used that money to start this studio, but I'm sure you're both in need of a home. I'm pretty certain you and Darcy would like some privacy." She gives a little wolfish grin as Darcy turns an adorable shade of pink. I'm pretty sure that she's a hair's breadth from tittering with glee that she did that to him.

I can't accept it, of course, as much as it would really help Darcy and me out. I'm not denying that our own space would be fantastic, but . . .

"It's too much, Gran. I can't accept it. Surely you need it, to sell or something for your own care?"

"My dear." She squeezes my hand again. "I have enough, and it's not your concern."

I still protest.

"But—"

"Nick." Darcy cuts in and sits on the chair next to me. "Do you remember a conversation we had a month ago, when I said that using your savings to start our own studio was too much and I didn't want you to?"

"Yes, of course I do." I'm not sure what he's getting at.

"Well, you were pretty stubborn about it." He gives my gran a look and then turns back to me. "I think your gran has the edge on you for stubbornness, and I also think you should let her have her way. Just like I let you have yours."

The sass pulls me out of my stupor.

"You let me have my own way?" I retort.

"Oh, I knew I'd love you." Gran cackles at Darcy with delight, then, in an aside to me, she whispers loudly, "Don't let this one go, Nicholas."

Like that was ever going to happen.

"Mrs Parker!" Darcy blushes again.

"I think you can call me Gran too now, don't you?" She tells him and his colour deepens.

"Is everything alright, love?" my mum asks, as she and Dad appear next to our table.

"Well, Mrs Parker has just given Nick her house," he says, breaking the news for me. I look up at my parents and they're smiling like it isn't a surprise.

"You knew?" I ask incredulously, but I already know the answer.

"We always knew she was going to leave it to you, Nick. She amended her will years ago. That she's doing it now, we also knew, but she wanted to be the one to surprise you."

"I'm surprised alright."

"Well," sniffs Gran. "So far, he hasn't said yes."

I look at my gran and her expectant face, the smiling faces of my parents, and then to Darcy, my beautiful Darcy. The thought of living alone with him and not having to share a space, fills me with a deep joy . . . and something else. But this is not the time or place to allow my horny ass to follow that route, so I look back at Gran, seeing from the look on her face that she knew what I was thinking. I almost blush myself, but instead, I give one of her wolfish grins back at her.

"Yes. Thank you." It seems an inadequate thing to say, but I can't think of what else, so I repeat it. "Thank you so much, Gran."

"I knew you'd see sense, with a little help from your man, of course." She tilts her head to Darcy, and when I knee bump him under the table, he bumps me back. She produces a pen. "Now, if you'll just sign the papers, I can give them back to the solicitors."

I dutifully sign them and hand them back over to her. I lean over and kiss her on the cheek and whisper, "Thank you, Gran. I mean it when I say you've made my year."

"Oh, I can't take the credit for all of that. I think it's mostly due to Darcy."

She's not wrong, and I turn to him to tell him that. He's looking over at the door. His face is ashen, all traces of the pretty pink shade obliterated. I follow his line of sight and see a figure framed in the doorway. His dad.

Chapter 41

Darcy

Icy dread plays her fingers along my bones when I see Dad in the doorway. It takes a couple of breaths to realise that the reaction isn't to him, but to the expectation that Mum would appear next to him. So far she hasn't and curiosity gets the better of me. I rise and walk over to him. A few seconds later Nick is by my side, his warm hand on my back helping to dispel the chill still keeping her hold on me. Claire appears on the other side, my protectors flanking me. I'm grateful to them. I'm tense and worried, but I don't make a move. He's come here for a reason and I'm not going to make it easy for him.

"Hello son," he states simply. I can't stand it any longer. I need to know.

"Where is she?" I demand, looking round my dad, expecting her to show up.

"Your mother?" My dad's shoulders sag a little. I notice he

looks older and worry lines crease his face. "Probably somewhere in the middle of the ocean by now."

"What?" I don't understand.

"She wanted to go on a cruise, follow her hero, Bruce de Silva. He'd told of it when we met him in London. She seemed happy, and I agreed to it, but . . ." He looks around, noticing how many people there are about. "Can we go somewhere a bit quieter?"

Nick leads the way into the kitchen, which is currently unoccupied. I'm sure someone will be in to fill another teapot soon, but for now we have it to ourselves. When the door closes behind us, my dad starts speaking again.

"I'm sorry." He looks between Claire and me. "To both of you, but especially you, Darcy. I shouldn't have allowed her to behave like that towards you. When it came time for us to get on the cruise ship, I realised I couldn't do it. I couldn't sit there night after night listening to her prattle on about her achievements at raising her children."

I hear Claire's small gasp beside me. My dad must have heard it too, as he turns to Claire. "She told everyone you were a high-powered marketing executive and how she'd encouraged and helped you to get there."

"Whaaa—" Claire screeches and then stops, letting out a huge puff of air. She speaks again, this time her voice quieter, but full of venom. "She never once encouraged me. She barely acknowledged what I did, and she certainly never told me she was proud of me. I did everything despite her!"

"When we were standing on the quayside, I couldn't do it. I knew that if I stepped foot on that ship I'd be condoning her behaviour—which I've done too much of already—and I knew that I'd blow any chances I might have of reconciliation with my children, and that seemed the most important thing to me. It is the *most* important thing to me now."

No one speaks at his words, as all of us are locked in our

own thoughts about what he's saying. My head is a jumble, then he continues.

"So I made her choose." He gives a small, sad shrug. "I said that I wanted to see my children, to have the chance to make it up to them and, if they'd let me, be a part of their future. I said that if she wanted that too, then she could come with me, but if she didn't, then she could get on the ship—but to not come looking for me when she got back."

It's my turn to gasp, but I think we're all stunned into silence.

My dad sighs. "She hesitated for about three seconds before turning away and walking up the gangway."

He presses his lips together in a grim look before letting out another sigh. "All I felt at the time was an overwhelming sense of relief."

"Oh, Dad," Claire says, her voice cracking, and she hugs him. I wipe my palms down my trousers. I want to hug him and forgive him, but there's a part of me that still hesitates.

"It's okay, Darcy," he says tensely. "I know I have to earn your trust and forgiveness."

I just nod, pleased he understands it isn't so easy for me to forgive, but I can make a start. "Please stay Dad, I'd like you to."

"Thanks, son." His voice sounds relieved.

We seat him next to Nick's gran, because Nick said that she would be the best person to keep him in line. Not that he needs it. He truly does look repentant. I have no idea what he plans to do, but that's for him to decide. I do feel glad that he's made the effort, and I know I'll be able to let him back into my life in time.

"You know that looks like a weird case of 'meet the parents,'" Nick says to me sometime later. I look over to the table where my dad and Nick's gran have been joined by Nick's parents. They're all laughing, which is a good sign.

They've all met before, years ago, but this is the first time since Nick and I have been together.

"They aren't discussing us, are they?" I ask, suddenly worried.

"Oh, probably." Nick laughs and drags me away to talk to Riley and Kieran, who have also shown up to lend some support. Now we've finished the renovations, we have a bit more spare time. Kieran wants to plan another outing and picnic in the Peak District, maybe with an overnight stop somewhere, which would be fun. I let him chatter on with his plans; his enthusiasm is always turned up to eleven. I tune him out as I look round the room. From Nick's friends, who are now my friends too, to our families, who are getting on really well. To new friends, such as Justin and Mark, and to the clients who have stood by us. We've lost a few, as Nick predicted, but he's right, we don't want their business, nor do we need it, as we have others more than willing to take their place. I feel blessed to have this. To have Nick, family, friends, and a future. I catch hold of Nick's hand, causing him to look down at our hands and then up at me with his most brilliant smile.

It's getting late, and we've just finished tidying up. Most of our family and friends stayed to help clean up, from putting away the chairs and tables, sweeping up, and washing the dishes. Nick's parents left a few minutes ago and we'll follow them when we've locked up.

I give a final look round in the kitchen and the changing room before heading into the studio where Nick is closing the folding doors out to the garden.

"Well, that was a day and a half," I say, as he meets me in the middle of the room.

"It was," he says. "I can't go through many days like that."

"But we've created something good, haven't we?" I ask.

"It's going to be amazing." He wraps one arm around my waist, touching his lips softly to mine.

I place my arms around his neck. "You have a house."

"*We* have a house." He huffs a little laugh, as if he still can't believe it. "Do you know what's the first thing we're going to buy for our house?"

"What's that?"

"A bed."

"A big bed?"

"Such a big-ass bed." He kisses me gently again and pulls me close. "And I'm not going to let you out of it for a week."

Excitement at the thought courses through me as I breathe, "Yes, please." And I fuse my mouth to his, slipping my tongue in, and deepening our connection. My hips have a life of their own as they grind into him, and I feel his reaction. I let a small laugh escape, and he nips at my lip, eliciting a groan I can't hold in, and he growls in response.

"How soon can they deliver one, do you think?" I ask, breaking the kiss.

"Sadly, not by the time we get home." He looks rueful. "But tomorrow, for sure." He gives me a cheeky grin.

Then he takes his phone out, and I see him scrolling until I hear the opening notes of "Open Arms" by Journey playing through the sound system.

"Darcy Franklin," he says softly. "Love of my life. Shall we dance?"

Epilogue

Darcy

Eleven months later
British National Ballroom Championships

This is what I live for. This is what I'm made for. This is my life.

This is *our* life.

I extend my hand to Nick, my best friend, my boyfriend, and my business partner. The man of a million smiles shares one of them with me as he takes my hand and we walk onto the dance floor.

Cheers greet us and I'm grateful for their support. Barry had arranged a coach to bring as many friends, family, and clients as he could cram into it.

The last year has been so busy we've hardly stopped. Neither of us thought the studio would be so successful, but it's turned out to be hugely popular and, because it's a safe and inclusive space, people come from all over the city to dance with us.

The events have also been a hit, and we've held a few different themed days and evenings, from different decades of dances to dances from different continents. We've also held, at the request of our clients, some queer-only events, and although we don't really want a reputation as a dating club, we know some romances have sprung up from people meeting at the studio.

As well as running the studio, we've been competing, and have had a few minor wins in regional competitions. All of that has brought us back to this point, dancing again at the Nationals, which this year are being held in Manchester.

The familiar strains of a waltz start, and Nick elegantly twirls from his extended starting position into my hold, and we move as one to the one-two-three, one-two-three beat. Nick has always been a good dancer, but as he's now dancing full time and, like me, puts one hundred and ten percent into everything, he is exceptional. He claims it's because he spent so long watching me and my ass shimmy across the dance floor.

I relax into the rhythm and the familiar movements of our choreography. We've practised this hundreds of times, and now we just add that little extra bit of showmanship. All the major dance competitions follow the same order of dances, so after a short rest while another category dances, we take to the floor for the tango.

It's always been a favourite of mine and I'm excited that soon I'll be able to try out the Argentine version. We've worked so hard for the last year that we agreed we needed a holiday. Along with starting up the studio, we've renovated the house. We modernised it, with stripped floors and simple colours. I never tire of waking up next to Nick in our huge bed, looking out at the stunning views across the valley and not quite believing how lucky I am. But I am looking forward to getting away for a while. It will be the first real holiday I've ever had. So after this competition, we're closing the school for a week and heading to Spain. It's not Buenos Aires, where I'd really love to go, but it's enough for now. I know we still need to be careful with money until the studio has been going for a few years. Something Nick, who with his typical Yorkshireman approach to finances, is adamant about. Buenos Aires has been promised for the future for an extended holiday, but Spain has its charms, especially since I found out about a queer tango club in Barcelona that we'll visit while we're there. We've been practising our Spanish, and when we take our final steps of the dance and finish in a move that has Nick low with his leg extended behind, and I support him, I look at him and whisper, "Mi amor."

Earning a whispered, "*Cariño*, my sweet, my honey," in response.

When we start the foxtrot in its elegant sophistication, it strikes me I no longer suffer from the demons of the previous year. Although hard, I now can look back at it as an event that created the opportunity for this life that I wouldn't swap for any other. Doing what I love with the person I love most of all in the world.

The Viennese waltz is fast paced compared to the slow waltz and we're constantly turning and whirling round the dance floor, only just managing to get our breath back for the quickstep. The quickstep is another fast-paced dance and we incorporate as many hops, jumps, and skips as we can into the sweeping movements, as we swish through the music.

I'm grateful for the break, and Nick and I head to the dressing rooms to change into our Latin clothes.

Once we're ready, he sits down and accepts the water I

hand him. I stand in front of him and he parts his legs so I can move closer between them.

"Do you think we have a chance this year?" he asks, his blond hair falling over his eyes. I resist the temptation to brush it back, knowing how particular he is about his hair.

"Well, we're dancing the best we ever have, but the competition is tough." It's not a lie. Last year's winners are dancing, as are Krystal and Andrew.

"Hmmm." He gives a non-committal response, apparently deep in thought. His hand caresses the back of my thigh, working its way to stroke my ass. The effect has my cock taking notice and I don't need that right now. Damn him and his magic hands.

"Babe?"

"Hmmm?" he responds.

"If you don't stop that, I'm going to find it difficult to dance."

That gets his attention, and he tips his head to smile up at me, a predatory look in his eyes. Dear God, he knows how much that look affects me.

"Don't we have time . . .?" He gives me a slow, seductive smile—it's not helping.

"No, we don't. We're due back on the dance floor in a few minutes."

He pouts slightly, and I have to smile.

"Get your horny ass out there."

"And later?"

"Later you can do whatever you want to mine," I promise and step out of his reach, turning away and adjusting myself, willing my semi away.

"I'll hold you to that promise." His voice is sexy and close to my ear as he's come up behind me. I turn my head to the side and capture his lips for a kiss, just as there's a knock on the door preventing me from deepening it, which is probably a good thing as my cock threatens to perk up again.

"Are you guys ready?" Claire is outside. She had offered to drive us to the competition, an offer we readily accepted as we'll be tired afterwards. And a sleep on the way home would be helpful as, whatever the outcome, a party has been arranged at the studio later. Again arranged by Barry, who has turned into one of our biggest supporters, much to the surprise of Nick and I.

We walk back to the hall with Claire while she gives us the results of the first half. Krystal and Andrew are currently leading the points table, and we're lying in second, with last year's winners in third, but it's very tight and it could be anyone's competition.

I start the cha-cha-cha nervous. I'd rather not have known the results. It's easier when you're not trying to win, but we're so close that we could actually do it. The dance passes quickly and the following samba is a blur. Last year I had something to prove, to show my family I could dance with whomever I chose, but this year I don't want to let Nick down. He understands me well enough to know something is bothering me.

"Are you alright, D?" Concern showing in the tightness of Nick's voice. The warmth of his hand on my back, his protective gesture, grounds me and I swallow to try curing the dryness in my mouth.

"How do you seem so calm?" I ask. Nothing seems to faze Nick.

"Because the result doesn't matter to me," he replies. "I'm doing something I love with you. That's a win for me, whatever the outcome."

I love his outlook on life and wish I could be the same instead of overthinking everything.

"Just enjoy this, D." He pulls me into a side hug. I relax

into his touch and take some deep breaths. "I need you to focus for the rumba so you don't drop me on my ass," he says quietly, and it makes me laugh; such a Nick thing to say.

I don't let him fall, and put everything I can into the dance, which is another favourite of mine. Nick's face as we leave the dance floor shows me he enjoyed it too, and we've found our form. There are only two dances to go.

We've changed our choreography of the paso doble to make the most of our strength—precise and complex footwork—rather than relying on the showiness of a dress we don't have. We hope to show the drama of the dance, depicted as the relationship of the bull and bullfighter, as best we can. We portray it with the chemistry of push and pull energy. It's a gamble, but it shows how we can dance within the rules of the ballroom federation, just as two guys. If we can pull it off, it might just put us ahead. The final notes die away and Nick grins at me from where he finished the dance—on the floor. His look tells me he also thinks it went well. The applause is deafening as we take a bow at the end of the dance. I don't know if it's for us or one of the other five couples in the final, but it feels good. The cheers and whistles continue long after we leave the dance floor.

"Wow. Just wow," Claire says, when we come off the floor for a few minutes. "That was incredible."

"Thanks. We weren't sure it was going to work."

"It was bold." She's smiling. "Even though I can't get close to the judges, I think you have the popular vote given the comments that have been going on around me."

A couple of people come over to tell us how much they enjoyed the dance, and by the time we take to the floor for the last dance—the jive—I find I don't mind what the result is. We've shown what we were capable of in the paso doble, and that was enough for me. Anything else is a bonus.

"How're you feeling now?" Nick asks as we take our

positions.

"I just want to dance with you," I reply, and when we start, I give myself over to the rhythm and dancing with Nick, and I truly enjoy the dance.

We finish and happiness floods through me. Whatever happens now is out of our hands.

We move to the small area for competitors as the judges make their minds up. Krystal comes to wish us well and I reply with the same sentiments, but I have nothing to say to her and Andrew. Claire waits with us, seemingly more excited than we are. My relationship with Claire has become a lot closer in the last year. She helped us out in the beginning; her marketing and media experience were really useful, and she helped us set up an Instagram account for the studio. Nick and I share videos of us dancing. Last month we topped a record of two hundred and fifty thousand followers, which I find quite bizarre really, but it certainly gets the studio name known. She often comes round to dinner with Nick and me, the last couple of times with Rich. He's a nice guy and they seem to get on well together. I think it's a big step that she wants to bring someone with her at all. She's even started coming to the studio to dance occasionally. I think she's always enjoyed it, but never wanted it forced on her, staying away in rebellion. The last time she brought Rich with her as well and taught him some steps.

I'm sitting next to Nick, our legs touching, but I'm talking to Claire when he leg-bumps me. I look at him and he indicates with his head past me. I turn and see my dad standing there.

Claire sees him at the same time and goes straight over and gives him a hug. I stand, but hang back a little.

"That was really special, son," he says. "I'm proud of you."

I haven't seen him in six months. He came to visit us a few times, but he never looked settled, like he'd lost his purpose.

He'd served divorce papers on Mum, and when that was finalised, he went off on a round-the-world trip. I didn't know he was back in the country. I've had no contact with my mum, nor do I want to. She's occasionally seen, photographed with Bruce, so there might be something there, but I don't much care. She can't hurt me anymore.

I look at my dad, and he seems happier than when I last saw him, though little lines of worry show round his mouth as he looks at me tensely. I think back to the bond I was starting to form with him when I first got together with Nick. I realise I would like to try to see if we could have that bond again.

I step forward and hug him. "I've missed you, Dad," I tell him, because it's true, and he squeezes me harder.

There's movement on the dance floor, and the presenter informs the audience that they're about to announce the winners. Despite not being too bothered about the results, I still need to wipe my sweaty palms on my trousers as my stomach flips.

We line up with the other five couples and they start by calling out Krystal and Andrew in third place. She looks a little peevish for a second before she plasters a smile on her face. Last year's winners are in second and while my heart starts hammering at the thought that we might have won, I remind myself of the three other couples who were dancing. The points were close all throughout the competition.

Then they're calling us out first. We've done it. The first time a same-sex couple has won the National Championships. The cheering is deafening and I can't quite believe it. Nick gives me the greatest grin and I jump into his arms, wrapping my legs around his waist. He spins me round and then kisses me, in front of the judges, the camera, everyone, and I don't care, as my world only exists in the deep blue eyes of the man I love.

Are you ready for some more?

Coming Soon - It Takes Three To Tango
Pre-order here: https://books2read.com/TTTTango

It was the need to shade from the hot sun that sent me down the shadowy alley shortly after midday.

It was the desire to slake my thirst that made me enter the small bar with the curious name and the soft music.

It was the hypnotic voice of the singer and the sensuous movements of the dancer that kept me there until after midnight.

What brought me back the next day I have still to discover, and yet here I am, book unopened on the table as I sit sipping coffee and trying not to contemplate the disaster that is my life.

Acknowledgements

Wow where to start for this project!

When I put forward the idea I was tentative about it as I didn't really know how many other people also loved a film which I consider permanently in my top 5.

But the response I was met with has been incredible.

First of all I need to thank my bookwriting bestie Hinsel Meyer, who without her constant support and messages half my words wouldn't get written I appreciate you daily - thank you loving my Darcy and Nick.

Thanks also to Rebecca Louise and JoJo Stone who form our author circle.

Huge thanks (which are truly inadequate) to Stephanie Dempsey who has been so enthusiastic for this project that I nearly heard her response from across the ocean. She's been by my side for every word, alpha reading, proof reading, providing her dance expertise, creating awesome graphics, merchandise, and the stunning covers. I'm not sure what I'd do without her.

Thanks to Jenn Green and Sam Buckley for knocking my rough vision into a readable form and Wren Vale and Helen Smith for beta reading and proofreading.

I also want to thank my Street Team who have shown their support by sharing and promoting this book - as well as helping choose character names.

Thanks also to the members of my readers group for their enthusiasm and support.

And final thanks to you the reader for picking this up and giving my boys Darcy and Nick a chance.

Also by Jem

Have you visited Larchdown Valley yet?

Putting Down Roots - Larchdown Valley Book 1

https://books2read.com/puttingdownroots

Jackson

Jackson's plan had been a simple one—fill the van with fuel and drive until it ran dry, then start his life all over again.

Luca

Luca's art career is on the rocks after a spiteful review from his art critic ex-lover.

* * *

Bridging the Gap - Larchdown Valley Book 2

https://books2read.com/bridgingthegap

Cole

I like my life the way it is—my job, having my family close, my animals—and contrary to what my brother thinks, I don't need to find love.

Johan

Going to England was my chance to bury memories of my cheating ex while following one simple rule: no dating. Despite my best efforts, that rule goes out the window the second I lay eyes on Cole, the gorgeous, smart-as-hell vet of Larchdown Valley.

Will I only get my heart broken again? Or will Cole find he does want to share his life with someone, and that someone could be me?

* * *

Carving out a Future - Larchdown Valley Book 3

https://books2read.com/carvingoutafuture

Thirty years can make strangers of the best of friends.

Harlen wears his sadness like a second skin, protecting it like a cornered animal. Duncan knows Harlen isn't all snarl and snap, and he's determined to find a way to peel back the layers to the real person beneath.

About the Author

Jem Wendel is a British author who lives on the East Coast. She survives on gallons of tea. She loves history and is never happier than when wondering round a stately home or castle. She has been writing since she was old enough to hold a pen and as well as novels, has published several short stories and magazine articles.

When she's not writing she is usually hanging out with her rescued dogs, horses and mule.

She specialises in M/M romances that are sweet, low angst with heat and a HEA.

Stay in Touch